The Hero of the Big House

This English edition is dedicated by the author to Iris Murdoch

Alvaro Pombo
The Hero of the Big House

*Translated from the Spanish by
Margaret Jull Costa*

Chatto & Windus
LONDON

The translator would like to thank the author, Annella McDermott, Robert Lacey at Chatto & Windus, Martin Jenkins, Margaret Downing and Montse Gomendio for all their help and advice.

Published in 1988 by
Chatto & Windus Limited
30 Bedford Square
London WC1B 3RP

All rights reserved. No part of this publication may be reproduced, stored in a retrieval system, or transmitted in any form, or by any means, electronic, mechanical, photocopying, recording or otherwise, without the prior permission of the publisher.

Spanish title *El héroe de las mansardas de Mansard*.
Originally published by Editorial Anagrama, Barcelona, 1983.

A CIP catalogue record for this book is available from the British Library.

ISBN 0 7011 3193 4

Copyright © 1983 Editorial Anagrama
Translation copyright © 1988 Margaret Jull Costa

Typeset by OPUS, Oxford

Printed in Great Britain by Redwood Burn Ltd, Trowbridge, Wiltshire

1

Most of the time the master and mistress were away, but when they were at home they more or less held open house. The job had real class: the big apartment in the French-style building with vast mansards that rose up among the clumps of chimneys; the bronze statues that lent an additional elegance to the balcony parapets; and the six glittering glassed-in balconies, perched high above the trees in the Plaza de San Andres, almost as dashing as the masts of the sailing ships moored by the yacht club in the shelter of the port.

The house stayed open all year, looked after by three servants, not counting the governess. Both the master and mistress were from families of considerable social standing, related by marriage to Bilbao's most exclusive set. You should have seen the nannies all got up in different coloured uniforms every day, promenading as proud as queens. And then there were the linen cupboards and crystal cabinets that lined the corridors. And the Manila tablecloths. And the jars of jam from England. But, it has to be said, the two families had married and remarried amongst themselves rather too much. 'The master and mistress,' the manageress of the Hotel Principe Alfonso had observed with an insinuating little cough into her white linen handkerchief, 'are practically consanguineous.' And in the manageress's opinion, papal dispensation or no papal dispensation, such indiscriminate intermingling of the family blood could not be good for the boy. She always made special mention of him. She had gone so far as to say that you only had to look at the Egyptian pharaohs to see that she was right. After all, hadn't they all been consumptive and for just the same reasons? The boy was so obviously the product of inbreeding. Fair-skinned enough to be taken for a foreigner, and with clear, blue feline eyes. With only a cat and the governess for company, he played by himself all day, with a whole division of toy soldiers and a squadron of battery-operated fighter-bombers, in a playroom with large gothic windows, while the governess read the papers and sucked bitter little marshmallow and lemon-flavoured sweets. She was a rather wizened old governess by now. According to the manageress, she ate neither bread nor cooked vegetables, breakfasted in her room, lunched alone, and dined at seven in the evening, with her tea and all, with the boy when he came home from school, on whatever they served as a main course (as long as it wasn't meatballs). Neither the boy nor the governess ever spoke Spanish, only English, morning and evening. The only native speaker there was the cat. And the servants, of course.

A fascinating job. He didn't know how else to put it. He didn't know how to thank her. He felt sweaty, tearful, a little ashamed and agitated, almost happy.

'I can't tell you how grateful. . .' he mumbled at last.

The manageress, who had been like a mother to him, but had considered the interview at an end some time ago and was fast losing patience, cut him short with: 'Well, if you can't tell me, don't say anything. It's almost eleven o'clock! Show your gratitude in deeds, not words, that's what I say. Instead of thanking me, just make sure you behave yourself. You know what I mean. . .' the white handkerchief reappeared, she gave another little cough, and her voice dropped to an even more knowing, censorious tone, 'don't you? That business is all over and done with. But if anything else happens, I won't answer for you again, so just you be careful. . . Just do your job and don't go thinking about anyone you shouldn't think about, agreed?'

When he went out into the street the light made his eyes water. He patted the breast pocket of his jacket lightly with his left hand, almost knowing beforehand that his dark glasses would not be there. He remembered having worn them that morning, just before going down to reception to say goodbye to the manageress. He was sure he hadn't packed them in the travelling bag which contained his few possessions and lay at his feet like a scruffy dog. There was no point looking for them now. He invariably left his dark glasses behind whenever he left a place and this last pair had just become the most recent addition to the ghostly ranks of lost objects which he vainly labelled in his memory, keeping them eternally on ice. As many pairs of dark glasses – which his chronic conjunctivitis made indispensable – as jobs. And, since they met in that theatre group, so many places, including the worst of all, the one before last, so many that... He dabbed at the streaming tears, his head thrown back a little, avoiding his half-closed eyelids, mastering a powerful desire to rub them. He'd been told that his face, spectacularly inflamed by the conjunctivitis, looked tragic. Troubled like a pool by apparently significant nervy ripples. The truth was, however, that he had become so used to the gritty discomfort in his eyes that any exacerbation of his condition seemed to him deliberate, simulated, somehow contrived by himself. He had an absurd idea, which nonetheless he couldn't dismiss, that his affliction came between himself and other people like a mask, that this uncontrollable outpouring, this weeping, like some prodigious talent for tears, was, in effect, his mask. He was convinced that every disguise reveals some profound truth about the person wearing it. It was as if one fine day in his youth, or even perhaps long before, as a kid, he had jokingly pulled over his face the invisible, unused skin of another which now, as it grew older, wore the expressions of that other person, that other life. The north-east wind shook the sunfilled tamarinds, rushing through the leafy branches like the wind in a forest. For an instant all the people in the street seemed irresolute, all desires unimportant. The sky was as silkily perfect as the pale leaves of the tamarinds. But very blue, briskly scooped clean and silvered by the wind and the rains of the last two weeks, which had turned the white petunias brown and bruised-looking and made the evenings seem shorter. Was it true about the toy soldiers? And the governess? Perhaps she wasn't as old and wizened as the manageress had said.

It was time he went. Bending to pick up his bag, he noticed two workmates shouting to him from the first-floor terrace. He turned towards them, suitcase in hand. With his left hand he waved a silent, mechanical goodbye. 'Goodbye for good,' he thought. He walked on a little but, fearing that a too-hasty farewell might reveal to them his abrupt decision to forget them all forever, he stopped, without putting down his bag, and looked back towards the terrace, cupping his ear with his free hand in an exaggerated mimicry of listening. They were both shouting at the same time now, as if repeating something; three or four words, no more; not even a sentence. The shouting and their wild gesticulations made the meaning, if there were any, so obscure as to obliterate or alter it. And what did it matter now anyway? They hovered like marionettes above the sounds they made. In fact, the distance between them was not that great. He could have understood them if he had wanted to. Instead he let the voices deafen him for a moment. The whole of that wing of the hotel seemed to have grown dark, with the white cane chairs taken in and the awnings taken down in readiness for the winter. The vast blue- and white-painted façade, the flight of steps and the damp garden with its gravelled paths surrounding the building, were, he thought, rapidly taking on the introspective air of the hotel's permanent guests, the leisurely winter residents who dined at eight each night. The two on the terrace had stopped shouting, but now they started up again, leaning right out over the balustrade. Again he raised his left hand in a half-wave then hurriedly made his escape down the garden. What had they wanted to tell him? And what, after all, did it matter? What did it matter now, at least, as he hurried along the path, the gravel crunching under his feet, towards the iron gates of the Hotel Principe Alfonso? None of it really bothered him, indeed it almost pleased him, the weight of his bag, his streaming eyes, the malicious eyes of the doorman who greeted him from the safety of his glass lodge as he passed by. But the memory of his return to work at the hotel after what had happened still rankled and made him turn his head away. Standing near the gates, the dramatic iron spikes casting a shadow on the gravel, he could see the doorman with his face pressed against the window of the tiny door to his lodge. The old gossip with his bulging, vinous eyes. He had asked for his papers, pretending not to recognise him, the evening he came back... Free at last from all that! No one could touch him now. His life would be as unimaginable to them as a stranger's, as unknowable as fate. And out of the well-intentioned but humiliating and impatient reach of the manageress too. In a few hours he would have vanished into the new house, safe... He stopped. He seemed to have covered four hundred yards in a flash. He put down his bag by the bus shelter on the seafront. The beautiful air. The waxy green leaves of the laurel bushes. A whole flank of the Parque Aguero (which belonged to the Sisters of the Adoration of the Convent of San Cosme) deserted and awash with sunlight. The hollow autumn sea, sprigged with foam, like a giant conch shell murmuring of powerful, remote passions. And if the governess did keep herself to herself, well... he'd try to make himself understood with his smattering of English, very respectfully of course, with the perfect manners which befitted his profession. It was probably true about the toy soldiers... The manageress, as far as he could remember, hadn't mentioned the boy's age. Younger or older, it didn't matter. He found either prospect equally amusing. A chance to forget everything. And not think about anyone he shouldn't think about – the manageress was right there. Perhaps they'd give him a single room with a bath, a bathroom just for himself, with bedroom adjoining. At this point the bus raced up to the stop. A blue bus, completely empty. It was long and wide with automatic doors and wooden flooring like a tram. It had caused a sensation that summer: a dreadfully dangerous, well-nigh uncontrollable vehicle, according to some; the ideal form of urban transport, according to others. One man acted as both driver and conductor and, on this occasion, being alone, he wore no cap. Julian went and sat right at the back so as not to have to make polite conversation. The bus pulled away sharply and his bag lurched and fell to the floor. As they took the first corner it slithered under the seats like a dog.

For once in his life, he thought, as he wiped away his tears again, things had turned out rather well.

2

They were already in the dining room. You could hear them from the play room. Julian had just served the hors d'oeuvres which had been prepared in a terrible rush after everybody had arrived. It was one of those wretched days. In the kitchen everyone had been in an impossible mood all morning. Even Julian was not his usual calm self, although just to watch him opening the swing doors with one foot whilst carrying a tray in each hand made such dreadful days worthwhile. Normally, with Julian, there was time for everything. When they were left alone, when the master and mistress had gone and would not be back for a month or more, and it didn't matter if things got done later or tomorrow or even the day after tomorrow, they would sit at their ease at the kitchen table, picking over lentils and talking about life; almost better were the weekday mornings, with Julian in shirtsleeves, smelling of shaving soap, and Kus-Kus missing classes with a sick note signed by Miss Hart on behalf of his parents, saying: 'He has been indisposed since yesterday and is in bed until the doctor orders otherwise.' Miss Adelaida Hart's Spanish prose never failed. Her grammatical mistakes actually added to the serious tone of the note. 'You see, Father Florentino, she's an Englishwoman. My parents have always trusted her completely to sign sick notes and so on, ever since I was a child.' And anyway, with Julian there, the desire not to go to school but to stay at home and chat was almost as intense and persistent as a real illness, so the note to which Miss Hart appended her signature and rubric 'By order of the student's parents' was, in a sense, true. Because with Julian there was time for everything. From changing the batteries of a torch to rolling a cigarette as smooth and firm as a cartridge, better than any machine-rolled one. Not like with Miss Hart, who was not the woman she had been. She couldn't keep up with Kus-Kus now and still insisted on holding his hand when they crossed the road; she didn't smoke or have a key-ring with a rifle-bullet as decoration and she didn't even suffer from conjunctivitis. Poor Miss Hart, all wrinkled and rouged. But today was one of those days he hated.

This time, as usual, it fell on a Sunday. They would be halfway through the hors d'oeuvres by now. It was time for Aunt Eugenia's visit. So as not to gain any more weight, she never ate hors d'oeuvres but took the opportunity instead to visit him before she saw anyone else. He crossed his arms as Julian did when something inevitable was about to happen. At that precise moment the drawing-room door opened, letting out a gust of chatter and cigarette smoke. The noise seemed very close, like an ever-present reminder that it was one of those hateful days. He pushed the door of the playroom to with his foot so that it looked shut. The handle had disappeared years ago and the resulting hole – which on ordinary days acted as an embrasure through which to spy on the cat or to aim the barrels of the muskets – was now carefully plugged in honour of the illustrious visitor. So that Aunt Eugenia could play her usual game. He stood just by the door though without touching it, with his hands on his hips, like the captain of a frigate. There was more than enough time. He heard a restless tapping of heels on the hall parquet. (Where the prairie of fringed carpet did not cover its steppe-like waxed wastes it sounded hollow. From autumn onwards and all through the winter it was like a glacier dividing the house in two.) They came nearer and nearer, up the carpeted slope of Miss Hart's corridor which led on to the playroom then split off to another three rooms separated both from the kitchen and the distant rooms behind, places of twilight and foreboding, by the gulf marked by the famous swing doors, and now, now was the moment to move away from the door. There came a muffled tapping that grew faster, then stopped. Finally, there was complete silence. Aunt Eugenia had arrived. At this point, once Aunt Eugenia was installed on the other side of the door, slightly flushed as she bent over to peer at the plugged hole of the handle, it was essential that utter silence should reign. Since time immemorial it had been a pause which each of the protagonists spent in reflection. The silence grew in intensity. Then, like a small animal, he climbed to the fanlight above the door. He had a flash of insight. It gleamed briefly. The official car had arrived at last. Inside rode Aunt Eugenia dazzling the whole of the uniformed fleet. The orderly's whistle. A good, long blast. The sailor at the foot of the stairs stood to attention. And Aunt Eugenia entered. Dazzling. She had never married because she had not wanted to. If she wanted, she could marry the richest man in Spain tomorrow. She'd been the talk of every town she'd visited ever since she was a girl. Always accompanied by well-groomed young men, hopeful suitors, who drove those yellow convertibles he'd seen photos of in the albums. Very pretty, very slim, her hair in an Eton crop, playing tennis and going to dances; during those summers when the King and Queen came with the princes and princesses, people talked of nothing else... Now a great silence reigned.

'What game are you playing now? What were you playing a moment ago? I've been spying on you for ages. What were you playing? Tell me.'

'I wasn't playing anything.'

Only her head was visible, with its recently curled hair. This time it was reddish, carrot-coloured, like the red on those testcards for the colour-blind. She was almost too big for the doorframe. A glandular disorder, according to his grandmother. But, glandular or not, she was too heavy for her still-slender legs.

'Aren't you playing anything now?'

'No, not now. You can see that. That's some haircut they've given you.'

'Do you like it? You do, don't you? It's terribly flattering, you know... In Cuba all the girls have it like this but they'd wear a flower too, morning glories most likely or lilies. That's how they wear it in Cuba but I didn't dare go the whole way, besides here in the north there are so few flowers and they droop so easily. In Cuba it was different, very different. What a difference! How do I look, Kus-Kus? What flowers should I put in my hair? Come on, be nice!'

'If it were up to me, Aunt, I'd choose chrysanthemums.'

'Kus-Kus, don't be cheeky. How you've changed in the short time since I last saw you. You were never like this before, far from it! You would never have made fun of your poor, silly, ugly aunt!'

'But I wasn't making fun of you. . . I meant it. Chrysanthemums are very decorative, you know. . . You said so yourself once.'

'I did? I don't remember. Are you sure I didn't say another flower?'

'No, no, chrysanthemums, it was chrysanthemums. . . they're very decorative you said, because they're so huge and yellow, and in China, surely you remember saying this, they give them to brides to ward off demons. . .'

'Did I say that? Goodness me, you shouldn't pay so much attention to what I say! Decorative, yes, well, they are decorative. . . And the Chinese are yellow themselves, maybe that's why I said it, I don't remember, but in China yellow goes with everything, not here though, here you'd never wear chrysanthemums in your hair, good heavens no, Kus-Kus, the things you come out with. Frankly, it's the sort of flower you'd give a widow. Now, what were you playing? What a pity you don't play like you used to. But of course you're growing up now. A pity, eh? When you were small, whenever I saw you, you were being someone different, you imagined yourself to be thousands of things. Do you remember the time just the two of us with Josema went out to La Cabra for the day in the speedboat? You must remember. And the whole time you were pretending we were I don't know who, throwing a little bit of string into the water, the plumbline, you said, with a lead weight on it and knots tied in it every foot or so, and you wouldn't let us moor on the little beach even though the water was clear as clear, no, there were coral reefs, sharp as knives, round the whole island and until we found a really safe, really deep channel, nobody could bathe, don't you remember? and not a flicker of a smile, you were so serious about it and, seeing how serious you were, I was too. And Josema, poor thing, kept coming and telling me not to lean out over the side so much, that we'd capsize, all because I wanted to be the one to find the channel, "We'll capsize, do be careful and let the boy do it." Poor Josema, he meant because I was so fat, though I'm thinner now, and from the stern we watched the wake, you did too, chasing us, dancing behind the boat, as if the only thing that existed was the sea, I thought, really that's what I thought, Kus-Kus, as if nothing else existed but the sea, beneath us, lapping around us, wishing us no harm, wishing... Now you never come up to have tea with me like before, now I'm alone. You don't like to watch the boats any more. When you were little you used to say that when you grew up you were going to be a merchant seaman, isn't that what you used to say? And you knew the flags of all the countries by heart...'

'I still do.'

'I suppose now you play that dreadful football, and shout in that awful way boys do...'

And that was it for today. It made one a bit sad to hear Aunt Eugenia talking the way she did, but not too sad, since she'd never been known to talk any other way: so fast, in that affected tone of voice grown a little husky from too many cigarettes, half-closing her bovine eyes and lowering her mascaraed eyelashes, seeming to imply that she could say more but that it was up to others to read between the lines of the snippets she gave them... The swing doors had swung to and fro twice. Julian had already announced lunch. Aunt Eugenia was leaving. She backed out of the room, smiling and talking a great deal as if she were saying goodbye forever. At the end of Miss Hart's corridor, from across the hall, the others could be heard leaving the drawing room and entering the dining room, all together.

'I must go. Come up any time, any time. I'm always at home in the afternoons.'

'But I have classes in the afternoons.'

'Every single afternoon? Kus-Kus, you'll make yourself ill with so much studying!'

'All the subjects in junior school are more difficult now,

every year they get harder and harder until you get to the seventh year and take the final exam... Although on Thursdays, on Thursdays there are no classes in the afternoon and they show a film after games...'

'Well, come up on Thursday, this Thursday coming. I'll remind Fräulein Hart about it by phone, the evening before.'

'I'll remember, Aunt. Between five and six next Thursday and, Aunt Eugenia, just one other thing...'

'I've got to go, Kus-Kus. On Thursday then, Thursday, between five and six, but nearer five would be better, you know... what other thing? You're not going to mess things up now, are you, Kus-Kus?'

'Just don't phone anyone, I'll be there, and don't call Miss Hart "Fräulein", she's English.'

'Oh, for heaven's sake, still insisting on calling her "Miss"! And you can take that scowl off your face, I won't phone! Well, see you on Thursday, then, Pichusqui. I'll be expecting you, and try to be nice on Thursday, you must try to be charming and then we can talk about everything. Adío. Kus-Kus!'

'Adío!'

'Adío,' according to Aunt Eugenia, was how one says 'adiós' in Bariloche: raising the tongue, closing the lips slightly, stressing, very subtly the 'i' but giving very little emphasis to the 'o' and dropping the 's' entirely. It was meant to take the edge off farewells. Now there was an elegant place, Bariloche, the spa town of San Carlos de Bariloche in Argentina, certainly a cut above Baden-Baden. Aunt Eugenia would hear of nowhere else, not Italy, not Switzerland, and certainly not France, La Belle France, which got commoner by the minute in every way, from the tiles in the baths to the towels that smelled of bleach. And however delightful the ideal place you said you'd found in Finland, forget it. No matter how far you travel, Kus-Kus, you will never find anywhere comparable, not even remotely comparable to

Bariloche. Those avenues full of morning sunlight and little pink hotels, that immense sky, streaked with clouds, so vivid above the huge pines that look blue one minute, amber the next or purple or orange according to the season or the time of day. And the little side-streets full of boutiques, all the same height and shape, so that the shade at midday was exactly the same up and down the street, like a Greek frieze. And at night Russian archduchesses would walk down the hotel stairs, each accompanied by a Slav companion, who walked bending forward, a little like a swan, two steps ahead of his archduchess to catch her should she faint suddenly, a real gigolo, all the way from the Urals. Why should she faint? Well, because in Bariloche, one just always assumes that all archduchesses are gravely ill. . . And a gigolo is a handsome male companion, Pichusqui, preferably Russian with a smattering of English and French, enough to be able to order breakfast without being an embarrassment to an archduchess. But that's enough silly questions! She would be extremely tall and wear a black evening gown, very décolleté, with a train, but very simple, very close-fitting at the front, not a zip-fastener or a tuck anywhere and no jewels except for a clip valued at 500,000 roubles. She would sit and he would always stand, always, very tall and with those high Mongol cheekbones: oriental, intense, Russian. The two of them so elegant, never moving from their table, never changing position, nothing, just playing cards until the sun came up. During the season at San Carlos de Bariloche – Aunt Eugenia would declare in those moments of Buenos Aires lyricism when she confided in her enthralled little nephew – the chic thing was to say one's goodbyes quickly and unemphatically, to leave, as in Bariloche, without the 's' of 'adiós'. Because true chic lay in considering everything open-ended, never entirely irreparable or altogether certain. It was knowing how to behave and keep up a conversation whatever happened, as if any completed action, by the simple reason of thus having become inevitable, was a gaffe, something unseemly and inappropriate. Kus-Kus could not help thinking, now that Aunt Eugenia had left and was about to enter the dining room with the other guests, how that ideal state contrasted with the ostentatious and always somewhat tragic goodbyes of the lady herself.

While, with unconfessed nervousness, he waited for lunch to finish so that he could go in and greet his family, Kus-Kus came to the conclusion that when they were in the house everything stopped being open-ended. Neither he nor Julian had time for anything, not even, as Aunt Eugenia would have said, a moment to powder one's nose before the future was upon one. Now the chic thing could not be, as it was in San Carlos de Bariloche, knowing how to divest an event of its importance – in fact, when they were home, it always felt as if something, usually something serious, had just happened – or knowing how to say goodbye nonchalantly or to say hello with the poise of someone who, having just arrived in a place knowing not a soul, still greets everyone in the room. Now the chic thing was rather to screw up one's courage and give each person, on greeting them, their due importance and, accordingly, either two kisses or one kiss or one's hand.

3

There was no sign of Aunt Eugenia when he went in. The packed room smelled of cigars. That afternoon's wintry half past four sun seemed, as it entered through the windows, to have become burnished and overheated by the warmth of the room. The kitchen boiler had been left on last night and the night before. It usually took a couple of days to warm up that part of the house. Outside, up by the balconies, the bony uppermost branches of the plane trees in the Plaza de San Andres shivered and chattered. There was unlikely to be anyone down there in the square; nor was there likely to be anyone beyond that in the Paseo de la Explanada which skirts the yacht club and extends, narrowing after the jetty, all the way to the Chapel for Shipwrecked Sailors, the interior of which, numb and empty in midwinter, echoes like the hold of a freighter, the bronze of its commemorative statues glinting at the sea. The statues were imposing even on calm days, and he seemed to see them now as he approached his smiling grandmother: a woman calling and holding out her arms; a crop-haired little boy wearing trousers with braces, clutching at her skirt. It was a question now of beginning with his grandmother, then, trying to keep to a certain order, working his way round the room until he reached the door again. Most people had sat down or seemed ready to sit down at any moment; others, coffee cup in one hand, stood chatting. He saw Julian standing at the back near the door that led straight into the dining room without going through the hall. He was serving a glass of anis to Aunt Eugenia. Seeing them together made him feel calmer, almost sure of himself again. His grandmother was sitting on the wing sofa; next to her stood another elderly woman, his so-called aunt, Maria del Carmen Villacantero. She and his grandmother were great friends and when, as now, one saw them together, even rather alike.

'Is the little boy, the little scrap, going to give his granny a kiss?' his grandmother was saying as her grandson approached dodging the feet and legs of relatives of lesser rank awaiting their turn to be kissed. It was a pity that instead of lining up in their categories and according to seniority, his family, when it was time for this round of greetings, tended to spread itself about the room as if they actually wanted to be left out.

'Well, goodness me! Just look at the boy!' exclaimed Maria del Carmen Villacantero, monopolising everyone's attention. 'Give me a kiss, sweetheart, goodness, Mercedes, what a darling grandson you've got, adorable, won't you give me a kiss, goodness, how tall you've grown!'

Kus-Kus turned to look at her and held out a stiff right hand. 'Is that all the greeting I get then? No kiss? Look, Mercedes, he doesn't want to give me a kiss, imagine that, he's already a bit shy about giving kisses, who'd have thought it!'

Everyone laughed at Maria del Carmen Villacantero's mock exclamations of infinite regret at not being kissed by Kus-Kus. And, as the offended party, she reproached Kus-Kus for it – calling him by his real name of Nicolas; Kus-Kus being one of the secret names Aunt Eugenia had invented – repeating how much poor Maria del Carmen loved him, more even than her little nephews. She reminded him of how, when he was small, she came all the way from Belgium loaded down, at the height of the Occupation, stayed overnight in Paris with Ferdinand, *l'equilibriste pointu*, just to give him a surprise, and how the Gestapo opened her suitcase, and just as well that thanks to the Blue Division and all that the Spanish were well in with the Axis, but they did give her a fright at the Gare d'Austerlitz at half past one at night, being very German, very insistent, wanting to know what Ferdinand was and why on earth she was hiding him beneath her overcoat. And if Ferdinand really was of no importance, as Fräulein Villacantero had alleged several times during the search, why had Fräulein Villacantero not declared him to the Kommandantur at the Franco-Belgian border... So Nicolas could see how Maria del Carmen Villacantero was, always putting him first, even smuggling in Ferdinand for him... which, in the opinion of the beneficiary of the exercise, though of course he said not a word, was the silliest of all that unfortunate woman's silly exploits – in time of war or peace:

smuggling in Ferdinand, on the way back from Brussels, making the whole trip seem so clandestine, just to make a big thing about being a friend of the family and what's more going and choosing the most grotesque doll in all the toy shops of Europe, a kind of gaudy dislocated trapeze artist on a trapeze that didn't even swing... But Maria del Carmen Villacantero, who rarely let slip an opportunity to say her piece, then said they should let him be, the poor child, he looked so furious, Nicolas mustn't look at her like that, dear God, what a child, but it was natural, being almost out of school, that he should not want to give her a kiss, but he must not look at her like that, why only a minute ago she'd felt something like a chill run right down her spine, well, he was at that awful shy age, why she herself in the Sacré Coeur had been just the same, she'd suffered agonies as a girl, feeling half grown up and yet still such a child, when her great grandmother Maria Francisca de la Villa came to visit, a great lady whom Mercedes, though of course Mercedes was much younger than her, than Maria del Carmen that is, must have known and seen, a great woman always immaculate even after fourteen children, well, perhaps not immaculate, what Maria del Carmen meant to say was impeccable, but she had got confused as she so often did lately, it was these ghastly migraines and the arthritis, just like Mercedes, what the two of them needed, the two of them together, was a short spell in some dry spot instead of the appalling damp you get by the sea which was not good for either of them, Mercedes or herself, which reminded her, what a coincidence their talking about Kus-Kus now, when just as she was coming to lunch here, and many thanks to everyone for inviting her just as if she were one of the family, and she did understand absolutely what that meant and never for a moment did she forget who they were and how they treated her, Our Lady of Carmen would remember them most especially for that, that's why the first time she went on a trip, just the four days, you could scarcely call it a journey, she brought back Ferdinand for Mercedes's little grandson, grandchildren are such a joy, anyway, as she was walking round from her house, because whenever possible she avoided taking the bus because the pension left by her poor father, rest his soul, a Lieutenant Colonel in the service corps, and with her mother, well, Mercedes knew all this because often one just had to unburden oneself with someone, completely incapacitated and what with the way servants are today, and the poor woman being so very eccentric, pampered and spoiled all her life, her father had indulged her every whim, everyone said so, not *her* father, though even he didn't begrudge her the occasional caprice, no, Maria del Carmen's father, the late husband of the invalid, who had only to ask for anything she wanted with the Lieutenant Colonel's two aides to do the shopping for her, why those two boys were pleased as punch to be coming and going all day on little errands for the wife of Maria del Carmen's late father, who naturally broke down completely after the funeral, her mother that is, seeing how things were going to be and so it turned out, as Mercedes knew, the unmarried daughter was left to cope with absolutely everything, every little thing, with no thanks and no pay, and that's why, pensions being what they are, if she could avoid it, though sometimes one can't, she never took the bus, and so as she was coming on foot from her house today she met Miss Hart in the doorway putting on a very pretty white raincoat and it seemed very strange to Maria del Carmen Villacantero, very strange indeed, that Miss Hart should have lunch out, she would have to eat somewhere if she didn't eat in the house, on a day like that, such a special day, it seemed to her very, very odd with the whole family gathered together like that and Miss Hart having nothing to do with it, blithely putting on her raincoat in the doorway, but then the English were so clever at pretending they didn't care, she and Mercedes had already discussed this, coming to

Spain all fastidiousness and fine airs and graces to look after our children and then making demands which were quite uncalled for, quite uncalled for, who in their country would treat them as they were treated here? as both she and Mercedes always said, when the parents weren't there, the natural thing was for the grandmother to take care of her grandson, after all he was her grandson, rather than have him spend the whole livelong day with governesses who, because the fact is that abroad, well, in practice, Protestantism is as good as having no religion at all, and in the case of Mercedes's grandson, how could one not be concerned especially as children, poor things, can't be considered reasoning beings until they make their first communion, well, they're like kittens who love whoever feeds them, it's only natural for the poor creatures, it didn't shock Maria del Carmen Villacantero in the least, not at all, so... who did Kus-Kus love more, who? his parents or Miss Hart? What could he say, the poor creature, what could he say, always alone amongst godless governesses! Who did he love, the poor child? Why Miss Hart of course! Who else? And to think that Mercedes's grandson...!

Mercedes's grandson managed at last to pay his respects to all his family and slip out of the room. Shut up in his bedroom, he reflected sombrely on life. After a quarter of an hour his reflections necessitated a felt hat and a pipe. And the putting on of an overcoat – something he was strictly forbidden to do by Miss Hart in the house – and the turning up of the coat collar of the overcoat – something he was strictly forbidden to do by Miss Hart in the street. Reflecting sombrely on life – which meant walking with a slight stoop around the whole playroom – was impossible with Miss Hart around. As was trying to look, even a little, even in his way of walking, like Giacomo Gattucci or Gattuccio, Aunt Eugenia's lover who had escaped over the pampa with three million pesos in leather bags stamped with the emblem of the Bank of

Entre Rios to visit her in Bariloche. He hadn't thought about Giacomo Gattucci for some time. Julian had successfully replaced him. But there he was still, full of life, with his black hat and his smoking pipe and his whole desperate fate. He could never talk to Miss Hart about Gattucci. Miss Hart was not romantic, according to Aunt Eugenia. Whereas to Mercedes's grandson Julian seemed romantic even in the mornings, in his shirtsleeves; he had something of Gattucci in his profile, in his shining, wavy hair. Miss Hart had, indeed, gone out. The obtuse Villacantero was right there. On days like these, Miss Hart always arranged to visit a friend, English like herself, another ageing Miss. And she never returned from these expeditions before half past ten, having already dined. They used to go to the cinema – Kus-Kus had discovered this after submitting Miss Hart to a rigorous third degree. Kus-Kus had got into the habit, once he was in bed, of having her tell him the plot of the film, and thus he discovered Miss Hart's strange story-telling abilities, or rather the strangeness of her cinematographic tastes. All the pictures Miss Hart went to see seemed to have been mutilated, with their love scenes either missing or just plain dull. It was clear that Miss Hart was no romantic. Julian went to the cinema once a week too, but he never told him about the films, and Kus-Kus would never have dared make him tell him as he did with Miss Hart who, it now occurred to him, was definitely ready to go to her final rest. It was no more than she deserved. He took the pipe out of his mouth, holding it for a moment in his left hand at chest level, in an attitude of brooding arrogance. Very Gattucci, that gesture, impeccably executed. A shame that Aunt Eugenia wasn't there to see. He regarded the bottle of isotonic vasoconstrictor, a present from Julian, which occupied a prominent place – although invisible to the eyes of the uninitiated – above the William books, the masked warriors, and *20,000 Leagues Under the Sea*. There was still almost half left. To all appearances it was just a little amber-coloured liquid. There was, after all, some truth behind the unfortunate Villacantero's troubling question. It was clear, as was only natural after so many years, that Miss Hart was very tired. She still insisted on accompanying him to school in the mornings, always getting somewhat left behind going up and down hills. It took very little for her to be found sitting, her head nodding, over her mid-morning sewing or, in the afternoons, over her elegant edition of the complete works of Jane Austen. It was evident that after so many years she deserved to go to her final rest. It would need only two drops of sulphanilate of zinc, dissolved in her tea, followed perhaps by a second dose four hours later in her bedside glass of water. Since it was administered orally, nothing could be easier. Some suppositories perhaps to reduce the fever on the first days; a day or so in bed right at the start. Then, nothing. According to Julian, you hardly felt a thing. Miss Adelaida Hart, who was after all a subject of Her Britannic Majesty, would feel absolutely nothing. And would, in this way, pass gently over to a better life.

Feeling more cheerful, and with the Villacantero woman and the ordeal of greeting his family quite forgotten, Mercedes's grandson took off his hat and coat. There would be time on Thursday at Aunt Eugenia's to discuss whether, as Kus-Kus believed, Julian in profile resembled Giacomo Gattucci or not, or whether Julian was not altogether rather taller and broader in the shoulders than Aunt Eugenia's lover and, since nothing more had been heard of the latter, whether Julian – though he had not as yet galloped off with any money – would not be a preferable lover. Kus-Kus would be ready next Thursday to affirm and swear by all that was holy that his own observations had led him to believe that Julian, in comparison with the disappeared Gattucci, was by far the better lover of the two. Everyone had gone. The hall was dark. On the other side of the swing doors he could hear Josefa and Maria Soterraña talking quietly. The other rooms were dark too, on the other side of the hall, the long rooms belonging to the master and mistress, the terrifying unused bathroom which gave on to an interior patio and had its own anteroom and corridor, and the study and the living room and the dining room, all the other rooms; dark and quiet, everything smelled of black-market Virginia tobacco. Kus-Kus took a few steps towards Miss Hart's corridor, but without going into the hall. From there he could see in the distance, through the open living-room door, the gleam of one of the lamps in the square, flecked with the drizzling rain that had begun as evening fell; there would be no one down there; nor would there be anyone beyond, on the jetty, by the slippery nocturnal bronze statues of the shipwrecked, beneath the overcast dark green sky, with the drizzle speckling the unresisting surface of the yacht club wharf, of the fishing boats, and of all the other harbours of the world...

4

It was almost eight o'clock, almost dark, darker still in the park near the bus stop on the seafront, under the overcast dark greenish sky. Now that it was winter only one bus did the whole run from ten in the morning to ten at night. After clearing up, Julian went out for a walk. It was drizzling so he threw a white raincoat over his shoulders; it was almost threadbare but still retained its good English cut and an air of having known better times. A present he never wanted to part with. He intended taking a short, brisk walk before supper and then getting an early night after that exhausting day. Out of pure laziness he caught the bus at the stop in the Plaza de

San Andres, as if the coincidence of its arriving at the exact moment he was leaving the house somehow obliged him to catch it. The driver looked him up and down. The bus was empty and Julian, when he sat down – right at the other end of the vehicle, so as not to have to chat – remembered how his suitcase had crouched under the seats like a dog that morning of north-east winds, three months before, when he left the Hotel Principe Alfonso and made his way – so full of confused hopes – to his new post, the new house. The bus started and the driver, eyeing Julian in his rear-view mirror, was already rehearsing under his breath what he would tell his wife two hours later about the suspicious-looking bloke in the secondhand raincoat. For in winter the Parque Aguero – which had belonged to the Sisters of the Adoration of the Convent of San Cosme – had something of a bad reputation. This was due on the one hand to the fact that from All Souls' Day on the Council tried to save on electricity so that, instead of perpetual light, as befitted the Sisters, at that time of year, with only one lamp in three working, much of the park was left in the shadow more suited to people of the night. On the other hand there were the circles of dense evergreens which the Sisters of the Adoration had planted fifty years before. And then there were the comings and goings of the riff-raff who emerged out of the wanton shadows. And then finally the tawny owl and the short-eared owl, the devil who, impervious to the geometric dankness of the box hedges, got up to a little of everything out of sheer boredom. 'I shouldn't have come this far,' Julian thought as he got off the bus. During the journey he'd been thinking about the little boy, Kus-Kus, the precocious child the manageress had made such a thing of and whom almost no one, not even Julian, called by his real name of Nicolas. And of how he, despite having known the boy – so very young and so full of infectious fantasy – for three long months, still did not know what name to use: whether Kus-Kus like Aunt Eugenia, or Chatibiris and Chatibarati like

Maria Soterraña, or Nicholas, like Miss Hart with the accent on the 'i' and with an English 'ch' pronounced like the 'k' in kilo. At the precise moment Julian got off the bus and went to sit on the semicircular Egyptian-style marble bench round the fountain erected to Constancia Leal – the eminent writer, who presides, a book half-open on her monumental lap, over the passing of the local rabble – Kus-Kus would be riding through the province of Rio Negro, having crossed the whole pampa, heading for Bariloche, a spa better by far than Baden-Baden, in the guise of Giacomo Gattucci, Conde Duque de Protervo, and Prince of Moscow. He could not but reflect with what staggering inaccuracy the blasted child, that child, had been described by the hotel manageress ... Nothing of what the manageress had said had been right. It had not been a happy ending. In fact that was just what this posh job had not been: the end of anything.

'Hey, Julian!' called a sudden loud voice from the other side of the fountain. Julian sprang to his feet. The dark, greenish sky, the shadowy labyrinths of box trees seemed to close round him like a death trap.

'Hey, it's me, don't be scared! I really made you jump!' – the figure which approached him, talking very fast but almost in a whisper as it skirted the fountain, turned out to be one of the hotel people. Julian, pulling himself together, regretted both his presence in the park at all and his own obvious discomfiture at being discovered there.

'What are you doing here?'

'Out for a breath of air. I was just going.'

'Just going?' the new arrival, by now very close, murmured incredulously.

Now everything would run its inevitable course. The subsequent conversation, the account – peppered with malicious innuendo – that the manageress would hear the following day ... it would all, just from that one unfortunate encounter, unwind with mechanical inevitability. Julian was terrified. He stepped back a little, just two steps, and then, before his betrayer could reach his side, he started to run, his eyes streaming, stumbling on the wire fences that protected the flower beds, cursing the inexcusable stupidity that had led him to catch the bus when he left the house, cursing himself as he cursed his luck . . . It was ten o'clock. The bus did not seem to have moved from the stop by the park . . . The same driver again looked him up and down as he gave him the ticket and again watched him in his rear-view mirror for the whole journey, his mouth twisted into a little mocking smile . . . It was the last bus, at least he'd been in luck there.

'Why did I run away?' Julian asked himself when he was alone in his room again, in bed, where he'd gone without even touching the supper they had put aside for him. 'I ran away because nothing has changed,' he had to admit, tossing and turning in his bed, unable to get to sleep until he curled himself up like a cat amongst the blankets.

You couldn't really judge the house from the outside. There were, in fact, apart from the governess but counting Julian, only the three servants. That, however, was the only thing the manageress had got right. After a couple of weeks Julian had discovered that she spoke only from hearsay. That being so, it was a mystery to him how, without moving from the hotel, she had got him the job. Not that he was disappointed, far from it. In no other job had Julian felt so at home right from the start. It was something else. Why did he run away? The question was rapidly taking on the certainty of a regret. What was it about the house? Julian sat up wide awake in the midst of a sweaty tangle of sheets and blankets, believing that he had found the answer. There was a torpor about the job; that was what it was. It was a torpor that the house itself induced in its occupants. Apart from the half dozen or so days like the last few when the master and mistress were at home, which were so frantic they took on an unreal quality – and, as with miracles, anything that unreal can usually be discounted – Julian could not remember ever having slept so well or for so long. Unable to sleep now, he recalled the siestas of the last three months, only interrupted by teatime. 'We're just here to do a job, no need to make things harder,' Josefa would say. She was the maidservant, a good-looking girl, already quite grown up and with a preference for boys who were equally grown up, according to what Maria Soterraña – possibly for Julian's benefit – told the Little Sister of the Poor who came to collect alms every Wednesday. 'There's enough suffering in this life without that!' Josefa would often declare over her sewing. And what suffering life might bring, Julian had come to think, only Josefa, with her draughtsman suitor married to a girl from Santurce, could know exactly. There was a friendly atmosphere. The friendliest he had known as an employee. And, yes, the main characteristic of this general friendliness was the sleepiness. The beatific torpor of the whole place and of its occupants. He began to grow drowsy, as if, simply by reflecting on the somnolent character of his new life, he unwittingly became a sleeper. And as if, as he fell asleep, he might discover – in some profound sense which sleep both suggested and obscured – why the sudden appearance of an ex-workmate in the park had so startled him that he ran away. He drifted further and further from the surface, more and more immersed in the role of sleeper, ever more convinced by the ease of that absolute explanation that left the notes unresolved, longings satisfied, as in a requiem. Even the fact that the languid passing of the days in the house tended rather to evoke than to erase thoughts of his troubled past with all its disquieting faces, acquired, in the irrevocable explanation imposed by sleep, powerful, glittering trappings, regal, pacific . . . The shudder of his door flying open woke him. It was the kid. In pyjamas. He looked very small. It was the first time he had appeared at such an hour in Julian's room.

'Why didn't you answer?' he asked, frowning.

'Do you know what time it is?'

'Miss Hart went to bed an hour ago. A whole hour.'

'What's Miss Hart got to do with it?' Julian put on his trousers over his pyjamas, annoyed.

'I heard you come in. I didn't think you'd gone to sleep yet.'

'I'd turned out the light. I was asleep. It's not the time of night to . . . '

'I'm sorry. If you like I'll go,' said the boy without moving.

The two looked at each other silently. 'I'm the one who should be in charge here. I should take the kid back to bed,' thought Julian. But he was filled with curiosity, like a vague itch, to know what the visit was about. He sat on the bed and lit a cigarette. He was half-aware of the blue eyes which watched, fascinated, his slightly trembling gestures; it wasn't the first time he'd noticed it. Like the smarting in his eyes, it was an irritant which, in the long run, proved stimulating. He distracted himself with a long pull on his cigarette. But this only reminded him of the unfortunate meeting, the uneasiness with which his ridiculous flight now filled him. What the devil was the boy jabbering on about, standing there in his bare feet at this hour. The master and mistress would be back at any moment. What the devil was it that they had to do without hurting Miss Hart's feelings? He had to make a real effort to pay attention. 'The years take their toll,' he heard the boy say, immediately adding that that was what Aunt Eugenia said. That sooner or later, for her own good, they would have to administer the isotonic vasoconstrictor of zinc sulphanilate to Miss Hart. So that she might go to her final rest. He could see no alternative. First it would be just two drops dissolved in her tea — Julian's help would be vital in carrying this out — then later, at 4 o'clock, two more drops dissolved in her bedside glass of water. And to do all this he needed Julian's help. Miss Hart wouldn't feel a thing. He repeated that several times. Some vitamin C to help her regain her appetite. Perhaps suppositories to lower the fever. Her temperature to be taken morning and evening. Then plenty of bedrest . . .

Julian stubbed out his cigarette in the ashtray. 'But, wait a minute, do you want to poison her or what?'

Julian was not responding as he should. He seemed distracted. Scarcely interested at all in whether Miss Hart should or should not go to a better life. No, it wasn't a case of poisoning her. What then?

'What's wrong with you, Julian?'

'Wrong? With me? What do you think's wrong?' he replied, irritated.

'You're not listening to me.'

'Not listening? You've been in here for an hour. You should be asleep.'

'See, you haven't been listening.' His voice was almost tearful.

They heard the main door in the hall open and the master and mistress enter. The boy gave a start. Julian switched off his bedside light. They stayed absolutely still, holding their breath, in the complicity of darkness. The footsteps and conversation stopped almost immediately afterwards. Julian switched on the light. The room had changed; as if a solution, which only sheer obtuseness had prevented them from seeing had imposed itself.

'What's all this about an isotonic constrictor?' asked Julian settling himself comfortably on the pillow at one end of the bed, his accomplice, at the other end, swinging his legs gently, as one does on a summer afternoon sitting fishing from a jetty. He took his time before answering. His voice, when he did, was perfectly serious. A voice suitable for outlining – broadly – a plan of action between partners in crime.

'It's called isotonic vasoconstrictor of zinc sulphanilate.'

It was two in the morning by the time all the details had been finalised. The master and mistress were leaving the next morning, Monday morning. The whole plan would be carried out at teatime. At exactly five past seven, Julian would phone from the bar downstairs and, putting on the voice of an English governess, ask to speak to Miss Hart. Josefa – who would not be in on the secret – would take the message, go in and say: 'Miss Hart, there's a call for you from your friend.' Miss Hart – who would just have finished pouring her first cup of tea – would leave the playroom, where tea was usually served, and go to the telephone. Kus-Kus would put two drops of the isotonic vasoconstrictor into the steaming cup. Miss Hart would find the line dead. She would return to the room, say something like: 'How odd, Nick, I got cut off,' and take a sip of tea. It had to be made clear to Julian that the isotonic vasoconstrictor of zinc sulphanilate was in a little bottle of eyedrops. When Julian learned that he hesitated for a moment like someone hesitating, Kus-Kus thought, between two identical doors in the Hall of Mirrors at a fair.

'Ah, well, if it's just a game, that's another matter,' he said at last, repeating it before Kus-Kus could answer, but changing the order of the words a little: 'It's quite another matter if it's just a game.'

'It's not a game!' exclaimed Kus-Kus sharply. Julian looked at him tearfully, raising his right hand as if about to rub his eyes, but without doing so (for an instant his whole body, the whole universe, seemed suspended, waiting for a final judgement). Then he said: 'What do you mean, it's not? What is it, then? Tell me what it is, if it isn't a game? It must be one or the other,' and Julian was about to add 'Kus-Kus,' but, without knowing why, he stopped himself, '. . . it must be one or the other, playing at poisoning her or really poisoning her, there's no alternative as far as I can see . . .'

'But it isn't a game, it isn't playing at anything, it's something else . . . !'

'Well, come on then, tell me, if it isn't a game and it isn't poisoning, what is it, tell me!' exclaimed Julian. Although he himself noticed the little note of triumph that had crept into his voice, he couldn't have said why he enjoyed confronting the kid with this dilemma, nor how bringing it up helped either of them.

'It's something else,' muttered Kus-Kus, cornered.

'Well then, tell me, what is poisoning someone if it's not murder and it's not a joke?'

'Something else.'

But he didn't know what to say now. Suddenly he was just a child in pyjamas, barefoot in the bedroom of an adult, whose questions he couldn't answer and didn't want to face up to. His eyes grew small and bleary, and so heavy he could hardly keep them open. He let himself be led to his bed, let himself be tucked in. Any desire he had had to come up with a third possibility to answer Julian with had vanished. Before turning out the bedside light, Julian covered the boy's feet, which were sticking out a little, with a blanket. He brushed one of them as he did so, and felt suddenly moved by a vestige of his own, poor childhood memories.

'I've let him down,' thought Julian as he closed the door of the room behind him. And he felt guilty of some vague, disproportionately grave error. He fell asleep instantly, thinking once more how wrong the manageress had been about everything, and that Miss Hart, though a woman of few words and rather curt manners, was capable of inspiring much more respect than the manageress ever could. So Julian would not help Kus-Kus the next day; he would not go down to the bar to telephone; he would not join in that game that could never be anything but a game. Mingled with this thought – as if sleep somehow permitted him a certain measure of resentment – was the wish that the kid should play on his own in future, without involving him in his games. Because Julian was convinced that games, like disguises, always mean something, and always define and label those who get involved in them. 'If he wants to play at murders, let him play his silly little rich kid's games on his own!' But he knew that was going too far (just as he knew his resentment was purely abstract), and didn't really conform to the flesh-and-blood Kus-Kus.

Kus-Kus too fell asleep, wrapped in the importance of having been talking to Julian until the small hours, and with the double expectation for the coming week of a radical change in his governess's existence and a visit to Aunt Eugenia in four days' time – Aunt Eugenia, it seems, had that afternoon regained her capacity to fascinate Kus-Kus, a capacity which had somewhat diminished in the last few months because of Julian's presence in the house.

There are more days than nights, many more. And the nights, made of green transparent down, only afterwards interleave themselves in the weeks to ensure that each week has seven days. And the nights are silent enough for the new moon to rise as it should and for the full moon to put ashore on the wharf used by the Harbour Police. And for the squid to sleep in the slippery, inky alleys of the high seas and for the wrasse and the sea-tortoise to sleep in the little hollows in the wall, amongst the limpets.

5

In spite of the kitchen staff's calculations, the master and mistress left on Tuesday afternoon, not Monday morning. Someone telephoned Julian twice. After each of these calls – especially after the second, during which he scarcely opened his mouth except to say 'yes' and 'no, really, please, it would be madness' – Julian walked about the house like a soul in torment. He forgot his gloves when serving at table, broke a plate – albeit only a pudding plate – and on Tuesday, according to Josefa, he made a long-distance telephone call as soon as the master and mistress had left the house, to some village whose name she couldn't make out on the outskirts of Madrid, where there was no sea and where, to judge by the half hour they took to answer, no one was ever in, particularly neither of the two people, a lady and a gentleman, for whom Julian asked so desperately. Infuriated at being unable to contact them, Julian put on his raincoat and went out – this would have been at about seven in the evening – and they didn't see him again until noon the next day, when he reappeared, looking furious, with dark rings under his eyes, demanding to know what time it was and devouring the two lots of fried eggs with bacon cooked by a sympathetic though angry Maria Soterraña, whilst an angry and not in the least sympathetic Josefa made her own long-distance telephone call to Madrid, to her married sister who had had a baby two months before and from whom, since *she* had not wanted to take advantage or abuse her position, Josefa had not heard for a year. Miss Hart hid in her room pleading the most frightful migraine while Josefa bellowed down the telephone. And Julian went to have a siesta (lasting until the following day) under the special protection, the more effective for being undeclared, of Maria Soterraña who, feeling her authority in the kitchen challenged by the offhand impudence of a mere spinster maidservant who didn't even know how to use a sewing machine and who took advantage of the departure of the master and mistress to spend the afternoon talking on the phone, took Julian's part and, hoping to find an ally, talked the matter over with Kus-Kus. The consequent postponement of the poisoning of Miss Adelaida Hart – whose frightful migraine that day had nothing to do with eyedrops – obliged Kus-Kus to retire to his winter quarters and to reflect, with his hat pulled down over his eyes like Giacomo Gattucci, on the strangeness of human behaviour. Thursday found Kus-Kus counting the minutes until a quarter to five when he could go up to Aunt Eugenia's apartment.

The time was really half past four when the hall clock (a veritable cathedral of a clock you had to stand on a stool to wind up and put right once a week, and which even Miss Hart thought very British in spite of its very Spanish habit of being unpredictably fast or slow) said twenty-five past. Aunt Eugenia had said 'between five and six', and he knew that meant 'better five than six and better still five minutes to five'. In Bariloche the chic thing was to separate by an hour the appointed time of meeting and the desired time. Kus-Kus, as he rang the doorbell and adjusted his tie – dark blue silk with white spots, a present from Aunt Eugenia – was thinking that any gigolo of reasonable good looks and with some degree of refinement would know he was expected to arrive five minutes before the arranged hour and greet his hostess thus: 'I'm *so* sorry, Eugenia, oh, but you're looking divine, forgive me for arriving late like this.' It was a double door, with moulded panelling, and a vertical rectangle of caramel-coloured glass as a spyhole. All the doors opening onto the staircase — including Kus-Kus's — were dark, except Aunt Eugenia's which was painted white.

It was the last door. On the landing the light, even on cloudy or rainy days, was dazzlingly bright, flooding in through a skylight built into the two sloping sides of the roof. On the raw, changeable mornings of early October, as the trees turned copper-coloured, whirlpools of plane leaves would accumulate there, like trapped seagulls. At any time of year those who, like Kus-Kus, took the stairs rather than the lift, felt as if they were climbing the tower of some gigantic observatory or lighthouse at whose distant feet shone the booming sea, the marvellous platinum ocean of trade winds and hellish slave-ships about which Aunt Eugenia was an inexhaustible source of information.

'I'm so sorry to be late, Aunt Eugenia!' Kus-Kus duly pronounced as she opened the door. 'I was detained downstairs ... some urgent business detained me ... you look extraordinarily pretty with your hair that carroty colour ... forgive me for being so late, do you forgive me? Please forgive me ... !'

'Heavens, Kus-Kus, it's not even time, nothing's ready and I haven't even changed yet ... !' Aunt Eugenia exclaimed in her turn, removing with her left hand as she said this a sort of mauve wrap from around her shoulders ... From then on, too, everything would follow the usual pattern. Kus-Kus assured her that her being behindhand with things was not of the slightest importance and that he was only sorry they weren't able to talk longer and that Aunt Eugenia shouldn't worry, he'd look after himself and get himself a drink ... Aunt Eugenia, on hearing this, would disappear, to return a quarter of an hour or so later, looking almost exactly the same but smelling of two different perfumes and pushing a three-tiered trolley bearing tea and cakes, all of which would be delicious.

Once alone, Kus-Kus made his way to the two living rooms Aunt Eugenia used. It was really one room curiously arranged to form two triangles, crammed with armchairs, flowers, large cushions and with all kinds of photographs and pictures covering every inch of wall. And there were little tables and writing desks on which the most disparate objects, each of which Kus-Kus knew individually, were displayed. They always spoke of the room as two rooms, partly because of its shape, but also because Aunt Eugenia had divided it with a couple of big screens of greenish lacquer painted with red and yellow dragons ... And then there was the light, the simple superfluity of light which the glass mounts of lithographs and engravings, the mirrors, the polished slippery surfaces of the screens, shelves, little tables and ornaments seemed to multiply, turning the place into a cave of visual delights, of sapphires ... Kus-Kus sank into one of the sofas, a cream-coloured, velvet sofa, almost as large as a bed, where, in fact, when he was still a little boy, he and his aunt had more than once taken their siesta together.

Miss Eugenia — Kus-Kus thought, while he waited for his aunt to enter with the tea trolley — did not have any servants, nor, amongst the kitchen staff, did she have a very good reputation. They said she received visits from men when she was alone, and as for the shop assistant from the Cubana grocery store (a boy with irresistible eyes like dark velvet, who wore tight trousers with a wide belt and a white shirt, whose reserve drove all the Josefas wild and who was, according to Kus-Kus's Josefa, 'very close', never giving anything away, so you never knew where you stood with him, nor, when it came down to it, whether he had a preference for one thing or the other), they said that when he came in the early morning with her order, Aunt Eugenia put on a black silk nightdress with slits up the side. But, as Kus-Kus reminded himself, they said all kinds of things about Aunt Eugenia: that if she didn't come from the family she did, she'd be a whore; mind you, given her upbringing it was only natural, especially seeing her father was a Republican who had died in a little villa with a garden on the outskirts of Toulouse refusing to say the Our Father ... What it came down to was that she had an itch that needed scratching, like all women, there was no reason why she should be any different, and what she should have done while she had the chance – which she no longer had – was to get married; and that now she'd got so fat from her continual, insatiable eating just to console herself for the lack of the other thing ... Because the fact was that when she was young Aunt Eugenia had had a fiancé. A rich South American, a very tall, dark, green-eyed boy, fell in love with her and with great style asked for her hand just like that, after knowing her for only a month and a half. And Aunt Eugenia had been madly in love with him too. They attracted attention wherever they went. But, life being what it is, her father – and we know how he ended up – put his foot down and sent the boy packing. They say he shouted after him that he'd sooner see his daughter dead or in a nunnery than paired up with some half-caste slaver with the scent of human blood still on his breath. And given the way he felt about nuns, him being such an atheist and a Voltairean, well, he must have meant it. August went by and the boat arrived, the liner, which it seems her father had been expecting since a month before the marriage proposal because they say he'd been seen going to the Transatlantic Company offices and at the yacht club reading the tidal charts on the noticeboard, not that, in this case, it helped the old fox. The ship was to make a three-day stopover, four days at most, something which the father had not bargained for because, coming as he did from the interior (from Guadalajara, in fact, where he became a notary and where he married the woman who was to become Aunt Eugenia's mother, after knowing her for only a month and half; this chilling coincidence in the chronology of the two courtships was enough to startle any decent person), he thought that ships came and went with as much freedom as the trains that crossed La Mancha. So, anchored as usual outside the port, right opposite the beautiful mansarded house where Aunt Eugenia would live years later, the liner rose and fell to the changeless rhythm of the tides. In the mornings it gleamed white; you could read its name without binoculars and make out the initials of the shipping company on the four funnels; in the evenings, surrounded by the sails of dinghies and by motorboats which, however large, looked tiny in comparison, the liner, magnified by the sunset that spread itself like a translucent amber albatross, seemed the nostalgic essence of some past, unrepeatable voyage; and at night, when it was lit up, it made the ladies think of the tears that at that very moment Aunt Eugenia would surely be shedding in the exotic arms of her desperate suitor. The truth is that no one gave much thought to the suitor himself. What caught their imagination was less and less the protagonists, and more and more the situation, the plot, the tragic imminent denouement. In fact, long before falling in love with Aunt Eugenia, the South American had intended travelling back on the ship, but, on falling in love with her, and finding his appetite for love whetted by their engagement, he decided, whatever happened, to convert the long return trip into a honeymoon, a nuptial voyage home, and to land in the Americas a married man. The decision, however, left him little time to go from ball to ball in search of a new fiancée. And so he got married, with no explanations and no wedding feast, the day before the ship weighed anchor, in the little chapel of San Cosme, to a young lady as small and round as a chickpea, quite a lot older than him, the oldest of a family of eight, but very capable, with a reputation as a marvellous cook. Aunt Eugenia spent that winter in Madrid. The following summer in France or Italy; and the next quite simply abroad. Then her father got involved in politics, then she met a German boy, then came the Civil War, and now . . .

When, twenty minutes later, Aunt Eugenia entered pushing the the tea trolley as she had on other occasions, Kus-Kus had the feeling that her orange hair seemed less bright and her eyes duller, as if something had happened in the rooms in the interior of the apartment, as if a phone call like the one Julian had received at the beginning of the week, or some other chance event, had first angered her and then left her disproportionately sad. Aunt Eugenia sat down next to him on the sofa as usual, but instead of pouring the tea she sat still without looking at Kus-Kus and without saying anything.

'What's wrong, Aunt?' asked the boy, who was feeling hungry.

As usual the tea-tray was piled high with plates of just the kind of biscuits and cakes that Kus-Kus liked. But his aunt's prolonged immobility was a novelty he had not reckoned with.

'No one loves me anymore, Pichusqui, I was mistaken.' Aunt Eugenia said at last.

'*I* love you, Aunt. What do you mean "mistaken"?'

'It's not the same as it used to be. Everyone has changed round here. Now they reproach me with things that before . . . the things I've always done are now considered wrong. Now they reproach me for saying and doing the things . . . I've always said and done.'

'I don't reproach you for anything.'

'You don't, no. But you're a child.'

'That's what you all say,' said Kus-Kus sharply, 'it's what Julian says too.'

Aunt Eugenia turned to look at him. He really was a child. She could not, should not, talk to him as if he were already a man. But why just on this Thursday, a Thursday when he'd come to tea as so often before when they'd been happy, did she have to tell him everything?

'I've always treated you like a grownup, Nicolas.' Kus-Kus opened his eyes wide. It was the first time Aunt Eugenia had said his name like that, without looking at him, her usually lilting voice barely loud enough to be heard. This was a sombre, muted Aunt Eugenia who contrasted in Kus-Kus's eyes (although he wasn't in a state to perceive the contrast very exactly) with the already opaline, nostalgic light that was flooding the room. Aunt Eugenia shifted her weight on to her right elbow and Kus-Kus felt her very close to him, this *other* Aunt Eugenia, one he had never noticed before, who didn't reveal herself in words, but in that act of leaning towards her nephew.

'The tea will get cold, Aunt Eugenia,' said Kus-Kus. And he thought that his aunt smelt a little of anis, as Julian did sometimes.

'The tea?' asked Aunt Eugenia, almost in a whisper. 'The next time I go to Bariloche I won't be coming back. Not this time.'

'I'll pour you a nice hot cup of tea,' said Kus-Kus. 'We could both do with it, couldn't we?'

'Am I very fat, Kus-Kus?'

'You look fine to me, Aunt. The same as always, more or less.'

'Last Tuesday, that is this Tuesday, I was waiting for you to come up. I was so looking forward to you coming and I had to go out for some shopping, you know I don't get out much, and they ignored me, they ignored me, I saw it quite clearly. I popped into the stationer's to buy some writing paper, they always keep some pale blue by for me, you know the sort, for airmail letters, that they don't have in other places, at least not in that colour, and they ignored me . . .'

'Who ignored you?' Kus-Kus fidgeted uncomfortably in his seat. He moved almost imperceptibly away from his aunt, who, almost leaning on him, was perspiring profusely and now smelt unmistakably of anis.

'Who? What does it matter who? You don't know them, I don't know all of them either, apart from one, in fact, who's the same age as me; we came out the same summer, she was unbearable. Now she's older she's a bit better, better at hiding how little charm she has always had, but that summer people talked only of me. Don't you believe me? No one believes me any more.'

'But Aunt,' exclaimed Kus-Kus, moving closer to her, almost brushing against her sad, worried head of reddish hair. The two-stranded beryl necklace, which was Kus-Kus's favourite and which really was magnificent, came undone. Perhaps Aunt Eugenia, in the rush to get everything ready that afternoon, had not fastened it properly. To Kus-Kus the escaping necklace, as it slid from Aunt Eugenia's neck, brushed the cushions of the sofa and at last fell to the carpet (even as it lay on the carpet, just for an instant) seemed caught between three kingdoms: the kingdom of stones that would normally be its own; the kingdom of restless vegetation, multicoloured and carnal; and the rushed, confused kingdom of the sensitive soul, of animal spirits and serpents, of disguises and every type of human clothing and finery. Until its transformations were extinguished in the carpet.

'But Aunt, I believe you, I'd believe anything you said, anything, honestly I would!'

'All we ever do is talk. Do you believe that?' demanded Aunt Eugenia, turning almost fiercely towards her nephew. Kus-Kus, distracted by thoughts of the ambiguous nature of the escaping necklace, said nothing. He thought, however, that this situation was completely unlike any they had shared before.

'All we ever do is talk. I ask him what he's been doing, he's young enough to be my son, after all. It's never him who starts, I give him an opening, of course, it's only natural, but those prigs, those goody-goodies, those hypocrites, don't understand that some women can't live, they can't, Kus-Kus, Nicolas, they can't, not without someone to admire them, someone who . . . who makes them feel, well, something you can't understand, Kus-Kus, you can't understand because you're still very young, though you're already quite the gallant; you're going to be like I was, aren't you? Giacomo was like that too. Yes, Giacomo was just like that. They're very alike, really they are . . .'

'I'm sorry, Aunt, but I don't understand you at all. Who are you talking about? Who are very alike?'

Aunt Eugenia seemed to come to. She sat up and looked hard at the boy in his blue tie with white polka dots, his dark grey jersey and short trousers in pale corduroy, showing his childishly bony knees. He had a scab on the right knee with still-fresh traces of iodine on it. She poured tea for both of them and, in silence, cut a big slice of newly baked fruitcake.

'Thank you, Aunt,' mumbled Kus-Kus, trusting that with that their meeting would return to more familiar channels. Now Aunt Eugenia seemed to be in doubt about something which, though really quite serious, might suddenly seem funny, take an irresponsible turn.

'Who are very alike? Why, Giacomo and Giacomo are as like as two peas!' Aunt Eugenia started laughing with all her old vivacity.

'Giacomo Gattucci?'

'Yes, the very man; he usually brings my order up first thing on Tuesday mornings, and the other day I asked if he had a girlfriend. "No Miss," he said, "They don't give you room to breathe, on at you all day about one thing or another; far better to stay single . . ." And, well, I was curious, yes, curious, only natural don't you think, after all there are weeks, some weeks, when he's the only person I see, you know I don't go out much now I'm so fat, I prefer to stay quietly at home and he, Giacomo, brings me everything, even fruit, the dear boy, though he doesn't sell it himself, he says it's no bother to him to buy it when I need it, and he never wants me to pay him the day before, I couldn't resist teasing him, he was so sweet, with those attentive eyes of his, like black velvet, and such a frank expression, you understand these things, Pichusqui, because you're sensitive like me, so very charming and sensitive to everything . . .'

Kus-Kus fidgeted in his seat again. He was disturbed by the mercurial, blue-yellow-pink crystals of the hexagonal dusk that climbed the uncurtained windows of this strange, double Aunt Eugenia. The sea and bay crouched like some restless beast in the dying light, as did all those things that, were he but to approach the windows, he would still be able to distinguish clearly, although from the other side now, shifting and precise, the perfect boats, the perfect voyagers, the opaline perfection of a city clean and empty as a conscience. Divine. Kus-Kus did not know what to do next. He took a sip of tea which had gone cold and had not been sugared. It left a sharp, somewhat disorienting aftertaste, like the shock when something doesn't taste as one had expected. To get rid of it, he put a small piece of the fruitcake in his mouth, the slice having disintegrated on his plate as if possessed by a destructive will of its own. Aunt Eugenia, having affirmed that Kus-Kus was as sensitive as she, had grown thoughtful, as if, after that bold declaration of their similarity, something in her mind stubbornly began to deny any possible resemblance between them. It was clear to Kus-Kus that that Thursday was going to degenerate into a confession – or confessions — all too exact and carnal. Even to his inexpert ear, what had gone before did not bode well. It was certainly nothing that, in Bariloche, could be considered chic, or could be talked about or listened to with nonchalance.

'Your necklace has fallen off, Aunt Eugenia,' said the boy, watching his aunt, who at that moment was absorbed in the task of removing a ring from one of her fingers. It occurred to him that that was the only thing to say in such circumstances, and that the appropriate action was not to pick up the necklace from the floor, but quite the opposite. Kus-Kus loosened his tie a little, because everything was becoming more and more of a riddle and riddles always discomfited and irritated him.

'I asked him if he had a girlfriend,' said Aunt Eugenia as if talking to herself. Kus-Kus pulled off a bit of loose skin from his thumb, an enormous hangnail that, almost as an afterthought, opened up a little channel of burning pain along the raw skin. At the same time, he had the feeling that Aunt Eugenia had said exactly the same thing only minutes before . . .

'I mean I asked Giacomo. It just happened, well, we've known each other for so long, at least by sight, and lately some days I get a bit lonely, he asked me why I wanted to know, that was the first thing he asked me, before saying that he didn't have one, and didn't want one, that we women were a terrible bore . . .'

'He said that? Well, he seems a bit rude this chap, if you ask me!'

Aunt Eugenia burst out laughing, and in doing so became her usual self again. 'You do get some funny ideas sometimes, Nicolas!' she said, clucking like a broody hen over the word Nicolas, which she pronounced as three distinct syllables. 'It wasn't rude at all! I was grateful to him, you see, for including me like that, so naturally, amongst all the boring tiresome women who pester him, it made me feel younger, you see, when he said that . . .'

'And then what? Then what?' asked the boy abruptly.

'We kissed each other.'

'But why?'

'Why?'

'You mean you just started right in kissing each other, just like that? In all the films Miss Hart sees, the kiss comes at the end, Aunt Eugenia; even Josefa waits till the end, at the door, to give her new boyfriend from across the way a big kiss; the last thing they do at the back door is kiss each other on the mouth, with their tongues touching, Josefa says he's just like

Errol Flynn. Wishful thinking I reckon, but anyway, how was it? Did you both just suddenly feel like kissing each other on the mouth like Josefa and Errol Flynn?'

Aunt Eugenia hadn't realised that it was already eight o'clock. And neither she nor Kus-Kus heard the telephone ringing in the hall. Aunt Eugenia had picked up the necklace by now and had put it back on, closing the clasp carefully this time. For lack of a glass, she served herself a cup of sherry from a blue, engraved decanter with a silver top while she listened to the chatter of her nephew, for whom kisses were mostly still a joke, something people did in films . . .

'We were in the hall at the back, the two of us . . . it was . . . it was the most natural thing to do, I think, don't you? Then he said did I want to see him again, he asked me if I wanted to see him, because just then he had to do his other deliveries and I was, you can imagine, completely stunned . . . I'm sure you'd find Giacomo delightful too, Kus-Kus, don't you think so?'

'I don't know.'

'What are you thinking? What were you thinking just now when you frowned? Tell me the truth!'

'Well, whether if after kissing each other you're engaged or not . . . Josefa says that kissing each other is the most important thing of all and that both of you get a sort of funny tingle all through your mouth and all over your face, right down to the nape of your neck. I gave Josefa a kiss to see but I didn't feel anything, she said I wasn't old enough and that I just made her mouth all full of saliva, that's what Josefa said, this chap, this . . . Giacomo, I expect he knows how to kiss well, doesn't he, Aunt Eugenia?'

'Giacomo? Really, the things you come out with!'

At that moment the front doorbell rang loudly. They leapt to their feet and, almost falling over each other, rushed to the hall. Kus-Kus went first. Aunt Eugenia followed behind, panting, her right hand on her prodigious heaving bosom. The doorbell rang again, two firm rings this time.

'It must be Miss Hart come up to fetch me. It must be quite late.'

It was indeed Miss Hart, who said simply: 'I hope he's behaved himself this time. Have you, Nick?' And they went downstairs, Kus-Kus remembering as they went Aunt Eugenia's final anxious warning before opening the door: 'Please, it's a secret between you and me, a secret!'

6

Maria del Carmen Villacantero assured everyone that both of them would feel much less alone if they divided the apartment, she and Eugenia. And that she wouldn't mind in the least renting a part of the mansards or even buying her part were they to divide them, because she was already used to sharing everything with her mother and, after all, that's what the daily lives of most ordinary normal mortals is about, sharing the things, however small, however large, that one had so that later one did not find oneself alone and unloved, affection plays such a big part in women's lives, well, it's what you'd expect, she'd be quite happy with the kitchen, the study, that little tiny bathroom and the other little room, that she seemed to remember even had a teeny weeny bedroom with a skylight that opened directly on to the terraces between the chimneys and the next house, and she could remember in the old days how they used to hang out the washing there, a wonderful place to hang clothes, well, they dried in an instant, sheets, towels, all the big things, it was even good for beating carpets, since one end of the line was attached to a main beam and you could hang a carpet over it, a whole one if you wanted and nothing would happen, a good spring clean, a good thorough clean, when needed, yes, that would be the best thing, give all the carpets in the house a general clean, if they divided the mansards . . .

Of course she didn't want to insist because, if she insisted, it would look as if she had some interest in it, well, how could she not have, it was only natural she should, what with her bedridden mother, completely crippled, with her nerves you know, but those cases were the worst kind, sometimes she was stubborn, like a capricious child, spoiled and capricious, that was what she was, and she'd had to put up with it all her life, and she was sure that Eugenia too, in the long term and the short term, both really, would be much better off, in a better position, much less exposed to things, not like she was now, a woman alone with no servants, exposed to all kinds of things; on the other hand with Maria del Carmen Villacantero on the other side of the wall, she'd just have to call, at a moment's notice, just call, she could be relied on, absolutely, nothing would stand in her way, just like her father, God rest his soul, a man who was solid as a rock, and to relax they could do their sewing together, the three of them, Eugenia, Maria del Carmen and Maria del Carmen's mother, why not? they could make some table linen for Mercedes, that you'd love, wouldn't you love that? linen's something you can never have too much of, and her mother, well the poor thing couldn't exactly help but she wouldn't be in the way either, how could she, the poor thing, get in the way, that is, no, and she liked a bit of company in the afternoons and Maria del Carmen Villacantero would make fried bread for tea for the three of them and if little Nicolas came up, for the four of them, and if Mercedes came up . . . well, imagine how lovely the five of them having tea together, she'd make hot chocolate, and use the best bread for frying. Much better than a thin loaf, a round loaf, good country bread, the best bread for frying, Eugenia with that sweet tooth of hers would just love Maria del Carmen's fried bread, because Maria del Carmen did not soak it in milk, never in milk, good heavens never in milk, because milk gives the bread a cakey taste and ruins the spongy texture, she had it all worked out, just leave the bread slices to soak in a little bit of water and then straight into the frying pan with them, cover them in oil, very hot oil, the very best you could get, of course, oh but oil was delicious, she just adored oil, like a cat with cream she was where oil was concerned, well, anyway, she loved it, so, you simply put them in the frying pan one by one until they were just turning golden and then served them immediately, dusted with masses of sugar, oh, how Eugenia would enjoy it if they divided the apartment, Maria del Carmen Villacantero would make do with the part Eugenia liked least, she wouldn't mind at all, and as regards costs and expenses they could be shared and, for example, Maria del Carmen Villacantero could do the shopping for the three of them, and what would three women on their own spend, hardly a thing, and the three of them would get on like a dream and it wouldn't be much trouble, even the construction work involved would not, after all, be that much trouble, and she'd take care of that, she wouldn't stand for any impertinence from some young whippersnapper, she'd give him a box round the ears, she would, you bet she would, a simple brick wall and that would be it, and how her mother, the poor thing, would enjoy it, being so eccentric, because her eccentricities all came from her having all her life been spoiled, who knows, she might even get thinner, because excess fat, of this Mercedes could be quite sure, the excess fat one put on after a certain age might well have a lot to do with the endocrine glands, she couldn't say for sure because she didn't have enough medical knowledge to come down on one side or the other, but a lot of it was due to being too much alone, you ate out of pure boredom, whether you had a thyroid problem or not, and Aunt Eugenia must on no account take thyroxine, dear God no, because she might well take it out of desperation at being such a fatty and then be unable to control herself and fall ill but then if, God forbid, if she did fall ill, she'd have two women there, and not have to depend on anyone, least of all on certain people, and then as for her mother, as for Maria del Carmen's mother, if they divided the mansards, the family would be performing a genuine act of charity, because her mother once quietly installed up there, if they divided the mansards, would be in seventh heaven and as both of them, both Maria del Carmen Villacantero and her mother, adored, were just mad about flowers and birds and as there was a little terrace, yes, Maria del Carmen Villacantero thought there was, yes, she was quite sure there was a little terrace at the back, because she remembered going up there in the old days, long before Aunt Eugenia moved into the mansards, because ever since she was a child she had always loved heights, yes, really loved them, even if it was only a little garret, a *guardilla,* to use a good Castilian word, Castile, conqueror of empires who let nothing stand in her way, nothing, what people, fine people who came to be the *non plus ultra* of the whole world, much more so than the United States today and with much more class, there was no comparison, and, of course, as Eugenia at the end of the Civil War was in a financial situation that for that time, imagine, was like being in the lap of luxury, and she, on the other hand, what with having to look after her mother, poor thing, a complete invalid, well, what was she to do, and she never said a word, never a word to anyone, not even to Mercedes, her best friend since childhood, no, she was silent as the grave, that's not for the likes of you, Maria del Carmen, she thought, you be satisfied with your little flat and give thanks to God that you've got three windows on to the street, even though you've only got a goldfinch and some little tiny flowerpots, no one can take them away from you, money doesn't buy everything, Maria del Carmen was quite prepared to declare to the world, her head held high, that there are some things that not even money, no amount of money, can help a woman keep as safe as they should be kept, but gracious, there she'd been talking all afternoon, Mercedes must have a headache from listening to her, ah, how sweet of her to say that her head didn't ache and to be so interested in everything, how good Mercedes was to her, that couldn't be repaid with money either and what superb, freshly made scones there always were in Mercedes's house, what a superb touch Mercedes had with any sort of baking and especially puff pastry, she remembered some puff pastry that she gave them once, quail vol-au-vents they were, what exquisite puff pastry, just exquisite, Maria del Carmen could remember it to this day and she must give her the recipe if they divided the mansards so that Maria del Carmen Villacantero could try it and see if it turned out as light for her, though how could it? well, it just wouldn't because that touch with pastry was something you either have in your blood or you don't, no cook male or female, no French chef could make puff pastry as light as that... What's more dividing the mansards was the best way, the only way, of putting a stop once and for all to that business, because things were getting very bad, very bad indeed...

Things were getting very bad and, in all conscience, she had no option but to tell Mercedes... in all conscience Maria del Carmen Villacantero had no option, it was all true what they said was happening, what was that, Mercedes? Mercedes must forgive Maria del Carmen but she hadn't heard her, absorbed as she was in the sound of her own voice, she must forgive her, she must... It seems that Mercedes, on the very day that Maria del Carmen and she were lunching in Kus-Kus's parents' house, had come across Eugenia looking very upset and, in Mercedes's opinion, God forgive her, frankly, not to mince words, inebriated, or at least drinking much more than is usual at such family gatherings. Something was wrong and she thought too that the poor thing was even fatter than the previous spring when Eugenia had turned up without warning at the mass for Federico Pizarro, and Cristina still in floods of tears every time Federico's name was mentioned in the prayers, what was that, Maria del Carmen? Had Mercedes heard correctly, because if she had heard what she thought she had heard, she could scarcely believe her ears ... so that *was* what she had said, eh? Well, you're quite wrong. Some people were as stupid, ignorant and dim-witted as mules and why this affectation of Maria del Carmen Villacantero's of being a tiny bit surprised at such a show of grief, was she calling Mercedes a liar to her face? because if that was the case, it was better to say so clearly, and not go beating about the bush, so come on, speak up, speak up, what was that? Maria del Carmen Villacantero shouldn't be so mealy-mouthed, Mercedes couldn't hear what she was saying, yes, mealy-mouthed, talking out of the corner of her mouth like that, the same awful way nuns talked amongst themselves and the way they did in the convent schools that produced those dim-witted girls, Maria del Carmen Villacantero should speak up, speak up, it was so much better in England, where the Church of England, the High Church, had some very clear ideas, all the little girls playing football, doing horse-riding, fit to burst their lungs and then going perspiring and exhausted to bed, that was healthy, that was elegant, not like these poor prim, affected prigs, who got broader and broader in the beam after sixteen years of sitting down all day doing nothing but gossip over their little bits of lace-making, with behinds as big as old sows', and what did she mean, Mercedes shouldn't get upset like that, like what? she'd get upset any way she wanted to, all right? anyway, had Maria del Carmen Villacantero heard her or would Mercedes have to repeat it all over again, even louder? and as to being surprised, that was nonsense, firstly, Maria del Carmen Villacantero didn't come to tea to be surprised by what Mercedes said, and secondly, Federico and Cristina had been a much closer couple than most, much closer, was Maria del Carmen listening? and Mercedes had known Cristina since she was a child and loved her like a daughter and she was sure she was deeply in love when she married and still was and would always be an inconsolable widow, that was all there was to it, neither more nor less, so Maria del Carmen Villacantero should give up these stupid ideas and suspicions, and stop acting like some silly little nun on visiting day . . .

Sorry, heavens, of course, she was just a poor provincial and of course Mercedes must forgive her at once, she realised how totally mistaken she had been about almost everything, no, not almost everything, but everything, everything, and she realised that she was a poor, foolish wretch, oh, how awful, oh dear, oh dear, would Mercedes please lower her voice, what would they think of Maria del Carmen, it would look as if Mercedes was telling her off, and after all what more could they ask for, that was just what they wanted, to see her scolded, insulted and unhappy . . . and that was no suspicion, no, it would be better to go into Mercedes's sitting room because in the dining room Maria del Carmen might so easily be overheard, misunderstood, misinterpreted, and if Mercedes wouldn't mind, couldn't they do what they did every afternoon after tea and go into her little living room so they could clear this all up and at the same time they could sit round the table with the electric heater on and the two of them would be more comfortable, get back to normal, because what Maria del Carmen Villacantero had meant to say was that she . . .

7

He went to wait for them at the station, afraid that both of them would turn up. He hadn't slept all night; neither had Josefa, or so she told him at breakfast. He'd tossed and turned, smoked cigarettes until he ran out of them at four in the morning, coughed and cursed, his eyes watering, and then gone to the bathroom for a drink of water and to take a piss, the rather murky piss of an insomniac. That detail, or the fact that he had thought so much about it during the night, seemed, now that he felt wearier and calmer, drinking coffee in the station buffet, the most typical symptom of days like the one that was just beginning. He'd been celibate for nearly three months, he thought, feeling sorry for himself and at the same time making fun of his old obsessions, and he'd felt fine, and now it was the same old thing starting up all over again ... He kept worrying about what would happen: whether he would have to confront both of them, or just one of them, and in that case, which one ... It had been over two years now. On the other hand, as always, there was something enjoyable about his nervousness, a certain carnal enjoyment, a quickened sense that the world was not passing away in the torpor of the refuge the manageress had found for him. The train was an hour late. He had arrived an hour early, at eight in the morning. The newspaper stand didn't open till ten; he bought cigarettes in the buffet, but they didn't have any matches, and he would never ask for a light in the street; he hated people asking him for a light in the street. It was a cold, sharp morning from which all the blue had withdrawn; he could hear the whistles of other trains; he saw groups of clammy travellers standing round suitcases, baskets, as if evacuating the city. Just then, exactly as the bus had raced up to the stop three months before, the train raced up to the platform, suddenly closing the circle and releasing him from the unease that had paralysed him until then. Which of them would it be? Wouldn't it be better to meet them both at once, to hear it all, once and for all, for them to get the whole thing off their consciences? He quickly put on his dark glasses and dabbed at his watering eyes, lifting the glasses a little as he ran his finger round his eyelids. From behind his glasses the darkened landscape all at once took on a certain bitter charm, had a warmer, summery, suntanned feel to it. The train, an express with a lot of carriages, stretched right along the platform. The porters ran towards the first-class coaches. They'll have come first class, if they came together. The crowds disconcerted him; he was standing almost next to the engine now, afraid he might miss them. He was sure of it now: they would both come. Would they have booked a hotel? Or a boarding house, or anything?

'You're looking good,' she said from behind him.

He didn't say anything when he turned round. He hoped she wouldn't notice that he looked around in vain for her companion. Ah, so that was it, after all. It was really him he wanted to see. He remembered the manageress, as one remembers the name of someone who has died, or, indistinctly, the smell of a certain place when speaking of that person to others. 'I won't answer for you again,' he remembered her saying. 'Don't go thinking about anyone you shouldn't think about.'

'No, he didn't come. I came on my own. Have you got a cigarette? Don't just stand there, let's go and have a coffee! What's wrong with you?'

He reacted in time and took her arm. She was wearing her

coat with the collar turned up. He remembered that collar, how it had sheltered him when he had kissed her, two years ago, in the Retiro Gardens in Madrid, in dressing rooms, in the corridors of boarding houses and trains, anywhere, as soon as they could get away from him, on any pretext, for just a moment.

'There's no need to hide. You know perfectly well he doesn't care,' she used to say. But Julian had never wanted him to see them embrace, see him kissing her. 'If he loves you he must suffer, like any normal person; if he loves you and sees us together, he must get jealous, like anyone else . . . I'd kill you, if it were me,' he argued. And she always replied the same way, always in the same tone of voice, quiet, cold, exciting. 'But it's obvious that you're just an ordinary man, jealous and ordinary, whereas he, he is a god.'

She let him take her arm; let herself be led far from the platform, far from the station, without their speaking to or looking at each other, until they reached the port. They were used to walking arm in arm. Very close together, with the same brisk stride. The body, he thought, remembers everything. And he thought there was one body made from their two which, when they separated, had become the longing of each of them. Or, at least, he – for she was unfathomable – felt the lack of that third, almost tangible body made from their two entwined bodies as if he had lost part of himself.

The gentle, shining beryl colours of the sea had turned green; a green that recalled the pale but pungent tones of a transfer stuck to the bathroom tiles. There was a rowing boat a few yards in front of them that floated, poised like a bird on its keel, and as it rose and fell monotonously on the restless surface of the jetty waters, it made little splashing noises.

'There are some fish swimming down there, can you see? Here they come,' she said.

She sounded like a little girl when she said that. He snatched off his dark glasses, hating her.

'Did you come here to see the sea?' he asked, letting go of her arm, but without moving away; they could both feel the still warm, slight awkwardness of mutual irritation.

'Among other things, yes, I did come to see the sea. I was born here, you know.'

'No, I didn't know,' he said, a shudder running through him.

He put his glasses on again. He could feel the tears caused by his chronic ailment building up in his eyes, deforming his whole face behind the glasses that afforded him some compassionate, bitter protection.

'They're very small,' she added, leaning out a little over the iridescent green of the waters.

There it was, he thought. It was clear now. The horrible truth. He wasn't a god. He wasn't even the opposite of a god. He was simply a bad lot, as the hotel manageress would have said. But the truth was there, in what he remembered of Esther, prefacing the words that she would doubtless soon speak. The ridiculous, abstract passion of all that talk about gods. The extravagant words, theatrical, inadequate. Yes, that was the worst thing: that the immensity of those supposedly divine qualities, bestowed with such monotonous regularity, helped to hide, in the collective consciousness of the three of them, the fact that there was nothing, however remote, that could substantiate them. At least he saw that clearly now. But too late. It was too late for such perceptions: he, the other he, his alter ego. To Julian, the sharper the contrast with those godlike qualities she attributed to Rafael, the more unforgettable and seductive he became. And he – his other self – had been seduced while he was seducing the other man's wife. It was a revenge that no one could have foreseen. A revenge taken by the situation itself, that took place behind the backs of the characters involved in it.

. . . him and him and her . . . The three monsters of a fable that seemed never to end. There was always something new

. . . like this last thing, the information Esther had just given him out of the blue. Now Esther was looking at him.

'I didn't know you came from here,' said Julian.

'Does it surprise you? You look surprised. Even I have to come from somewhere.'

'I suppose so. You never talk . . . never talked about yourself . . . then . . .'

'There's not much to say.'

'You like to keep a few tricks up your sleeve, is that it?'

'Tricks? You're imagining things.'

'We hate each other now.'

'Really?'

'You know perfectly well it's true.'

'I didn't know you hated me.'

'This is all a stupid farce. Tell me once and for all why you've come. It's over two years now. I didn't want it to go on, you know that . . .'

'It's our duty to remind the faithful flock that God exists, don't you think? Give me a cigarette. You didn't hear me at the station, or you pretended not to.'

'How long do you intend staying?'

'A while. But I don't know where yet . . . I should visit my family, don't you think?'

'What are you plotting?'

'Rafael needs ten thousand pesetas by the end of the month. Lend it to him. You've got nearly a fortnight to get it . . . and what's more you've got a job, no expenses, no troublesome friends, you're far from Madrid . . . very far . . . You've come a long way!'

'A year in prison. Rafael cost me a year in prison . . . and I was lucky. I was lucky twice: when they gave me my sentence and when I came out after serving it . . .'

'So I heard. It seems old ladies like to look after you. You don't seem the type. But then there's no accounting for taste . . . Don't look so gloomy! Let's go . . . that's enough sea for today.'

'I haven't got ten thousand pesetas. I wouldn't lend it to you if I had, let's get that quite clear. I'm through with you both.'

'I don't know if you'll be able to live without me, Julian. Without Rafael. You remember Rafael?'

'I suppose so. I have to, don't I?'

'Of course you do. More and more. He's been ill. Seriously ill this time.'

'What do you want me to do about it? Why does he want ten thousand pesetas? It's a lot of money. A lot. What has he done? He didn't tell me anything on the phone . . .'

'It didn't seem wise . . . on the phone. You went crazy, he said. He said he had to repeat everything two or three times, because you just couldn't grasp it . . . How much do you earn?'

'Are you thinking of staying around until I get paid? It's not exactly your style. You'd get bored here. It's a quiet place. I go out very little. To a film once a week. And for walks . . . not much else.'

'How much do you earn?'

'Not even a tenth of what Rafael is asking. I'm quite content with the job. Gives me plenty of free time.'

'My parents were in service – is that what you call it? – in service for years in the same house you're in now. I imagine it must have been for the grandparents. I'm not sure. I was already in Madrid. Until the Civil War started. They managed to get the whole family into Portugal. My father had informed on one of the boys, and he got bumped off. It was a foul thing to do. My father was a coward. A repulsive coward. Franco's men shot the boy right away, the very night they liberated the town; he was stupid too, he didn't even try to hide for a couple of months, or run off to the mountains . . . nothing, the stupid fool.'

They found themselves in the business part of town, in the gloomy, noisy, rather steep streets behind the port. The quality of the buildings had noticeably deteriorated. Undistinguished blocks of flats whose façades, covered balconies and verandahs had nothing dashing or maritime about them. They belonged to the interior, far from the absolute nobility of the ocean.

He felt tired, and much more worried than he looked. He must try to affect indifference, confidence ... He sighed, knowing that with Esther, alone with her, it was a wasted effort. Everything was useless now, he thought desperately, feeling, at the same time as his desperation grew like a fever, or like the subliminal effect of a shot of whisky, sexually – albeit vaguely – aroused. Nothing had changed. The manageress at the hotel would have been horrified. At least, thought Julian bitterly, she can have the satisfaction of having been right about everything. They sat down in the corner of a bar. It was Esther who was leading him now. If she could see her, thought Julian, if she could just see her dragging me, linking me forever to her unbelievable failure, if she could see us like God sees us going into this bar, sitting down, ordering two white coffees. I'm speaking from memory, from hearsay, because I don't know if there is a God or not, and I don't care, thought Julian, saying out loud: 'I haven't got ten thousand pesetas, Esther, that goes without saying; I haven't got it ... Couldn't it be a bit less?'

'Now that's more like it!'

'What is?' asked Julian almost mechanically, feeling defeated.

'That last question, about whether it couldn't be a bit less. It shows you're open to discussion ... Well, Julian, Rafael really does need exactly ten thousand ... But it could be a bit less ... Yes, it could be a bit less ... Why not? A little bit less, anyway, not much ...'

'It will have to be a lot less, less than half. It'll have to be a quarter of the ten thousand ... or nothing, Esther. I haven't got a penny saved ... And what about you, are you going to contribute? It would be a nice way of making amends...'

'I don't look after the money side, darling. I'm the Holy Virgin, remember. Money's your business, men's business. I shouldn't even be here in this filthy café you've brought me to ... I'm an actress, or have you forgotten that too? Give me a cigarette. You came without bothering to shave ... unforgivable, darling, unforgivable ... here am I, a leading lady, a superb, immaculate star ... and you haven't shaved! Am I making you suffer? Two years ago you found suffering exciting; Rafael made you suffer a lot. You really needed it, suffering suited you if I remember rightly; poor Julian, neither of us ever loved you ... perhaps I did, at first, a little bit, out of curiosity, out of vengeance. Why did you persist in that role of juvenile lead? You weren't young even two years ago, Julian, and you're a bit repulsive with that conjunctivitis, with your eyes always watering; I remember how you seemed older to me naked ... and then you could have done with being circumcised ... you don't look so good in the nude, you really don't look so good ... and that trouble with your foreskin ... you should have had it seen to ... anyway, there was something a bit disgusting about you, you were like a little boy ... and we never did really fuck, remember, never ... we began and had to stop because you couldn't get its little head to poke out properly...'

'How long are you staying?'

'Not long. Not long at all, in fact. I find the sea oppressive; I hate it ... you haven't said a single nice word to me all the time we've been together ... what time is it? Give me a cigarette, I want to go. Pay for the coffees ... didn't you have a whole packet a while ago? Rafael loves you, you know. In his way. I know. I never leave his side, maternal instinct I suppose it must be. I know that he loves you. He understands you, Julian. He *understands* you, don't you see? And you're not the easiest of people, half-impotent as you've become through disuse. Does that wretched foreskin really hurt so much? If I was a man in that state at your age, I'd cut it off myself, it must be less bother than having an abortion, for example. Haven't you got a razor handy at home?'

'What did we do to you, Esther, to make you hate me so much?' he murmured at last as, almost with a jump, he stood up, asking the waiter for the bill, dredging up as if from his own body, that third, incorporeal body, the only one now, the strength to get away from the insane, level, monotonous gaze that held him; his own eyes, perhaps, looking out at him, from that incomprehensible woman whom he had kissed, when Rafael's back was turned, before he loved him, in the Retiro, in dressing rooms, in corridors, in theatre toilets, everywhere because, because . . .

She was looking at him, frowning a little, her eyes slightly closed as if she were in a bright light. They were in the street now. Staring at each other without saying a word. Was Esther pretty? Was she a pretty woman? Was she a beautiful creature, in any sense – human or otherwise – of the word 'beautiful'? Julian had never known.

'He needs ten thousand pesetas, Julian. It could be less, but it really has to be ten thousand. Do it for Rafael. He's dying. I'm telling you the truth now, I wasn't before, but now I am. I'm an actress, remember, don't pay any attention to me; Julian, he's desperate and he's counting on you . . . I think I'll stay here for a few days, the sea calms me a lot, I've loved it ever since I was a child, in secret; you know, the vastness of the sea is soothing, the sea is God, I think; in His way God is like a strong current from the Pacific Ocean, don't you think, a kind of Gulf Stream. I'm going . . . I'll phone you tomorrow.'

The houses and the streets behind the port were like the livid transfers of a reflected consciousness that could not, as it was reflected, contain itself, or love itself, or cease to contemplate itself . . . Julian's eyes were streaming by the time he got home.

8

It's impossible to say if his eyes were merely watering or if he was crying. It could have been either of the two. After all, both were chronic conditions, his conjunctivitis and his grief. Ever since he was a child. As far back as he could remember. Whenever reality let him down he had always had one of two reactions – either he would cry or his eyes would start to water. As a child Julian had identified with the selflessness of his mother, giving way beneath the tyranny of his father's questions, and in his eyes she had always stood by him like a guardian angel. The ridiculous images of guardian angels in the popular religion of the time had irritated him. His mother was, like the house in which they lived, that pokey little second-floor apartment in a working-class area of Madrid, the point from which he took his bearings. He came and he went, got together with friends, or played truant, knowing that that woman would never give anyone else his place in the damp apartment in Cuatro Caminos, and that he didn't even have to make any special effort to keep it. When his mother died and her husband, Julian's father, a figure of some influence in the porter's lodge of a bank, insisted on milking his grief for all it was worth at work, Julian fled the house – he hid in the home of some cousins with whom his father was not on speaking terms – and he would have fled consciousness and life itself. He was only sixteen then. Without realising it, the cousins – two girls and a boy of about Julian's age – saved his life. He didn't go back to that house in Cuatro Caminos.

He didn't attend the miserable funeral his father organised. He managed to get a job as a bell-boy in a hotel on the main avenue of Madrid. He'd always been lucky with jobs. He spent six years there. He had been a tall, thin boy and the manager had taken to him. Julian could still remember him solemnly, greedily lighting a cigar after each meal. It was in the first-floor linen cupboard that Julian had masturbated for the first time. He could remember every detail; the smell of the linen, the cramped space, the shelves piled with spare bedlinen, almost like an extension of his own body. And the damp mark the semen left on his trouser leg, which for weeks had made him the butt of malicious jokes in the kitchen . . . 'You'd be better off doing that in the bog, where no one will see you. Just bolt the door and away you go,' said one of the kitchen hands, who was a couple of years older than him and who, amongst the younger hotel employees, was thought to be a bit of a lad. 'But, listen, don't overdo it, you can go mad if you go at it at all hours, like a bloke I knew, a real mangy bugger . . . do it with someone else, it's healthier.' And Julian did it with the kitchen hand who, as well as being known as a bit of a lad, was also said to be queer.

Safe in his room that afternoon, Julian smiled. Why should those adolescent memories surface now? Because he couldn't rid himself of the physical presence of Esther that morning, nor of the memory – horribly intensified – of Rafael. It was supper time. Since coming in he had not left his room. Josefa came to call him a couple of times as supper approached, putting on her finest, most affected telephone voice, just in case. Kus-Kus appeared after supper. And Julian, without knowing why, opened the door to him.

'This is from all of us,' the boy announced, offering Julian a fried-egg sandwich. 'Josefa told me to come when Miss Hart had gone to bed and now she has. Josefa said you were more likely to open the door to me than to her and that she was going to cry herself to sleep, and she said that before she wasn't calling you because anything was wrong and that she loves you like a sister although I already told her that you didn't have any sisters, several times I had to tell her that.' Kus-Kus installed himself on the bed to see if Julian would eat the sandwich. It was rather touching in a way. And it must have touched Julian; or perhaps Kus-Kus just appeared at one of those fragile, painful points in our lives when, so as not to be crushed by our sadness, we unburden ourselves to whoever happens to be there. Julian recounted to Kus-Kus the whole of his interview with Esther that morning, together with much else that came out by the by, running – so to speak – along the gutters of the story. He told the whole tale like a blind man, like someone who flees from what he tells and keeps on telling it in order to flee from it, without looking back, without the remotest idea, when the tale is told, of whether he has given the essentials or just a part or if he has utterly bared his soul to an irresponsible audience. Julian just knew that when he finished his mouth was dry, his tongue was leaden, there was some whitish saliva in the corners of his mouth, as Kus-Kus kindly informed him, and the remains of the sandwich lay on his plate. Apparently he'd been eating and talking at the same time. When he tried to remember, he found himself answering the boy instead.

'Of course I've got a mother . . .' said Julian to Kus-Kus, who by now had been in his room for an hour and who, in the light of what had been revealed, and concerned by his accomplice's evident anxiety, wanted to know why Julian did not ask his mother for the ten thousand pesetas. 'But Julian, surely you've got a mother!' Kus-Kus had exclaimed a moment before, feeling, to judge by the extravagant things he said and did, almost angry to see his fellow-conspirator so trapped and powerless to get what he wanted.

'Of course I've got a mother . . .' Julian repeated, '. . . or did have, which comes to the same thing. What do you mean?' and added, 'This is no time for joking.'

'I'm not joking. I thought your mother was alive. If she were alive you could ask her for it . . . after all, it's not that much . . .'

He was a child. Julian suddenly saw the situation as it really was. He'd been telling all that to a child, hoping for advice about things for which a grown-up would have had no answers. What's more, he was a child who had understood nothing. Or maybe he'd understood and was making fun of him? Standing there in his pyjamas, he looked like an elf. Like some very finely drawn and lacquered gnome, straight off a piece of porcelain on which, having jumped free, he left a little empty space in the dubious subterranean pastoral scene: what did I tell him? I don't think I told him everything, thought Julian, and said, unwittingly echoing Aunt Eugenia's words, 'What I just told you is a secret. It's a secret . . . a secret between two members, like you and me . . . of the same gang. We're part of the gang, you and me, and there are others too who you'll meet some day . . . We're a very important gang in Madrid, a secret one and, well . . . we swear an oath when we join, in blood . . .'

'I haven't sworn any oath,' said Kus-Kus, with unexpected sharpness.

Julian was startled. 'You're not going to tell on me?' he said, using the expression, so inadequate now, which all through his youth had most terrified him.

'I'll have to swear the oath too, won't I? To join the gang, I mean.'

'Of course, the oath, of course you will, you swear the oath to join, we all do, in blood, you have to swear in blood . . .' said Julian, seeing that the boy had not in fact understood anything and wasn't laughing at him. After all, to this child ten thousand pesetas was not very much. Lucky child, Julian thought, a hundred pesetas probably seems more money to him. Still, what he had told him, however much or little, couldn't be unsaid. Julian couldn't remember if he'd told him everything, or only a little, given him only a general outline. He had mentioned the names of Esther and Rafael, of that much he was sure . . . but what could they mean to a child?

'Who do you love most, Julian, Esther or Rafael?' asked the boy.

'I love them both equally, both the same. Why? Why do you ask?'

'I don't know . . . it's just that it's Rafael you talk about all the time, that's why I asked . . .'

'Are you sure that's the only reason?'

'Why else would I ask? It's Rafael you talked about most. Is he nice? It's hard to tell from what you say . . . Sometimes he seems a bit arrogant . . . the sort who cares a lot what girls say about him, that sort of thing . . . What does he look like? Is he handsome like Giacomo Gattucci? To be a gigolo you have to be handsome; Aunt Eugenia says I'm going to be a really good gigolo when I grow up, that's what she says, because you have to be handsome. Am I handsome, do you think? You are . . . I think you're much more handsome than Errol Flynn, with that little moustache . . . have you seen *Robin Hood*? It was on for three whole weeks last winter at the Alameda. Miss Hart didn't want to take me because she said the film was unsuitable for children just because there's a bit of kissing in it, you see Miss Hart had already seen the film with her friend and she didn't tell me about the part where the boy and the girl kiss but I saw it on the posters. There was no way I could persuade her to take me even when I promised her I'd close my eyes during the kissing parts if she wanted, I didn't care if I didn't see those bits, I've seen it millions of times anyway, it's no big deal . . . Do you and Rafael kiss? Aunt Eugenia kissed the boy from the shop last Tuesday, she said they just couldn't help themselves.'

'What would I be doing kissing a man? I didn't say anything about that, I didn't say that, that's disgusting . . .'

'I don't see why . . . if you love him that much,' said Kus-Kus.

Julian watched Kus-Kus out of the corner of his eye now, wondering if that child – whom the manageress at the Hotel Principe Alfonso had made such a thing of – was not, after all, going to turn out to be some sort of sprite, some powerful, evil elf or, almost worse, the opposite: an innocent, the only innocent creature in the story. While he watched him, he realised that the child had just said something odd about the aunt, the fat redhead who lived in the mansards; something about her kissing or not kissing someone; he didn't feel any curiosity, but as drowsiness overtook him the conversation had removed a lot of the obsessive urgency that Esther had given her story. The fact that Esther was so near, on a folding bed in some modest flat in the backstreets of a dark city of which the façade, the maritime city, knows nothing, that she would be gathering information, preparing some plan, some revenge, if Julian didn't get the money by the agreed date, this vague, worrying fact shifted, with the child's rather inconsequential chatter, to the middle distance, then to the background. So what the boy had just said about that aunt of his seemed worth hearing again, this time with more attention.

'Who did you say your aunt kissed? I didn't quite catch the name.'

'I don't know his name . . . anyway, it's a secret, she told me in secret.'

'And you don't want to betray her. That's good, very good . . . I'd do the same. Secrets, all secrets, are sacred . . . the only thing is, well, it's up to you, but in the gang, in this gang of mine I told you about, we don't have secrets . . . among ourselves I mean . . . I've been completely honest with you, I just think you should be the same with me . . .'

'But I don't know what this boy's called, really I don't. Aunt Eugenia calls him Giacomo because she says he looks like a lover she once had called Giacomo, Giacomo Gattucci.'

'Oh, right,' said Julian, yawning.

'It's the boy from the grocer's, a stocky chap, who delivers to the houses. He comes here sometimes. Do you know the one I mean?'

It was nearly midnight. The boy's chatter had made him sleepy. What did it all matter? What did it matter who the fat woman's boyfriend was, if she really did have a boyfriend. What did Rafael matter? thought Julian, surprising himself with the thought, as if falling asleep was like entering a dense forest, after which the heart might be able to forget. The forest of forgetting was a little story Esther used to tell the two of them when they were all inseparable, not like now. He woke with a start two hours later, shivering. The clock in the hall struck three. He got dressed as if he had to go out at once. He'd been dreaming that he'd met Rafael at Irun Station and that they were crossing the border in a little Fiat and they were laughing. They reached St Jean de Luz and the weather was very good; although it was summer the shop windows and the streets and the pretty little French houses with shutters painted pale blue looked blurred, dull, washed out like in autumn when the sky clouds over, and the plane trees were just like the sparse, dripping plane trees in the Plaza de San Andres that Julian had seen . . . perhaps the day before, before catching the train; in spite of all that it was hot and they went swimming just in their underpants, playing amongst the foaming waves that broke in silence, and then they lay down on the little empty beach, where an alsatian was barking at them, keeping its distance, and again he couldn't quite hear it . . . and then the police, in plain clothes, rushed down on them barking out insults . . . A kick in the stomach woke him . . . Getting dressed when he woke up was almost like a defensive reflex action which, now he was awake, prolonged the anxiety of the dream. 'Where am I going to get hold of ten thousand pesetas? I can't even steal it,' he was thinking. There was nothing of value in the house, he thought, nothing that might just disappear and be sold for a quick profit. Would it be worth asking Miss Hart? Amongst the kitchen staff Miss Hart had a reputation for being thrifty, even tightfisted. A reputation for being well-off because, according to Maria Soterraña, they even paid her wages direct into her bank account, which, again according to Maria Soterraña, was a sure sign that she had many, many, thousands; banks being what they are were not going to let her open an account if she wasn't going to start depositing a fair bit of money. And she must earn a decent salary, although nobody had ever dared to ask exactly how much. It was all in the bank. It all went straight into that vast account of hers, without Miss Hart, so Maria Soterraña said, ever seeing the whole amount together, let alone spending it, poor woman. She'd probably have to send a bit to her family in England, to the widowed mother she spoke about occasionally, and who sometimes sent her postcards of the Royal Family or letters in little envelopes, very pretty ones, with Miss Hart's name and address neatly written in the same round writing as Miss Hart, only shakier. There was no way of stealing anything from her because she had nothing on her; she just took out a little at a time for her expenses two or three times a month. And Julian, who respected the good woman and who, moreover, had scarcely spoken to her, couldn't possibly ask her to lend him the money, especially not such a large amount. Ask for a loan? But how could he ask it of her when, out of sheer respect for the woman, Julian exchanged barely half a dozen words with her each day? To speak to her of the matter would be almost as violent as robbing her. And what about borrowing from the master and mistress?

Julian had left his room. He found himself in the lounge. It was a large, rectangular room, pretty but with nothing of value in it. He sat down in an armchair. The curtains weren't drawn. They had taken down the net curtains to be washed a few days ago. The bare panes seemed scarcely to separate the room from the greenish shadow of the square below, or from the gusts of wind which made the branches of the plane trees tap against each other; by now they'd turned off the street lamps. It was drizzling. The continual sound of the branches knocking together made him feel lonely again, left alone to face Esther and Rafael, whose immediate need to get hold of ten thousand pesetas Julian could not doubt. Where would Esther be now? What did she want from him? I must speak to Rafael myself, he thought. It was already daylight when he got up from the armchair and tiptoed back to his room.

9

Kus-Kus climbed the stairs two at a time, scarcely taking a breath. He stopped, panting, outside his aunt's door. It was late. Gone six. The skylight, almost completely obscured, had the dull sheen of a squally, windy night. It was Thursday. Aunt Eugenia had given no sign of life since that strange Thursday a fortnight ago when Kus-Kus had felt himself to be in the presence of another Aunt Eugenia, a lonely woman substituting the brilliant heroes of Bariloche for perplexing characters of flesh and blood. There had been frequent allusions in the kitchen to 'the couple upstairs' and, contrary to the established custom of considering Kus-Kus as one of them and talking about everything in front of him, an embarrassed silence greeted the child every time he appeared and the subject of Aunt Eugenia was up for discussion. It was very annoying. It was the first time such a thing had happened. When he came back from school, Kus-Kus would shut himself in his room, his feelings swinging violently between self-pity and fury. It was obvious they were talking about Aunt Eugenia; it was obvious they didn't want him to know what they were saying; Kus-Kus had felt very alone during those two weeks; even Miss Hart, who never joined in the gossip, had intervened once, after having listened for a good long while, to recommend that Josefa and Maria Soterraña stop talking about things they neither knew about nor understood, a recommendation as well-intentioned as it was ill-conceived, since they said, almost in unison, that if there was one thing they did know about and understand it was what was going on upstairs, Miss Adelaida Hart could be quite sure about that. Julian, on the other hand, had become almost unapproachable since that late-night confession. He tried whenever possible to avoid Kus-Kus's company. Moreover, he spent a large part of the afternoon out of the house, another matter which caused speculation in the kitchen and was also, it seemed, considered inappropriate for the ears of a minor. They all seemed to have been swept up on a great tide of censoriousness, with much wagging of index fingers and shaking of the head each time some fresh bit of news provoked them into showing by some such gesture: 'It can't go on, it can't.'

Kus-Kus, who hadn't been invited up this evening, had decided to go up anyway because, in his eyes as well, although for reasons of his own, the situation was becoming unbearable. The master and mistress had announced that they would arrive the next day, and would stay Saturday, Sunday and perhaps Monday. Kus-Kus needed to talk to someone. And only Aunt Eugenia would do in the circumstances. It was the first time he'd gone up uninvited, and he felt uncomfortable about it. That's why he had taken the stairs two at a time: to get over as quickly as possible the uncomfortable feeling of not knowing whether Aunt Eugenia wanted to see him. When he arrived at the door, however, he stopped, realising that to suddenly present himself at his aunt's door was justifiable only in an emergency, like a fire for example, or if he had something important to tell her, something that couldn't wait until the next day, something serious . . . He'd got his breath back now. He'd stopped sweating. He felt a whole hour must have gone by while he stood there on the landing and contemplated, without really taking it in, the windy, phosphorescent skylight which looked, Kus-Kus now thought, as if it were covered with a very fine layer of frost. He heard the clock in Aunt Eugenia's hall strike the half hour. Was it half past seven already? He rested his right hand on the door, about to ring the bell . . . The door opened of its own accord, as if silently obeying a magic password, like in *Ali Baba and the Forty Thieves*. It stood ajar. Kus-Kus slipped through the gap. The hall was in total darkness, not even the little red-shaded light that was usually lit in front of the statuette of the Virgin was on. Neither of the two doors which led off from the hall was open. Nevertheless, once inside that hall he could hear disconnected sounds whose source he couldn't at once determine. He felt his way to one of the two doors which gave on to the curious angular living room. He heard Aunt Eugenia's laugh. If Kus-Kus hadn't been convinced that only Aunt Eugenia could be in that room at that hour, he couldn't have said for sure if it was a man's laugh or a woman's. That was one thing. If he hadn't been convinced that it was his aunt's laugh he would have thought it had a certain shameless energy. Why are the lights off? he wondered. The fuses must have blown. The fact that the fuses often blew in that house was an inexhaustible source of enjoyment for Kus-Kus. He turned the handle rather sharply because he had to stretch a little to reach it, and he found it awkward and irritating having to open and close doors. The door-handles in the mansard apartment were placed at a height worthy of Versailles. The door opened. All the lights inside were out except for one above Aunt Eugenia. She looked frightful. Dishevelled and in her dressing gown, this time she really did seem a different woman. An enormous bare calf and a foot stuck up over the arm of the sofa as if making some extravagant gesture. It looked like a scene from a play, arranged with deliberate exaggeration in order to shock the spectator. Kus-Kus regretted having entered without knocking. He even took a step back. But he had been seen. Once his eyes got used to the half-light of the room he made out a crouching figure next to the sofa, that rose at once swiftly and slowly, contradicting any previous idea Kus-Kus might have had about the significance of that figure or of what it was doing squatting there. 'What the hell's going on?' it said.

If Kus-Kus had not automatically associated the exclamation with the person he had seen crouching when he came in, who was now moving hesitantly towards him, he might have mistaken it for Aunt Eugenia's voice, a rather gruff, tipsy voice, a little too brusque to be pleasant.

'Good evening,' said the little boy, as clearly and courteously as he could. After all, he thought, he was the one who should do the explaining and who was at fault. The other two occupants of the room, when all was said and done, were in their own home. Kus-Kus felt that he was the one who was out of place, an intruder, a snooper.

'Good evening, Aunt Eugenia,' he repeated, in view of the silence that had followed his first greeting.

'Who's this?' asked the young man loudly. He was clearly visible now, and had retreated a few steps to stand next to Aunt Eugenia. She had wrapped her dressing gown around her and seemed to be smiling. Or rather she had twisted her mouth up to one side, a bit, thought Kus-Kus, like the bream in the fish market.

'This . . . this is Nicolas, my nephew, Nicolas, who lives downstairs and has come up to visit me today, as he does every Thursday, isn't that so, Kus-Kus?'

'Well, I . . .' murmured the boy. He felt ridiculous and his blushing to the roots made him feel even more uncomfortable. More straitlaced too. Almost ready to disapprove of the situation his aunt found herself in. But what exactly was that situation?

'Well, you might have given a bit of warning, you nearly caught me in the altogether!' exclaimed the young man.

When she heard this, Aunt Eugenia laughed again, her laugh less forced this time. The words were said with a lack of inhibition, a spontaneity that removed any coarseness, as if he had merely said some such thing as 'I was just about to have tea.' Aunt Eugenia seemed happy now to see her nephew.

'I have to go,' said the young man.

'Why don't the two of you sit down? We could play something together. We could play a hand of cards. Yes, why not?'

'Why not? We can play bezique, or pontoon, if you like . . . you can play what you want, you're in your own house, after all. Anyway, I have to go, but don't let me stop you two playing.'

'It wouldn't be the same. Without you it would be different, it wouldn't be half as nice, would it, Kus-Kus?'

'I don't know,' said Kus-Kus, shrugging his shoulders, 'I don't feel like playing anything and certainly not cards, and anyway, I don't know how . . .'

'You know, my nephew is already quite a writer and a poet of remarkable sensibility . . .'

'Who, him?' the young man mumbled distractedly. 'I wonder what time it is. When I came up it was getting dark. I had the afternoon off, that's why I came up so early; my mate and me take turns having a half-day off each week, as well as Sundays that is . . .'

'How dreadful! They really keep you at it!'

'I'm going,' said Kus-Kus.

Aunt Eugenia didn't seem to be in control of the situation, Kus-Kus thought. Part of her charm lay in persistently — if only slightly — infringing the rules and mores which most of the people among whom she moved accepted unquestioningly.

With the young man there, however, Aunt Eugenia didn't seem at all original but, thought Kus-Kus, rather affected and obsequious.

This was perhaps more surprising even than Aunt Eugenia letting herself be seen in her dressing gown like that by a stranger, however young he was. Moreover, he wasn't as young as Kus-Kus had assumed a delivery boy would be.

Neither of them had sat down. Both had announced they were going, but neither of them seemed prepared to be the first to go. The situation had grown less tense. Aunt Eugenia made to reach for a bottle of sherry that was on the table. Both of them rushed to help her. Aunt Eugenia twittered. In the hall the clock struck eight. What's going to happen now? wondered Kus-Kus. He felt as if he were on a switchback, trapped on a rollercoaster, being too continually bumped and thrown from one side to another to recover himself, to distance himself from his own feelings, from his own fear... of the next moment. And he thought that perhaps that was what Aunt Eugenia too was feeling now: afraid of stumbling over the pothole of the next moment and falling flat, finding that everything had become incomprehensible.

Aunt Eugenia had continued drinking straight from the bottle all this time, without speaking, looking from one companion to the other, as if hypnotised. The young man was standing at ease as if in a gymnastics class, his arms by his side. Then he began to rub his right arm with his left hand, observing as he did so how his muscles flexed. It was a methodical movement, repetitive and infectious. Kus-Kus felt hypnotised by its mechanical tenderness. The three of them stayed like that for a long time. Aunt Eugenia was the only one who moved as she raised the bottle to her lips or moved her head. When she burst out talking she startled her two companions.

What were the two of them doing standing there, looking at her as if she were a monster, what were they doing? they should sit down or go to hell, to hell, yes, better they went to hell if they were going anywhere, if all they could do was look at her as if she were a monster, the two of them standing there, like two dumb animals, what did the stupid boy think was happening, eh? come on, what did he think he'd seen? he was the worst of the whole family, the dirtiest of them all, the biggest gossip, the least sincere of the lot, whereas poor Manolo was just a poor uneducated boy, a poor boy who had to spend the day carting baskets around, and don't come the innocent with her, he was the worst of the lot, yes, the worst, they should either go or stay, it didn't matter now, but they should sit down if they were going to stay, it made her neck ache having to look up at them, he was the worst of the lot, the little boy, running with tales to his grandmother, to the servants, to anyone, just to have something to tell, just to make out he was someone important, he was capable of anything, any cruelty, just to make himself seem interesting, ah, now he was putting on a sad face, trying to put the blame on other people, he was only a child, he was only a child, I'm a poor innocent little child, I only repeat what others say, what my aunt says, my aunt who's half-drunk, half-naked, I've seen her with my own eyes, half-naked giving tea to the boy from the shop, go to the servants with that tale, go and tell the priests, and don't look at her with those eyes, that was all she needed, him pouting and crying, so that he could do even more harm than he had already by bursting into tears and making his aunt feel even more of a whore, was he listening? and if he thought that tell-tales ever came to any good he knew now it wasn't so, now he could see they didn't, now he could see for himself how this tale ended, hadn't he wanted to see what his aunt and that boy did upstairs? well, now that he knew, was he any the wiser? where had it got him? at least the other boy had a heart and treated her with affection but him, he just wanted another story to tell the servants, the grandmothers, the priests at school, he was just the same as the rest of them, worse in fact just because of that, because he seemed to be what he wasn't and he got by because of that, the others might be stupid but they were honest, whereas he was intelligent but deceitful, give her a stupid person rather than a deceitful one any day, rather than a lying deceiver, and if on top of that he was going to cry, that was just malicious, trying to make her feel guilty and old ... he was the old one, him, him, yes, he was a bitter old man, a horrible bitter little boy, a *revenant*, Manolo must forgive her, she only wanted what was best for him, she hadn't expected to fall in love the way she had, but it wouldn't last long, she didn't have much longer, please, Manolo, the two of you, go, please go, don't take any notice of me, I'm tired, and please, tomorrow don't talk to me about this, take the little boy, my nephew, when I die you'll know why I didn't marry the South American, it was me who didn't want to, my head's spinning terribly now, probably one afternoon the three of us can go out together for a ride in the motorboat, if Josema can take us, as far as the island of La Cabra, we'd probably get there, even though it's winter, you can go if the sea's calm, it all depends on the sea ...

They went down the stairs in silence, without turning on the lights on the landings. Kus-Kus went ahead, sliding his right hand gently down the banister. 'It's a secret between you and me,' he recalled her saying, the distorted voice of a fortnight ago intercut with the hysterical voice he had just heard, unfairly accusing him of telling tales to the servants and the priests. His mouth felt dry and bitter. And when he covered his ears and shouted up the stairwell so that Aunt Eugenia would hear him, so that that young man would hear and never forget: 'I haven't been telling tales to anyone!' tears started to his eyes.

10

'You have to help me,' he'd said, accosting him on the steep corner at the exit of the school, on the Calle del Piru. It was pouring with rain. His dark glasses and white raincoat looked startling, like the disguise of a gangster. And his hair was flattened to his head, dripping. It was an afternoon in mid-April, and when he came out of school the rain was pelting down. The streets were already dark at four o'clock. It had smelled of grass in the Geography classroom and the air contained the seeds of the Easter holidays. 'Don't be frightened,' he said, his hair drenched; he pushed him towards the sliding door of a garage where there was enough space for them to stand next to each other, both facing forward, as if standing to attention on parade. The only thing lacking for him to really look like a gangster was the hat.

'Don't be frightened,' he said again. He had to tell him that he wasn't in the least frightened, not a bit; no, he was just surprised and, well, very pleased to see him . . . after so many months, a bit surprised, yes . . . But it didn't seem to get through to him; he said again: 'Don't be afraid, I'm not going to do anything to you, don't be frightened,' as if infected by the repetitiveness of the rain. And then he said: 'Hide me,' repeating the words several times before explaining exactly what he meant. 'Hide me. Just for a few days. Then I'll make for France. I can cross the frontier on foot. There are routes you can take. Just for a few days, a couple of days, until the money arrives.' He couldn't move until the money arrived. He had to help him. It was pitiful to see him there, soaked to the skin, unable to find the words he was looking for or to say exactly what he meant. It seemed an age from January to that afternoon. After his disappearance, at midday, everything had changed in a lot of ways at once. The master and mistress had come and gone several times. That was the only thing that was still almost the same as before. And not even that was really. The first month had been so bizarre that everything that had been upset by Julian's disappearance had stayed that way, as if in commemoration. An inspector from the police station came. He fascinated Josefa and Maria de Soterraña. During the search of the room and the questioning of each member of the staff in turn, Maria cried intermittently as if at a funeral. The inspector had a little notebook with squared paper and a little tiny diary pencil that he chewed each time her snivelling grew louder. He was a man of few words. Just once, when he was nearly finished, he mumbled: 'Stop crying, woman, *you* haven't done anything, this is nothing to do with you!' which, as one can imagine, heightened the criminal, penitential aspect of the whole thing. They also questioned Miss Hart, who declared that she was a British subject, that she thought Julian a good man and was very upset and wanted to see the British Consul before saying anything, and that she was most distressed; all of which the inspector listened to without taking notes, his eyes very round, saying, 'Forgive me for troubling you, Miss, but we have to find the lad, it's just routine.' He can't have found out much. He phoned the hotel from the house to say he was going there. It appears the manageress had phoned the police station, even before any charge was brought, to help in the hunt and capture of the thief. It seems she had indicated over the phone that she was in possession of numerous relevant facts about the criminal, and even had the addresses of several people in Madrid who knew him. The manageress – who, by the way, had not made a good impression on the inspector – had declared that nobody was going to make a fool out of her. The search of Julian's room was over in a trice. Kus-Kus watched it from the door. There was nothing in the room, which now had the appearance of a monk's cell. The shaving brush and the razor were gone. And the key-ring with the bullet on it. Nothing of value was missing from the house; not even Maria de Soterraña's gold wristwatch which, it turned out, hadn't been stolen after all, but left by its owner on some out of the way little shelf in the WC. The only thing he left when he fled was a pair of dark glasses, which the inspector forgot to take and which Kus-Kus hid in a cupboard next to the little bottle of eyedrops. The empty cell gave off an icy atmosphere that distanced Kus-Kus from the kitchen staff. They sat in permanent judgement on the faults of the guilty party. The first month, full of reminders of the past, took an age to pass. The next two slipped by as fast as water snakes. Almost nothing was heard of Aunt Eugenia during those three months.

A couple of new school friends had kept Kus-Kus behind until supper time. It was pouring with rain, Julian's voice was wintry, Kus-Kus remembered, as if dreaming all the details with the flowery, silvered clarity of the young faltering spring; Kus-Kus, he himself recognised, was a little cruel, not very moved either by the memory of what had happened or by Julian's presence next to him. Could Aunt Eugenia be right? he wondered.

How easy it had been! And there was no way he could have planned it beforehand, because the idea of cashing that cheque had come to him at the last minute. The master and mistress were leaving on a trip that afternoon. 'Just pop down to the bank and cash this cheque. Ask for it in thousand peseta notes.' It was a cheque for twenty thousand pesetas. To get to the bank, cash the cheque and come back would take at most an hour. Julian left at eleven in the morning and, by lunchtime, a little before two in the afternoon, he still hadn't returned. No one suspected anything. They all thought he must have had an accident. They telephoned the first-aid post. They telephoned the police station. They thought he might have gone on some errand for Miss Hart and they asked her if that was the case. They telephoned Mercedes, the grandmother, who sometimes, when the master and mistress were away, made use of his services in the mornings. They thought of Aunt Eugenia who, being a bit eccentric, had probably met him on the stairs and embroiled him in conversation and he, not daring to interrupt Miss Eugenia, would still be there with one hand on the banister, one foot higher than the other waiting to continue up the stairs. They went out to the staircase and listened attentively at the stairwell. They listened for the lift. The master and mistress sat down at the table. Josefa served lunch. They talked about how it looked as though it was going to turn out to be a nice afternoon. They talked about their trip. They ignored the fact that Josefa made the same mistake, on removing the plates, three times in a row. They sipped their water and sipped their wine and carefully washed their grapes in the water provided as if nothing were amiss. They coughed and said: 'Julian seems to have been delayed.' In the kitchen the oil caught fire once and very nearly twice, sending up huge flames. And Maria de Soterraña burned her left hand. They made a paste of flour and water to prevent any blistering. They applied the paste, and Maria de Soterraña scoured the pans with one hand behind her back, which gave her a rather Napoleonic air. The clock struck three. They served the coffee. The time for them to leave came round. They called the police station again. The police asked how much the cheque was for and, when they learned the amount, there was a rather loud though respectful whistle. Kus-Kus thought from the start that Julian had run off with the cash, like Giacomo Gattucci. He thought this without malice, but also without doubt, although he didn't say anything, because since the scene in Aunt Eugenia's apartment he had felt wary and grown up. He had noticed, however, that after only an hour, the amount on the wretched cheque had flashed just for an instant, like lightning, before everybody's eyes. To allow three hours to pass between realising that they had been robbed and reporting it was a slightly absurd refinement, a half-elegant squeamishness – very Bariloche, as Aunt Eugenia would have said – and incomprehensible to the inspector who took charge of the case. Once the loss had been reported, everything came to a halt, a stunned silence lay like a fall of snow over the whole house. The temperature seemed to plunge to zero. Then, at the same moment, everyone got going again and the master and mistress left on their trip as planned. Kus-Kus remembered the story Julian had told him that night in his room. Or, to be exact, he realised that the two stories fitted together without much difficulty. But he wasn't going to spoil a good farce like this for the simple pleasure of putting two and two together!

'You have to help me. Hide me. Just till the money arrives.'

'Hide you? Where?'

'Hide me at home, in your house, I mean . . . I mean, if you don't mind . . .'

'I don't know if I mind or not. Do you think I should mind?'

'It wasn't my fault. It was a matter of life and death. Don't you remember me telling you all about it?'

Some boys from Kus-Kus's year ran past, shouting hello to him, and, as they ran off in the rain, looking back at him and Julian.

'Why don't you take your glasses off? You're too conspicuous with them on. Where have you been all this time?'

'I hid in a few places,' said Julian, taking off his glasses and putting them in his raincoat pocket . . . 'Do you know if the master and mistress brought any charges in the end? The police haven't bothered me, haven't looked for me anywhere

... it wouldn't have been difficult to find me, especially at first. That really surprises me.'

'The police came to the house and there was a lot of fuss the first few days. Have you spent it all?'

'It wasn't for me. I lent it to a friend, to Rafael ... Don't you remember I told you about Rafael that night?'

'Yes, I remember. Is it Rafael who's going to send you the money?'

'Well, no, not Rafael. Someone else.' Julian's voice grew suddenly husky. 'The police are probably looking for me now though.'

'Why now?'

'A bloke was killed in Rafael's boarding house, in Madrid. Rafael has disappeared.'

'With all the money?' asked Kus-Kus, turning to look at him. Julian avoided the boy's eyes and put his glasses on again.

'Will you hide me? Yes or no? I have nowhere else, nowhere.'

'It would have to be upstairs ... I don't know where else apart from there.'

'Where upstairs?'

'In Aunt Eugenia's apartment. In the mansards. There's plenty of room. I'll speak to her first, of course ...'

'Your aunt's sure to turn me in.'

'Maybe. But I'd be surprised. I won't know until tonight ... Come to the back door tonight at eleven. They close it then and the porter goes downstairs for his supper ... It's the best time.'

'At the back door tonight?'

'It's the safest bet. Don't go wandering round the streets. You look terrible, go to the cinema; then you can tell me about the film later.'

They took leave of each other at the garage. The rain had proved a better cover than any hiding place. Kus-Kus ran all the way home. He had never felt so excited. Now, he thought, the long-hidden hero would appear. Giacomo the hero. He couldn't eat anything at tea. Miss Hart, who had lately taken to treating Kus-Kus with a certain mocking solemnity, and who was already installed at the tea table when Kus-Kus entered the playroom, raised her eyebrows slightly and, beginning to pour, remarked: 'The tea's getting cold, Nick. Let me know next time if you're going to be late.'

'I'm sorry,' said Kus-Kus, without looking at her.

'That's quite all right, dear. I know you're a very busy person.' He drank two cups of tea one after the other, with obvious difficulty. His mouth was dry and his shirt, soaked in sweat, stuck to his body.

'Don't you feel well, Nick? You're sweating a lot.'

'The tea's hot,' he mumbled.

'Well, it should be, shouldn't it?' said the admirable Miss Hart.

Once he was alone, Kus-Kus strode back to his room. There was no need for disguises this time. This time there would be no talk, from him or Julian, of a third possibility that was neither playing at hiding a fugitive from justice nor actually hiding one. Kus-Kus remembered the triumphantly sarcastic tone in which Julian had put the question to him on the occasion of the failed poisoning of Miss Hart. Now, he thought, he'll see that it wasn't a proper question – the boy stopped in the middle of the room, his face flushed with a feeling which, given his age, it would have been excessive to consider simply pride – now he'll see there was no distinction to be made, because I *am* playing . . . I'm just playing. If he wasn't so stupid, Julian would be grateful to me for having nothing to do with reality, that's just a boring jungle he was rash enough to plunge into with his thieving and his illusions about true love and innocence. These reflections absorbed him for a long time. The clock in the hall struck ten. Then eleven. He remembered that if Julian was to be hidden in the mansards he had to prepare Aunt Eugenia, and to get her to agree. Now it was too late for that. Julian would be downstairs. The house was still. The ticking of the clock was like the pounding of a heart. Like a victorious heart. Like a sign that the borders between reality and play had gone. He went down to the back door, leaving his own door ajar. In that house, in the rear part of the entrance hall, there was a sort of second entrance which allowed direct access to the stables. One reached this second door by going down three big marble steps. The place was always dark, even in the daytime – it was where Josefa and Errol Flynn used to kiss – and sitting there was a great bronze dog with hollowed-out sockets for eyes in which in the summer, as a child, Kus-Kus used to place two cherry stones. In passing he rested his hand on the dog's head and, unable to resist the impulse, put his arms round the animal's neck, letting himself be invaded by the chill of its rigid fidelity. He opened the door. It was still raining in the echoing, yellow-lit, solitary street. Julian wasn't there. The air was redolent of ancient memories. It smelt of the grasses of adventures from an earlier century. It smelt of the nearby sea. Kus-Kus went out into the street and, in the shelter of a shop window, could make out the whitish ghost of the fugitive who, seeing him come out, left his hiding place and hurried across the puddled street.

'I thought you weren't coming down,' Julian said, wiping his feet on the doormat. 'My feet are soaked. I didn't know what to do. I thought you weren't coming down, I thought you weren't coming down . . .'

'And I thought we were friends. If you don't trust me, if you're not going to trust me from now on, if you're going to be thinking stupid things all the time, we'd better forget it . . .' He spoke with some irritation, feeling hurt.

'I'm sorry, there's no reason why you should do anything for me, I let you down . . .'

'Don't talk so much. Someone might come. We'd better take the lift, it's safer.'

Julian followed the boy to the bottom of the corridor, where there was a lift to one side of the main staircase. While they were going up, he murmured: 'Has she agreed to it? Have you told her?' And Kus-Kus again told him not to talk so much and that from now on he should get used to trusting to fate because they had now crossed the boundaries of normal behaviour. From now on the two of them would have to play things by ear. Julian said nothing. Kus-Kus thought that he smelt bad, like a tiger, and that his face seemed disfigured, defeated. The only thing Julian said, before following Kus-Kus's instructions to hide himself in a corner of Aunt Eugenia's landing while the boy rang the bell, was, 'I'm sorry to put your aunt to so much trouble.' Julian had been informed, a moment before the lift stopped, that Aunt Eugenia knew nothing of the matter.

11

When she heard the bell Aunt Eugenia got to her feet with some difficulty. Though she wasn't expecting anyone, that sudden ring at such a late hour did not startle her. There was a second ring, the same as before except that, unlike the first which had been merely abrupt, this second ring contained, coming as it did much sooner than the normal interval a visitor leaves between rings, especially when they aren't expected and it's almost midnight, an ill-tempered note of impatience, haste or violence. The third ring, after almost no interval, sounded in Aunt Eugenia's ears just as, with extreme difficulty, she was leaving the sofa and making her way to the hall. On that evening, knowing that Manolo wouldn't be coming, she had dressed with great care so as not to fall prey to melancholy. The pain in her kidneys made her press her hands into the small of her back as she walked. Her head throbbed dully, though it wasn't exactly a headache, and her vision was blurred. She switched on the light by the door. From the other side of the door there came the murmur of interrupted conversation. As she opened the door she had the impression of a shadow dissolving into translucence beyond the glass. She found Kus-Kus standing there, looking at her in a way which, in another person, she would have termed insolent. The boy moved towards his aunt, almost forcing her to step back.

'Good evening, Aunt Eugenia,' he muttered, and advanced further, pushing the door to behind him as he did so.

'Kus-Kus!'

'I missed you, Aunt. Without you I don't know how to play anything. I don't play any games any more, because you don't come to watch me, so . . .'

'It's very late, isn't it?'

'It's not even midnight. You go to bed late anyway, don't you?'

'No, I suppose it's not so late, if it's only about eleven. I thought . . . I don't notice what time it is, the time passes more slowly when one's alone, I don't notice the time . . .'

'You're not alone now,' said the boy winking.

'Yes, that's true. Come in! But what do you mean exactly?'

They had nearly reached the living room, and were both leaning on the frame of the open door. Kus-Kus answered, prefacing his reply with a broad, semi-circular gesture that took in the whole room, the windows with their still undrawn curtains, and, beyond, the black sail-less sea which could be guessed at through the windows on which the rain drummed.

'Now, I mean. You're not alone now. That was before, Aunt. You used to be. You only had me to play with, but I'm the worst of the whole family, that's what you said the other day, loud and clear, didn't you? Too bad. Still, that doesn't matter to you now that you're not alone. Quite the contrary...'

'I don't quite understand you. But why are we standing here chattering away when we could be making ourselves comfortable? It's too funny us standing here when we could... well, when we could *not* be standing!'

Aunt Eugenia went to sit down, and Kus-Kus leaned his arm on the left-hand side of the door frame, resting his forehead on his arm. He stared fixedly at the floor. His aunt, seated uncomfortably on the edge of the sofa with her hands folded in her lap, like someone scrupulously carrying out a duty visit, called to him to come closer and to sit down. The boy spoke now in a low but clearly audible voice, without looking at her. He was tracing a semi-circle on the floor with his right foot – he was still in short trousers and his thick school socks had slipped down over his boots – his wavering between ease and insolence growing ever faster and more abrupt.

'You look pretty. You're a bit thinner, aren't you?'

'Do you think so, Kus-Kus? You're always joking. Now that you're older you're getting cheeky... Do you really think I look thinner? I scarcely drink at all, drink makes one so bloated, but do you really mean it?'

'Absolutely, Aunt. Anyone can see that you're not on your own any more and that you take a little more care of yourself than when you only had me to charm, isn't that so?'

'You're acting very strangely. You never said such things before. You're strange...'

'Are you still seeing that boy?'

'I'm sorry I offended you that time. I'd drunk a little too much.'

'A skinful more like. Do you still see him?'

'Why have you come up here so late? Miss Hart will worry if she doesn't know where you are. Does Miss Hart know you're here? We should phone . . . Does Miss Hart know?'

'Miss Hart died suddenly at midday today.'

Shocked, Aunt Eugenia stood up. 'Good God!' she exclaimed. Kus-Kus watched her now from beneath his propped forearm. He remained in the same position, but had stopped swinging his right foot back and forth.

'Nothing to be done about it,' he said. 'She's gone to a better world now; she was an admirable woman but rather unromantic, isn't that what you said, Aunt Eugenia? You, on the other hand, *are* romantic, right, Aunt Eugenia? That boy the other day didn't seem very romantic to me, he seemed common, but you like him, for lack of anything better, I suppose . . . Hadn't you better sit down before you fall down from shock? You deserve a more romantic boyfriend, Aunt Eugenia, someone more like the Prince of Moscow, like Giacomo, have you forgotten Giacomo?'

Kus-Kus went out into the hall. Aunt Eugenia heard the creak of the front door which, she remembered now, had not been shut properly. 'Kus-Kus!' she shouted, 'Kus-Kus!' She heard the door slam shut and then two pairs of footsteps in the icy hall. Kus-Kus reappeared at the living-room door and, stepping aside, allowed his companion to pass into the room. Aunt Eugenia raised her trembling hands to her breast. The room had taken on a bluish, greenish tinge, like a nightmare. She saw before her, wearing a white raincoat that dripped water, the servant who, so they said, had run off with a load of money three months ago. 'Forgive me, Miss Eugenia,' she heard the man say. 'The boy, the boy said . . . that I could probably stay here, spend the night, if it's no trouble to you. The boy, well, I was the one who approached him, I waited at the gate this afternoon, you know. I approached him, I mean, I waited at the school gate to ask him to help me, Miss, I've nowhere to go, Miss Eugenia, until the money arrives . . .'

Julian was trembling as if suddenly gripped by a terrible fever. Aunt Eugenia went up so close she almost touched him, and stayed there, looking at him, while with her right hand she played with the beryls on the necklace she had put on that evening to dispel the pink and mauve melancholy of the twilight, the sadness of a life, her own life, undone in an instant. Then she turned to her nephew, who was watching them in his new guise of gnome and old man, his hands sunk in the pockets of his pale corduroy trousers, unsmiling, like someone looking on as a toy train is set in motion for the first time, a very expensive toy, too expensive for a child . . .

'You heard him, Aunt Eugenia; here's Julian, the old Julian who used to serve you glasses of Marie Brizard, he's come back; you know it suits you, that gesture . . . how can I put it, that very elegant gesture of, well, surprise. You'll have to hide Julian discreetly, just for a few nights until the money arrives and he can get away to France with the cash, just like one of your gigolos, eh? Julian suits you better than that common chap the other evening. You make a better-looking couple, and he knows how to do all that stuff too, crouching down or whatever. What *was* that chap doing squatting by the sofa when I came in? Now Aunt Eugenia, ask Julian if he'd like anything, to wash his hands, tidy himself up a bit, take off his wet raincoat, you know how to do all that so well, don't you?'

'Forgive me, Miss Eugenia, I'm truly sorry . . .' mumbled Julian, passing a hand over his watery eyes.

'Get out of this house this minute! I'm going to call the police, I'm going to phone downstairs! It's disgusting to take advantage of a child like this!'

'I'm sorry, Aunt Eugenia. At school I've heard some of the older ones talking, they say that women like men to lick their cunts, that's what the older ones say, they even made a drawing of a fat woman with her legs open and a man kneeling by her, it's very well done in charcoal, in the fifth-year toilets. Is that what the man from the shop was doing to you the other day? You phoned me so that I could come up and watch you doing it. If you call the police or whoever, I'll tell them everything the two of you showed me that evening. I'm not kidding. If you inform against me, I'll inform against you first and my charge is much more serious, or perhaps you don't realise that. Now, where is Julian going to sleep?'

Aunt Eugenia remained silent for a moment, as if considering her answer. Then she opened her eyes, half-closed until then, and, scarcely changing the expression on her face or her tone of voice – always a little shaky and hesitant, even when she was relaxed and in a good mood – said, looking towards Julian and her nephew, although without, it seemed, really seeing them: 'We could put him in the small bedroom, the one with the little study adjoining. Does that seem a good idea to you? He'll be comfortable there until the money arrives, don't you think?'

12

He threw himself on the bed, feeling exhausted, thinking he would sleep like a log all night. But after only a couple of hours he woke with a start between those slippery linen sheets, part of Aunt Eugenia's parents' trousseau. He dropped off once more, then woke again, and this time the need to piss wouldn't let him get back to sleep. From his bed, in the meditative gleam of the night-light, he examined the room. It was small and square, with two doors. The ceiling, which sloped so steeply it almost touched the bedhead, was done in *toile de Jouy* like the walls, and had a vague, rosy, calming effect on his nerves. He rubbed his reddened eyes, thinking that it ought to be easy to fall asleep looking at that garret-like ceiling, peopled with the soothing presences of faraway designs, like a bedroom in a cottage in a forest. The bed took up almost the whole of the left-hand corner of the room. Just above the bedside table he noticed the recess made by a small window behind a pale velvet curtain. One of the two doors, the smaller one, was opposite the foot of the bed. The other was in the highest wall of the room. On opening it in search of a bathroom, he found himself in a carpeted corridor, apparently at the back of the house, which ended in an abrupt corner. He made his way on tiptoe towards that corner, not daring to put on the light, guiding himself by the diffuse light from the bedroom. All the neat gold-handled doors looked exactly the same. He decided to open the one opposite his. Entering the tiny bathroom, he had the feeling of having stepped through a looking-glass. The cistern made scarcely any noise. He pissed in the dark, leaving the door open. Then he put the light on, shut the door and ran his hand carefully round the lavatory bowl. Turning the tap in the wash-basin just enough to allow a trickle of water, he washed his face, hands and neck. The towels, crisp and freshly ironed, looked as if they'd just been put on the towel rail, especially for him. He chose a small towel and, once he'd used it, folded it exactly as it had been. When he saw the blackish ring left around the wash-basin by the soapy water he felt dirty. Back in his room again, he parted the curtains and opened the window. A couple of yards above his head, almost wrapping itself about the blackened chimneys, was the heavy, racing sky of that strange dawn. After taking a few deep breaths he felt better, more awake and less ill at ease. He shut the window again and drew the curtains. The pale velvet gleamed briefly white as it fell in folds, like the dense matt fur of some unknown animal. With barely conscious curiosity he ran his fingers, like a blind man, over the hem of the curtain, perfectly finished, as if oversewn by a tailor. That was when he noticed the curtain lining, lemon-coloured satin, reminding him of sleet or mist. And then he remembered his mother; her cracked, reddened hands, twisted like roots. He walked round the room thinking of her, until the memory, barely tinged with emotion, dissolved entirely. The early morning air had sharpened his senses, especially his sense of smell. To his surprise he found himself sniffing the new room, like a cat. The perfect fragrant beauty; the coherence of all that sensory information; the fragile aroma of an empty cologne bottle: subtle and deep like an old man's conscience. He remained there for some time, he couldn't have said for how long; until the damp, smudged sun of the spring day sparkled on the slate tiles of the mansard roof. Only then did he decide to gently turn the slightly yellowed porcelain door handle, with its design of little green, red and purple flowers. Among the petals and stems were little specks of gold, perhaps representing pollen, a vague golden constellation, microscopic, microcosmic, which belonged to and at the same time did not quite form part of the flowers. The enamel was slightly raised and rough to the touch. The door opened very easily. It was white and, seen from the bed or from anywhere else in the room, seemed larger. Close to, however, he had the impression that the door was shrinking, until the frame only came up to his chest, like some tiny, slightly vaulted door discovered in the least frequented, most shadowy part of a wall. So strong was this impression that, before opening the door completely, Julian took a couple of steps back to convince himself of its true dimensions, from the original perspective of the bed. 'I'll have to crawl through on all fours,' he thought, but he crossed the threshold and entered the next room with no difficulty whatsoever. Once there he felt cheated. It was another square room with the same sloping ceiling, the same *toile de Jouy* paper, only in pale green this time. It was a sparsely furnished sitting room, somewhat bigger than the bedroom. The objects all had a glassy metallic brilliance, as on a stage set, conspiring with the rainy light that invaded the room, setting a seal on it all. Julian had the feeling that something had been said in that room just before he entered. He sat down rather warily in the armchair near the big window. Unlike the bedroom, this room, absorbed in the austere tones of its colours and furnishings, moved one to reflection, to contemplation. Julian tried to remember last night, yesterday afternoon, the squally morning spent watching for Kus-Kus at the school gate. And that rain, like a tropical storm, deafening, disfiguring and hiding them in that garage entrance, like two lovers, or the intrepid duo, Roberto Alcazar and Pedrin. He leaned out over the balcony, trying to show only his head, as if he were in the trenches. The street, the port down below, looked unreal, like a model. He went back to the armchair, leaving the window half-open, listening for some sign of life within the house. A seagull passed, screeching, only a few feet away. He felt as if he were alone in a country house; concealed in an attic room, listening to the cooing of the doves. Not a sound came from the street below or from the port. He thought it must be about seven in the morning, and that what he would most like was a big cup of really hot black coffee, with plenty of sugar in it. Then he thought: 'I wonder what will happen today? They'll turn me in, no doubt about it. The kid will turn me in, or she will. More than likely she telephoned the police straight away last night. Or now, this morning. Perhaps she spoke to the police just a moment ago, and they're coming for me now. They'll be very quiet about it, so as not to make a row so early in the morning. It's only natural that they should turn me in. Or perhaps they've told her to keep calm and to wait, that I'm not dangerous, and to pretend she knows nothing about me, because at this hour there would be a scene if I put up a struggle, and it would be better to wait until tonight, that they'll come and arrest me tonight, that as I'm not dangerous, she should keep calm.' He sighed, thinking that, in fact, the one person he felt sorry for was Miss Eugenia, who had always treated him kindly. It surprised him that at that moment he couldn't manage to recall her with any clarity; nor even what had happened yesterday. The thought suddenly occurred to him that perhaps what had happened had not happened, or that it wasn't important, that his struggle to remember it was in fact simply his struggle to invent it. Scarcely six hours had passed since last night, but all he could remember was the rain soaking him to the skin as darkness fell, and his desire to spend the night under cover. What time was it? He leaned out over the balcony. The little yellow and blue port had become considerably livelier. Three or four people were waiting at the bus stop. 'I must prepare myself,' he thought, coming in from the balcony and closing the doors. He felt like pissing again; it seemed unnecessary to go through his bedroom when he could use the door of the room in which he found himself, which would probably open on to the little carpeted passage. He turned the handle, which gave gently without opening. They'd locked it. He stepped back, electrified, galvanised by that obstacle. Ready to defend himself, to flee. And what if they'd locked the bedroom door too? In an instant he was there; he was panting a little when he found himself once more in the corridor. Just as well. He'd leave right now. To hell with the lot of them. To hell with the money. The front door, where was the front door? Not bothering now whether he made any noise or not, he opened the door at the end of the corridor. The hall. He had just enough money to catch a train, any train anywhere. He'd go unnoticed, it wouldn't be the first time. His wallet, where had he left his wallet? He rushed back to the bedroom. There, on top of the bed, among the tangle of sheets and blankets, was his raincoat. There was nothing to keep him now. How much money did he actually have left? He opened the front door. 'I'll just have to make do,' he thought. Hearing a door open behind him, he turned round.

'Aren't you going to have breakfast, sir? There's coffee and toast all ready in the living room. I've left the tray there,' Aunt Eugenia announced all in one breath.

Julian closed the front door and went into the living room, the door of which Aunt Eugenia — who, to judge by the dark shadows under her eyes, had also had a bad night — had opened wide.

13

'Like Eduardo,' shuddered Kus-Kus, 'who disappeared without trace.'

'What's the matter, dear?' he heard Miss Hart, who was sitting beside him, ask. He pretended not to have heard her; and he thought that perhaps Miss Hart was also pretending not to notice that he was pretending. The events of yesterday and last night didn't allow him to enjoy the tram journey calmly. What was happening upstairs? Was Julian still in Aunt Eugenia's apartment? He would know nothing until he went home after tea, when it would be almost night. And even then, only after having supper and knowing for certain that Miss Hart had gone to bed and fallen asleep after reading for a good while, a good half an hour. Until half past ten, or even eleven, it would be impossible to find out anything. From the corner of his eye he watched Miss Hart's hands, lying with the fingers lightly interlaced on her handbag, like two small animals asleep. It was the afternoon of the first whole day Julian had spent in the mansards. Kus-Kus and Miss Hart were going to have tea at his grandmother Mercedes's house. An unforeseen and, in the circumstances, extremely inconvenient invitation. 'Like Eduardo,' repeated Kus-Kus mentally, fidgeting in his seat.

'Miss Hart and the boy are to come today.' That was the message Josefa passed on at lunch time. Neither the invitation nor the manner of it was in any way unusual. His grandmother's invitations were always like that: 'They are to come today.' Always to the point. And always impossible to refuse. If the message said they were to come, they had to, regardless. There would be a magnificent tea to be sure, although there were always likely to be some unpleasant surprises. His grandmother – whose fearsome gaze would have petrified anyone who dared to suggest she was 'original' or 'eccentric' or 'unpredictable' – was, in Kus-Kus's opinion, with the exception of Aunt Eugenia and himself, the most brilliant, fascinating and strange member of the whole family. She was mad as a hatter, a curious anglophile cross between an empress and a police sergeant. Normally during those ample teas, which occurred more or less twice a month, Kus-Kus enjoyed watching her. Now, however, things had changed completely. They had really changed with Julian's return, much more quickly and more profoundly than the surprising theft and his disappearance three months before. But, this afternoon at least, Kus-Kus was in no condition to ponder exactly *how* things had changed; whether the change was caused by Julian's reappearance or by Kus-Kus himself, who, without a doubt, was also changing (above all ever since the unexpected and disquieting turn his relationship with Aunt Eugenia had taken). He could feel that he was changing, and felt at times irrevocably disfigured, at others transfigured, a thousand times better than before, and this was happening as spring, Easter and the end of year exams were all tumultuously upon him.

They would soon be out of the tunnel of plane trees, up the hill and at the stop where they usually got out. The vault of the tunnel, which closed over completely during summer, still admitted, in the early hours of that spring afternoon, a pale green light that seemed to rejuvenate Miss Hart's skin and surround her completely, like in an adventure story, with the shifting, transparent aura of an islander. 'Like Eduardo,' Kus-Kus thought again, without a shudder this time, but closing his eyes, as if he had suddenly entered a place lit by too strong a light. The memory of Eduardo's disappearance took hold of him with increased force as they approached the end of their journey. He had a sensation of pins and needles spreading over his whole body from his leg, which had gone to sleep in the three-quarters of an hour that he had been sitting still. 'What's the matter, dear?' Miss Hart asked again. 'Can't you sit properly? We're nearly there.' At last they were out of the tunnel; the tram, on the flat now, accelerated noisily. They reached the small square. Miss Hart got up and rang the bell (something she always did, although she knew perfectly well that it was a compulsory stop), and they got off and started to walk the half mile or so to his grandmother's house. 'It can't just be a coincidence. It's the same room. The same two rooms, the bedroom and the other one. Eduardo's room. She must have realised it last night when she suggested putting Julian there. I didn't remember, but she must have. She did it on purpose, so that he'll disappear like Eduardo. It's the same room.'

Mercedes's house was very large – too large, according to the rest of the family – just for her, however many servants she had, 'And she certainly has them: a whole regiment of gardeners and idle chauffeurs by the dozen for the one day in a million that she goes visiting.' And it had been built – against everyone's better judgement, against the good taste of the architect who drew up the plans and against the express wishes of her late husband, Kus-Kus's grandfather from Bilbao – right in the middle of a pretty park of some size, which was dwarfed by the gigantic edifice. They had had to cut down all the trees, move earth, dig enormous trenches. The result was a large building set in a now almost puny garden, where Mercedes was gradually replacing the flower beds with asparagus and where she was raising her one pig, thousands of hens and six ducks. As usual, they had to wait a long time for the door to be opened. Eduardo's room. Kus-Kus remembered clearly now, in a whirl of insights, that Aunt Eugenia always referred to those two rooms like that; although it was possible – under the circumstances – that last night she might have called the room by another name. If she had done so, it might have been deliberate, in order to deceive Kus-Kus, to confuse him. But why? Aunt Eugenia had assured him that she had never told anyone that story, only him, because he was 'special'. Aunt Eugenia said that she had never told anyone about Eduardo 'because it isn't a story, Kus-Kus. It isn't a story. It's the truth.' And to tell the truth, as Kus-Kus recalled now, as a sudden wave of bitterness rose in his throat, to tell the truth, according to Aunt Eugenia, was in very bad taste in Bariloche.

'. . . as it was about you know who, you understand, as it was about her, I didn't dare ask any more, you know how people are, oh, but here they come . . .' Maria del Carmen Villacantero was saying as they entered the dining room. The two of them were alone, she and his grandmother; they had already started tea. It was at an oval table, normally covered with a green cloth, where his grandmother played solitaire or whist with the caretaker's wife or son, when she couldn't sleep. Now the cloth was covered by a cream linen one. The table did not go with the rest of the furniture. The armchair his grandmother was sitting in didn't go with the rest of the chairs. Even the curtains didn't really match. That dining room was Mercedes's headquarters; there she discussed the price of eggs with the eggseller; there she did her sewing; there, once a month, she received the parish priest to discuss his sermons with him; there with Maria del Carmen Villacantero, she reviewed recent events. Kus-Kus's place was reserved for him opposite his grandmother, who sat in the middle. Maria del Carmen, at the end near the door to the study, had put her grey crochet shawl round her shoulders, against the draughts. It was the usual scene, but Kus-Kus had the feeling that Maria del Carmen was looking at him more inquisitively than usual and was talking less, or at least less loudly, than at other times. Miss Hart withdrew, as usual, after exchanging greetings. Aunt Eugenia's tale was a terrifying one. Incredible really. It's impossible to disappear without trace. 'Poor Eduardo, it was as if the room had swallowed him up,' was the rather melodramatic phrase she had used. 'Not even you can believe that, Aunt,' Kus-Kus remembered saying to her. 'I told you you wouldn't like it. It's the absolute truth.' Was it because it was true that the story seemed so sinister? His grandmother's voice made him jump.

'I said, "How is Eugenia," Nicolas. Are you deaf? We haven't heard a thing from her for months.'

'Aunt Eugenia? She's fine. Why?' murmured Kus-Kus.

'We haven't heard from her for a long time. I'll pour you a cup of tea, Maria del Carmen.'

'The boy's lost his appetite,' said Maria del Carmen, her face flushed. As she helped herself to a slice of toast and two spoonfuls of marmalade, one after the other, she added, 'Your marmalade always turns out so well, Mercedes, a little on the bitter side, just like the genuine English marmalade, exactly like it, exactly!'

'It's exactly like English marmalade because it *is* English, Maria del Carmen. Don't be so silly. You know perfectly well I'm not up to making marmalade any more.'

'Fancy, it tasted to me exactly like yours, that perfect touch of yours, exactly like yours, really. Goodness, what a shame you don't make marmalade any more when yours always turned out so well.'

Mercedes did not seem disposed to conversation that afternoon. Kus-Kus knew that, sprawled in her armchair, she had been staring at him, as if waiting for him to say something.

'Don't you feel like eating, Nicolas? You've been playing with that bread and butter for an hour.'

'Yes, grandmother, I do, but I'm eating slowly to aid my digestion.'

'What a darling little grandson, Mercedes! "To aid his digestion," he says, what a darling child!'

'Children these days are such liars,' pronounced Mercedes, stirring the water in the teapot violently. 'Dreadful liars. I don't know why that should be . . . This tea's stone cold! Genoveva! What's wrong with you, Maria del Carmen, has the cat got your tongue? Genoveva! Stone, freezing, icy cold! Genoveva! Where's the fool got to? Have the fuses blown again? Doesn't the bell work? Genoveva!'

'. . . well just today, Mercedes, as I was telling you, from two people, from two quite different sources, nothing to do with each other, they don't even know each other, and they said the same thing, that the sister, his sister, the boy's sister, well, she had also come down for the express purpose, just imagine, how dreadful, for the express purpose of seeing him to find out what was going on, well obviously when she's twenty years older than him, old enough to be his mother, imagine how dreadful, well to see what was going on, how on earth it was possible, from two different sources, I'm telling you, but as it was about you know who, my lips were sealed, I, you know me, oh really, a lot of fuss about nothing, goodness how ridiculous, but of course, I was stunned, saying to myself, I must tell Mercedes about this, I must tell Mercedes, I must tell Mercedes, because I . . .'

'Would you mind shutting up, Maria del Carmen, I can't hear what Genoveva's saying.'

The crisis over the cold tea lasted long enough for Maria del Carmen Villacantero to change her place and sit next to Kus-Kus, whispering. Was the little cat well? she wanted to know. Kus-Kus, with his mouth full and without looking at his interlocutor, said that it was. The dreadful woman seemed to believe that the cat is a mammal entirely lacking in the masculine gender, because when she spoke of cats she always used the feminine form, '*gatas*' or '*gatitas*', ignoring any evidence that might suggest otherwise. His grandmother was very upset today, she whispered, because she hadn't heard from her grandson, and she was worried because at certain ages you couldn't be too careful and had to watch who you went around with, older people, especially older girls, who were probably already experiencing certain changes, just things that happen, nothing of importance, of course, absolutely no importance, none, none, but they acted strangely, became nervous, didn't they, probably Nicolas had noticed it too, hadn't he, they got nervous, poor things, it was something that happened to girls, nothing to do with boys, he wasn't to take any notice if he saw something that puzzled him, that seemed wrong to him, it made Maria del Carmen feel rather odd just saying it, but he already knew, with those huge great blue eyes of his, he knew it all, Maria del Carmen was such a ninny, so innocent and so silly, and how she loved all her friends, all of them, she loved all of them so much, she was so sentimental and silly, and her with her mother completely paralysed, completely, as Kus-Kus knew, in a weeny little flat hardly big enough for a mouse, you know they couldn't even have a little bird, even goldfinches died of grief there, they couldn't even have a little goldfinch, nothing at all, in their little living room with the three-piece suite and the sideboard and the two of them they had to positively crouch because there simply wasn't room, now she, Maria del Carmen, had always had a lot of friends when she was young and she still did, loads and loads of them, too many really, and she'd been so silly, such a silly thing when she was young, giving everything to her friends, and her best friend, her absolutely best and closest friend, the one she shared letters from boyfriends with and everything, was Eugenia, how often they'd cried together, not once but many times, as sure as she was talking to Kus-Kus now, as sure as anything, Eugenia and she were the closest of friends, and she, Maria del Carmen, loved her, not like a mother, no, like a sister, no, more, more than a sister, who would believe it, but now she had changed so much, goodness how she'd changed, how Eugenia had changed, for example one day something happened which, well, she didn't understand, perhaps Nicolas would understand, see if he could because she couldn't, well, one day she went up to have tea in Aunt Eugenia's house, Aunt Eugenia had invited her up to see about some building work she wanted doing, well she'd always had such perfect taste in houses, how to make them comfortable, she made them just lovely, if she had no other talent she certainly had taste in decorating, thank God, she knew how to make the most of a *petit coin*, knew how to give it charm, and Eugenia wanted to divide the apartment in two, all it needed was a couple of walls, a few bricks, nothing much, because it didn't involve much, the division wasn't going to cost anything, hardly a thing, because she, Maria del Carmen, had had quite enough of construction work and bricklayers, so why didn't she come up any day for tea, to take tea with her, with Eugenia, come up any afternoon and then they could talk about dividing the apartment and about everything and how nice that would be, as she was rather lonely and that with these turns she'd been having, women's troubles, at her age she felt lonely and Maria del Carmen should come up, well they had been best friends, she should come up for tea any afternoon and they'd talk about it all, dividing the apartment, loneliness, and everything and well, and this is what Kus-Kus wouldn't believe, he'd never believe it, never, a young man was there, a stranger, like the man of the house, did Nicolas know about it, and what did he think, what did he think of that dreadful situation, his grandmother knew and had got very upset, terribly upset just thinking about it, thinking and thinking about it like mad, going over and over it in her head all day. Now what did he think about it?

By then, Maria del Carmen Villacantero was no longer whispering because it was impossible for her to whisper for such a long time without choking or raising her voice. She had, in fact, been sitting next to Kus-Kus for some time, giving every appearance of whispering but in fact saying everything in a good loud voice. And Mercedes, for her part, considering the episode of the teapot closed, and sprawling again in her armchair, was listening silently.

'I don't think anything,' answered Kus-Kus. 'What should I think?'

'Mercedes, I was just saying to your grandson what close friends Eugenia and I have been all our lives . . .'

'I know that. And what do you say, Nicolas, eh?'

'Me? Nothing. I didn't understand half of it. If she and Eugenia are good friends, that's fine, what do you expect me to say?'

'Children today are such liars. I don't know what the priests do to them. Look here, I'm your grandmother and I'm responsible for you while your parents are away . . .'

'But what do you want me to say, grandmother? I don't know!' Kus-Kus felt strong now, quite safe, shielding Aunt Eugenia from the curiosity of his grandmother and Maria del Carmen and the rest of them. They didn't manage to find out anything. And Mercedes ended up getting annoyed with Maria del Carmen, as Kus-Kus had expected. By then it was already late. Nearly supper time. Miss Hart came in to collect him. The chauffeur would drive them back, Maria del Carmen and the two of them. Kus-Kus tried to say goodbye in a friendly manner. It was essential that he appear tired, so that Miss Hart would let him go to bed immediately after supper. Another two hours before eleven o'clock. What would have happened upstairs? What would be happening right now? When Miss Hart and Kus-Kus went in the front door, the night had taken possession of the port and the nearby streets, sowing them with shifting velvet petals of shameless dark green.

14

He had supper and went to his room. He lay down on the bed in his pyjamas, to wait for the clock to strike eleven. He woke, thinking that not much more than an hour could have passed, and found it was already dawn. When he got back from school he found that the master and mistress had returned and intended spending a couple of days in the house. Three days later, when they had gone, Kus-Kus no longer felt like going up to the mansards.

He missed the way things used to be, his friendly relationship with Aunt Eugenia; that lost childhood. He had no memories of his childhood; or at least he didn't refer to the memories he had as such. But he also had the feeling that he had left behind, partly through his own fault, partly through Aunt Eugenia's, an unexplored kingdom of emotions and discoveries that were less raw and insecure and infinitely more touching than those of his present existence. The presence of the master and mistress in the house during those three days contributed more than a little to the impression he had of having left his childhood behind him for ever. For the first time he had lunch at table. He had the (possibly inexact, but irresistible) feeling that for the first time his father treated him as an equal and that they could talk together about life (rather as he and Julian used to do in the kitchen as they picked over the lentils, but now it was with more solemnity and propriety, and in the study, which seemed to him almost unrecognisable with the pale spring sun pouring in, its rays wreathed in mesmerising clouds of cigar smoke, whose rich aroma made him think of those shadowy Americas on his globe, on the other side of a gleaming Atlantic). He found himself thinking, 'Aunt Eugenia is to blame for everything.' He found himself formulating this thought word by word. He even got as far as writing it down in his Geography book: 'Aunt Eugenia is to blame for everything.' The sentence, once written, reared up like a snake, and although he ended up by tearing out the page, what he had written kept on coiling and uncoiling in the empty space that remained. The space was like a crevice, marking the spot through which the snake had escaped, unharmed, a crack through which it could reappear. On the last day of his parents' visit, he and his father found themselves alone together in the dining room after lunch; they had had coffee there and a contagious euphoria, like a need to prolong and seal the trust and camaraderie which seemed to be growing between them, almost led Kus-Kus into a betrayal. His father had said: 'As you'll soon find out, there's no understanding women. You can't live with them or without them.' And he had laughed at his own words and added, chuckling: 'Let me put that another way. Don't take me too literally and go telling everyone that I don't like women, then we'd be in trouble! What I mean is, well, what I said, as you'll find out soon enough for yourself, that you can't live with them or without them.' Kus-Kus was on the point of saying that he knew that all too well and that the reason he knew that was because of what had happened with Aunt Eugenia. But the idea of bringing Aunt Eugenia's name into the conversation brought with it all the old anxieties and threw into disquieting relief the idea of disloyalty and betrayal which Kus-Kus instinctively hated and condemned. Consequently, he stopped himself in time and simply said, imitating his father's tone of voice, and mixing it unintentionally with an expression that one of his grandmother's chauffeurs was always using and which he had already tried out, alone, and in various contexts: 'God knows what makes women tick.' At which point his mother came into the dining room and wanted to know what sort of language was that to be using and what were they talking about anyway. The situation changed completely. The camaraderie was lost. Aunt Eugenia's name was mentioned a little later that afternoon anyway, when his mother was talking on the telephone to a friend, perhaps to his grandmother (the conversation took place in the little room next to the study that led into his parents' bedroom, and Kus-Kus, who was in the study with his father, couldn't follow it all). But the mere mention of her name echoed round the room, casting a pall over it, and making Kus-Kus reflect sadly on how much his life had changed. 'Women are to blame for everything, isn't that right, Papa? That's what you were saying before, isn't it?'

His father laughed again and said, lowering his voice a little: 'I don't know about *everything*, son! No human being, man or woman, can be to blame for everything, not all on their own, no. Guilt always presupposes two or more people . . . And I'm not sure if it's right to call them guilty or simply victims. It's never one person who's to blame, it's everyone. Why do you ask?' Kus-Kus didn't answer because his father had already got up with the air of someone who had said the last word on the subject, and because, in Kus-Kus's eyes, any answer now would again have involved some disloyalty.

When the master and mistress left, the house returned to its customary peace (a peace which, to Kus-Kus, seemed suddenly dull, like a trivial game to kill time on a rainy afternoon); the peace brought with it its opposite, a lack of peace sown by his troubled conscience. In a way, in spite of what his father had said, it was impossible not to feel himself entirely to blame for everything that had happened. The peace in the house became unbearable, and Kus-Kus began to feel embarrassed and inhibited at the thought of going up to see what was happening (although, ironically, not going up didn't lessen his almost obsessive curiosity).

It was night. Kus-Kus had gone to bed. He had put out the light but couldn't get to sleep. On tiptoes, in his pyjamas, he went as far as the study. Without putting the lights on, he sat down in his father's armchair, but didn't make himself comfortable, just sat, almost without moving. They hadn't tidied up yet. First thing tomorrow Josefa would open the windows wide. But now, and all through the night, thought Kus-Kus, the room would smell of cigar smoke, of the strong cologne his father used, of the sudden camaraderie that had been born between them, and, paradoxically, of his abrupt deprivation of it all. That night, in the darkness of the study, he believed he could make out the beginnings of a possibility as new as it was ambiguous, and thought resentfully: 'I'll have to sort it out alone. Just as well I didn't say anything. Whatever my father says, I'm the only one to blame. I'll just have to sort it out on my own, as usual.'

He didn't even feel any surprise. It was — Julian resisted using the word which, nevertheless, kept coming to his lips — it was, yes, like a romance, like a love affair with no precise object. It was the first time he'd been in love like this, and he hadn't fully absorbed the astonishment that these emotions provoked in him. He was letting himself be carried along, but where? It didn't much matter. The novelty was itself too surprising for him to be thinking about the future. As is the case in love affairs, only the moment existed; the present moment, the previous one, the next one, became a pure present that coloured the infinitely variable light of the mansards. His conjunctivitis scarcely bothered him; when he went out on to the terrace or leaned out of the windows (something he was always doing) he didn't even put on his dark glasses. For the first time in his life he spent long periods watching the silky sea, which, as it shimmered down below, took on in his mind all the attributes of a loved one. When it came down to it, was it all just a sort of ecstasy brought on by the view? Julian didn't want to believe that. The other thing, that remained when, high up in that lighthouse of an apartment, he stopped watching or thinking about the sea, was Miss Eugenia herself and her extraordinary behaviour. Julian scarcely saw her. Only at meals, which she served him in the living room, with the respectful attitude, the diligence and precision of an expert maid. The first day, during lunch, Julian thought, almost convinced himself, that it was a joke. In fact, when he was caught in the hallway on the point of escaping, he had thought he would try to gain time by playing along with the eccentric woman; for that reason, overcoming an impulse to explain what had happened the previous night, he simply answered the questions Aunt Eugenia put to him, saying that he had indeed slept very well and that he did indeed prefer coffee to tea with his breakfast. Since she seemed satisfied with these replies and made no reference to what had happened, Julian had ventured into the kitchen after breakfast, where it seemed Miss Eugenia had chosen to shut herself up, and asked for a razor if she happened to have one in the house. She gave him one and said that, once he was washed and dressed, he could make himself comfortable in the living room if he wanted, or in his own room, where he would find a bell to ring if he wanted a drink, a glass of sherry perhaps, or anything else, before lunch.

After lunch he settled down in the little sitting room next to his bedroom and, leaving the window wide open, sat down in the armchair. About mid-afternoon he was woken by the front doorbell. And he surprised himself by simply closing his eyes again without feeling in the least frightened. He made out the sound of low voices in conversation, a man's voice, and the sound of the kitchen door closing. Then he forgot all about it. What occupied his whole consciousness was the sea, illuminated, as the afternoon advanced, by tender motes of light like airy vegetation caught up by a rain shower, and by the changes in the wind he had never noticed on land. At supper time, Aunt Eugenia asked if he had needed anything during the afternoon and if the doorbell had disturbed him. Julian said not. Two, perhaps three days passed in this way. Now when he woke early in the morning and opened his bedroom window, Julian discovered that the idea of escaping to France, the fear of being pursued if he left the house or of being trapped if he remained there, the increasingly obvious fact that Rafael had once again betrayed him, and thence the knowledge that the promised money would never reach him, all that, together with the humiliations and miseries which had marked his life until then, had ceased to have any importance. He did wonder what had happened to Kus-Kus, since his fate did, after all, lie in the boy's hands. But he thought about it as one thinks of something that might happen to someone else. The only important thing now, the only thing that quickened his senses and kept his mind constantly on the alert, was the mystery of that room, of those two rooms and the sea, to which the servile attitude of Miss Eugenia seemed to be related, and which were, he was sure, on the point of telling him something about himself.

15

'If only I could talk to someone about this . . .' It was the afternoon of the fourth day. It felt as if a century had passed. But who could Kus-Kus talk to? He would have had to explain so much before he could even begin that whenever he was about to start he always stopped short. With Julian? Why hadn't he thought of Julian before? While he was up there in Aunt Eugenia's apartment, he was the answer. Kus-Kus went to sleep thinking that he would talk to Julian and that everything would go back to the way it was ... He had confused dreams about Aunt Eugenia that night. In each one her figure appeared, but always indistinct, as if on the point of disappearing if he didn't instantly manage to say or do the right thing. And the right thing was to speak. To utter a word, or sometimes an interminably long sentence which he had to get out all in one go. When he got out of bed he felt strange ... not ill exactly, but what Miss Hart called 'off colour'. He would stay at home. It was a rainy morning. An unexpected storm. The whole house boomed, creaked, shuddered like a cabin in the middle of a forest. The wild weather seemed set to return at any moment, malignant and vengeful, like a blind fit of rage from the dark gods of the cloud-covered mountains on the other side of the bay. Huddled between the sheets after eating the breakfast brought by Josefa, who grumbled abstractedly about people staying in their nice warm beds instead of going to work, Kus-Kus felt as exultant as if he had safely traversed a dangerous forest infested with beasts as fierce and persistent as the rain that thudded against the windows. He felt safe and, as it were, absolved. Today he would go up and see Julian.

In the kitchen, too, there was tremendous curiosity about what was going on upstairs. What with one thing and another, nearly a month had passed without news, with no new developments, without any apparent comings and goings. The people upstairs seemed to have vanished into thin air, to have become invisible. It was still generally thought that Kus-Kus was the only one to have anything to do with them. 'Them' was, of course, Manolo and Miss Eugenia. Of Julian, long since forgotten, they knew nothing.

Kus-Kus got up about one o'clock and, still in his pyjamas, went for a walk about the house. In the dining room Josefa was flicking a feather duster over the sideboard and its tarnished mirror which only half-reflected the dull, blackened, dirty silver tea service. The old topic of animals came up and Josefa, just to provoke him, said that cats were ugly beasts. 'I don't care what you say, cats are just ugly beasts, nasty, ugly beasts, that's all there is to it.'

'And you're an ugly beast too, a nasty, ugly beast,' said Kus-Kus, almost angry now.

'Well, it takes one to know one . . .'

'And you're a tart too,' said Kus-Kus sharply.

'Listen to the pot calling the kettle black . . . !'

Kus-Kus gave her an almighty kick, wanting to kill her. Red as a beetroot, Josefa turned round, crouched down, and exclaimed in a hoarse voice: 'You little bugger! You've laddered my stocking!'

'You're the bugger. Stupid cow,' murmured Kus-Kus mechanically, not wanting to continue the fight, but not wanting to be the loser either; not understanding why Josefa had brought up the business about cats, not knowing why he had reacted so brutally.

'I'm sorry, Josefa.'

'I don't know what you do up there all day, I don't know what you get up to in Aunt Eugenia's apartment, you and the rest of them . . .'

'There's only Aunt Eugenia and me,' Kus-Kus said quickly, in a slightly sharper tone than before.

'And what about Manolo and that little sister of his that's turned up. Some little sister – with that hair she must get through a bottle of dye a day if I'm any judge, because it's pure peroxide, you can't fool me. I wonder if she really *is* his sister or what . . . you men are such innocents . . .'

'And you women are silly cows,' murmured Kus-Kus, disconcerted. What was this about a sister? What was going on upstairs?

'Don't get angry. You and I get on fine. Do you want to try giving me a kiss? Let's see if you've learned how, now you've grown up a bit. It's amazing how you've grown in such a short time. You've really shot up this winter, you're as tall as I am . . .'

'I must be really dumpy then! Who's this sister you were talking about?'

'Manolo's sister, of course! Who else? That peroxide blonde. Does she go up to see your aunt?'

'How should I know?' murmured Kus-Kus, feeling shaken by the information he'd just received. Josefa was in a talkative mood. She noticed the boy's uncertainty, which gave her confidence.

'What I say is, what can you expect from a shop assistant? I don't know how Miss Eugenia could have stooped so low. Honestly, getting involved with the boy from the shop!'

'Well, you wouldn't have said no! It used to be embarrassing watching you go to the door to pick up the order!' It was a minor victory, Kus-Kus knew, which left Josefa unabashed.

'So what? It's one thing for me to do that but quite another for a lady; when Lady Muck gets a taste for the same turnips as the maid it's enough to make a cat laugh! I must get my hair done this week, without fail, except I'd save money if I didn't . . .' said Josefa, changing tack and looking at herself in the sideboard mirror while watching Kus-Kus obscurely reflected behind her. He really had grown that winter. He was quite the young man already, almost attractive, she thought, not a child any more. Standing there in his pyjamas, behind her, with his long legs, she could see that his body was beginning to fill out. In a little while he'd be quite something. He already was. Still too young, of course, though he was filling out nicely . . . Josefa continued fixing her hair in front of the mirror, her curiosity about the goings-on upstairs now mixed with curiosity about Kus-Kus – '. . . except I'd save money by not going, and if you saw the queue, all the maids together, it reeks of maids there, and you should see Chati, her nephew, Juli, the hairdresser's nephew, she didn't have children, Juli, so they adopted this nephew, well, I don't know about adopt exactly, but if you saw this nephew you'd laugh, the expressions on his face, the way he ponces about when he's doing our hair, honestly, some of his gestures . . . if he isn't queer I don't know who is, you should just see the prissy way he moves around . . . do you know who else I think was queer? Well, it's only what I think, but Julian, I don't know for certain, you know, but I just got that feeling, nothing I could put my finger on, it's nothing he did, at least not in the house, but he seemed to me . . . I don't know, just the sort to be one of those secret queers, always on his own, I don't know, he seemed to me . . .'

'What's Julian got to do with it?' interrupted Kus-Kus, reddening, partly because of her manner and the allusions she made and partly because of the proximity of the object of those slanders. He must go up without fail this afternoon.

'What do you mean? I'm not saying he's got anything to do with anything, I'm not saying it's true and I'm not saying it isn't, I just mean probably, I'm saying that probably . . . anyway, you saw what he did, he's a thief, you can't deny that. A queer, probably; but a thief, definitely. What a turn-up him going off like that, I couldn't believe it, couldn't believe it!'

'Hello,' he said. It was going to be more difficult than he thought. Aunt Eugenia had opened the door and was looking at him without saying anything. She had changed. She was dressed differently, all in black. Kus-Kus couldn't remember ever having seen his aunt dressed like that, or known her to open the door like that, with no exclamations, without rushing to give him a kiss, without smelling of two perfumes at once. It was going to be difficult. He felt deeply sorry. He didn't know what to say. He didn't dare look Aunt Eugenia in the face. He was on the point of turning and escaping down the stairs. She didn't seem the same woman. Faced with this unknown Aunt Eugenia there was no way he could greet her nonchalantly, as one would in Bariloche. It was going to be impossible not to take her seriousness seriously. It was all going to be much more difficult than ever before. Much more unpleasant even than the last time.

'Hello,' he said again.

'Come in, Kus-Kus, good afternoon. Julian is in his room. He'll be pleased you've come, after so many days without seeing you.'

He knocked on the door of Eduardo's room. Aunt Eugenia had gone back into the kitchen without saying anything more. Julian didn't open the door. Kus-Kus couldn't hear anyone moving inside, not a sound. 'Can he have run off?' he thought. 'What am I going to say to him?' He felt nervous, as if he were knocking at the door of some important, enigmatic personage. It was like knocking at the headmaster's door at school. Would he have got the money? Then he remembered that no one knew where he was. He knocked again. Another silence. He didn't dare try the door to see if it was bolted from the inside. He knocked again.

'I didn't hear you. I was out on the terrace. You can get to it from outside. Did you know that? You go out through the window in the little living room and around the roof, it's much quicker that way, going round the outside rather than the inside. I spend all day on the terrace. How are you? How's everyone downstairs? Are they well? How are things? Come on, say something!'

'I'm fine, I'm fine, and I can see you are.'

'Does it show that much? What a stupid question! Sometimes up here, I talk out loud to myself, and say stupid things just for the hell of it, I don't know why that should be. I only heard you by chance. Had you been knocking for long?'

'Not long. A while.'

'You should have come in. You needn't have knocked. I was on the living-room terrace. Did you know you could get there via the roof? Ah, but I just asked you that! That's why I didn't hear you. Next time come in without knocking . . . it was pure chance that I heard you.'

'There probably won't be a next time.'

'Why not? What do you mean, no next time . . . ?'

'You obviously like the apartment, even the rooftops . . .'

'Yes, I do like it. Thanks, by the way. Thanks a lot. I should have said that at the start. I owe all this to you, don't think I haven't thought of you these past few days . . .'

'You're treated well here. Aunt Eugenia, I mean, she treats you well, doesn't she?'

'Well? Couldn't be better. She treats me very well; couldn't treat me better, really. Really very, very well . . .'

'I'm glad.'

Julian walked up and down while he talked. He moved calmly, almost slowly, in contrast to the speed with which he talked. Kus-Kus couldn't remember seeing him so talkative and animated before. They had just gone through the little door which led to the bedroom. Julian sat on the bed, lit a cigarette, and inhaled the smoke with evident pleasure. 'I'm smoking much less,' he murmured, as if talking to himself. He was in shirtsleeves. A shirt with thin blue stripes, freshly ironed, Kus-Kus noted. They remained silent, looking at each other.

'Do you remember how you wanted to poison Miss Hart? Why did you want to do that? Don't you remember? You came to my room one night . . . like now in a way.'

'A bit like now . . . yes, I remember. It was a joke, I mean a game.'

'That's what I thought, that it was a game. I didn't take it seriously. Why would you want to poison her?'

'I already told you. So she could go to her final rest.'

'That's it, so she could go to her final rest, that's what you said.'

'Only it wasn't a game, that's the only . . .'

'It wasn't? Of course it was a game! Or rather a joke, you said so yourself just now.'

'Me? I've hardly said a word. You haven't stopped talking.'

'Sorry, I didn't realise. Sometimes I just don't realise what I'm doing.'

'Sometimes it certainly seems you don't realise what you're doing. It often seems that way.'

'I'm sorry.'

'And sometimes you also don't seem to realise that you owe my parents ten thousand pesetas, that you cashed the cheque and ran off, just like that, you don't seem to realise that either . . .'

'I'm sorry. Of course I do.'

'I don't think so; you don't really. If you really did, you wouldn't be hiding up here for a start. For a start you wouldn't have asked me to hide you. You also don't seem to realise that you either give back the ten thousand pesetas to my parents or you go to gaol.'

'It wasn't ten thousand, as you know. It was a little bit less. I know it comes to the same thing, but it was less, quite a lot less.'

'Aren't you sorry? You should be sorry . . .'

'Sorry?'

'You're obviously not. If you were sorry, you wouldn't be happily chattering away here, in my aunt's apartment.'

'I'm sorry I let you down, I really am.'

'What's that got to do with it? I'm talking about being really sorry. Sorry for having stolen ten thousand pesetas from my father. Are you sorry for that?'

'No.'

'Well, I take it you know you've got to return it or they'll put you in prison, for twenty years probably, or more. For that amount of money probably twice as long. Did you know that? It's a lot of money . . . So, are you sorry or not? I've told you how long in prison you'd get, more or less, of course, I can't know exactly. But I do know that twenty years is on the low side for what they usually hand out to people for theft involving breach of trust, that's what it's called, breach of trust. So what do you say? You either give it back or get twenty years in prison. Are you sorry now, or not?'

'I can't give it back. I haven't got it.'

'Have you spent it all already? It was a lot ... You must have half left, at least half ...'

'It isn't that I've spent it. I gave it to friend. Don't you remember? I had to give it to a friend. I explained it all to you ...'

'So first you go and rob my father and then you give it all to a friend ... He must be a very good friend. Come off it, you can't have given it all to him. Not all of it.'

'I gave it all to Rafael. I explained that to you, I told you. Don't you remember me telling you?'

'You didn't tell me anything about that. You said something about some friend of yours, I don't remember now.'

They had scarcely moved while they were talking, although the distance between them had grown considerably. Julian was still sitting on the bed, but he had stopped smoking, and was no longer reclining but gripped the bedstead with one hand, sometimes both, his voice huskier and quieter than before. Kus-Kus walked up and down, his hands behind his back, his eyes fixed on the floor, not looking at his companion, but raising his head each time he said something. Then Julian seemed to relax; leaning over the mahogany bedhead as if over the rail of a pulpit or a prisoner's dock, he lit a cigarette and sighed deeply. 'In short, you want to go back on your word and you're going to turn me in. Is that it?'

'You think that's what I'm saying?'

'Well, yes, I do, frankly. That's what you've come to tell me, isn't it? That's more or less it ... Isn't it?'

'I come up here because there's something I have to talk to

you about, something important that I wanted to talk to you about, and you think I'm going to go back on my word . . .'

'Well, yes . . . Yes, isn't that what it comes to?'

'You haven't been listening to me.'

'Not listening to you? You've been here an hour, or two hours, I don't know how long, going over the same thing again and again, and then you say I haven't been listening to you.'

'You haven't been listening properly.'

'Perhaps not. I thought I had been. I'm sorry.'

'You're going to be even sorrier when I tell you that my parents have been and that they stayed three days and went off again yesterday afternoon.'

'I thought they were away.'

'Why do you think I haven't been up here for three days? Why haven't I been up? Come on, tell me.'

'I've been here nearly five days. It is five, isn't it? From that afternoon outside the school until today, exactly five days. The truth is that I hadn't realised. I've just this minute realised it!'

'You mean you've been living for free up here for five days and you didn't even realise? What a nerve!'

'Not until just now, no, I didn't.'

'So you're so snug and cosy, not a care in the world, nothing but the best, having such a great time, that you don't even notice the days passing . . .'

'I didn't notice, no. You don't notice time passing in this place.'

'And I suppose you've made yourself so much at home you've forgotten it was me who brought you here. You're only here thanks to me.'

'I haven't forgotten that for one moment; I'm very grateful to you.'

'You may be very grateful, but it makes no difference to you whether I come up or not, you couldn't care less.'

'Listen, I'm very pleased to see you, to talk to you, you know that. I don't mean just now, we've always got on well, you and me, from the start. I'm sorry not to have known the master and mistress were at home, I would have liked to talk to the master, I would have liked to talk to him, to take advantage of . . .'

'Take advantage of what?'

'I meant take advantage of their being in the house at the same time as me. Well, to take the opportunity to talk to the master and mistress, that's what I meant.'

'And what did you want to talk about, if you don't mind my asking?'

'About all this. I don't know, to see what could be done . . .'

'I'll tell you what can be done, you don't have to talk to anyone else. The first thing you can do is give back the ten thousand pesetas.'

'It wasn't ten thousand.'

'You're not sorry. You're not a bit sorry. You don't mean to give back one peseta of it.'

'I can't. I'm broke. All I've got is a thousand pesetas, I think.'

'You don't intend giving back anything to anyone and you want to talk to my father, just like that, say hello and tell him he can kiss his money goodbye, just in case he was harbouring any fond hopes of seeing it again. Do you think that's funny?'

'I think the way you put it is funny. I don't think it's funny, it's funny the way you say it. I didn't think the wretched money mattered to you that much!'

'My father knows you're here. I told him.'

'I don't believe you. If you'd told him, the police would have been here by now.'

'I told him you'd hidden the money and it was better not to make a fuss, that you wanted to give it back. Do you believe me or not? That's why he didn't call the police. Do you think I'm joking?'

'No. I don't think it's entirely a joke. I think it's like a game for you. Like poisoning Miss Hart.'

'So, you think it's true that I told him, you don't think it's a joke.'

'I think it's true that you told him because I think it was very important for you to tell him, it was very important for the game. But I don't know if they'll have believed you or not, because I don't know if the master and mistress, or anyone, knows exactly what your game is. I don't think even Miss Eugenia really knows. If anyone knew, she would.'

'Before you came to work at the house, she was the only one who knew. For a long time she was the only person who really understood my games. But that's all over now. We're not such good friends any more. Now no one knows.'

Night had fallen without either of them noticing. In the darkness their two figures had been slowly dissolving, until all that remained were their voices, carrying on a disembodied dialogue. Kus-Kus didn't say that he'd come up specially to talk to Julian about Aunt Eugenia because, after the aggressive tone which had, unfortunately slipped into the conversation, his self-respect, or perhaps his sense of the ridiculous, prevented him from acknowledging that he wanted Julian's help, or perhaps simply somebody's comfort; Julian didn't say, or didn't repeat, that the only thing he regretted was having let Kus-Kus down, because, after the talk, it seemed to him that such a declaration would smack of defiance. They looked at each other thoughtfully, each wishing perhaps that they had talked of other things and in a different tone of voice. 'Don't be upset. The only thing I regret is having let you down; but don't be upset. Try to understand me; at least in this,' Julian finally said. And while he was saying it he felt sorry for the kid standing before him, who seemed at times to be a child, at times an adult, but who never remained in either state long enough to take from it what was beautiful. He saw him suddenly as a very old little boy in an adult's room, small and unformed, guilty, having lost his innocence as Julian had lost his own, purely from lack of time to allow it to flower. And he remembered that other time when Kus-Kus had turned up in his room at midnight, how when he took him back to his bed, before turning out the bedside lamp, when he pulled the blankets down to cover the boy's feet, he had brushed against one of them, and had been moved by the numb clarity of some vestige of his own childhood.

They heard footsteps, then heard the front door open. Kus-Kus looked at Julian questioningly, and Julian said that probably, given the hour, it was the visitor his aunt received every evening, a male visitor Julian had never actually laid eyes on. The sound of whispering reached them, and they heard a door close. The kitchen door, thought Julian. It was the same ritual every evening. Julian felt not the slightest curiosity; once again he limited himself to registering the fact and including it in the list of incomprehensible information with which that house furnished him.

'I suppose it must be Manolo,' said Kus-Kus, suddenly coming out of his reverie. 'Haven't you ever seen him?'

'I don't know who Manolo is; I call him the visitor.'

'A very common sort, Aunt Eugenia's friend. I didn't know he came up every evening. You must know him.'

'It probably isn't him. I thought I heard a man's voice the other evening, but I'm probably mistaken. I didn't pay much attention, to be honest.'

'He's called Manolo. He's my aunt's new gigolo, he works in the grocer's. Surely you heard about him when you were in the house. Josefa talks about him all the time, he's the sort of man women like . . . What are you laughing at?'

'The way you talk makes me laugh. What do you know about what women like?'

'They like Manolo, I know that. He seems common to me.'

'I think I know who you mean, if it's the same Manolo. It must be . . . Yes, the one from the grocer's, a good-looking boy, I remember him well . . .'

'Did you like him too?'

'You've got some funny ideas today!'

'Josefa says she's almost sure you're queer.'

'Have you been talking to Josefa about me?'

'I haven't, no. She said it in passing, I don't know why. She doesn't know you're here, no one knows.'

'Before, you said your parents knew. Which is it to be?'

'Don't start on that again! We've talked enough about that. I'll take care of you now, don't worry.'

'You'll have to go, it's late. What are you going to do about me?'

'You're all right here, aren't you? As far as I'm concerned you can leave if you want . . .'

'Do you want me to go?'

'It's all the same to me.'

He went with him into the hall. The light was on in the kitchen. Julian felt as though he were sleepwalking. It was like accompanying a nephew to the door, like saying goodbye to him after a quiet evening at home. The kid didn't seem aware of the unreality of the situation, thought Julian, worried now about how late it was. Julian went back to his room. For a moment he was tempted to eavesdrop on the couple in the kitchen. Then he went to the window and, opening it, breathed in the bracing sea air, the marvellous, lucid velvet of the racing sky. 'Tomorrow's another day,' he thought. 'I don't know what it will bring, and I don't care.'

16

If she was going to die, Kus-Kus remembered her saying, of an illness, or was taking a long time to die, she would prefer to go to the hospital and die there, where the Little Sisters would take care of her, but if she had a choice she'd prefer to die suddenly, just to drop dead one day without having to explain anything. And she said that here women still lived in the Dark Ages, thinking that their fate was either to get married or to become a nun, and that was why old maids were frowned upon, because here people would always be provincials, and you had to put up with it or leave, and they didn't understand people like her, Aunt Eugenia, or like him, Kus-Kus, who had lived in other places and seen other things and had points of comparison and dreams and imagination and ideas and were always coming up with something different to do or say or think, not the trivia and prattle of the girls who had been her friends before they married, some of whom still had nothing more on their minds than what dress to wear or what was the latest fashion, and that was how they stayed, never getting beyond that stage, because there was nothing more to them, and what they called among themselves a 'good girl' amounted to nothing but a coward really. Kus-Kus mustn't let himself be fooled, but must learn to call a spade a spade. It was fear of finding themselves alone, because, here in the provinces, the price you paid for being like her or Kus-Kus, for being full of life and having marvellous ideas and dreams, the price you paid was loneliness . . .

He remembered all Aunt Eugenia's words, as if he had just heard them; and they still fascinated him. He mouthed them to himself without entirely understanding why, for example, it should be cowardice on the part of her friends to get married instead of staying single. 'I'm going to stay single, Aunt Eugenia, and I'll come and live with you and we'll go on honeymoon wherever you want, even to Bariloche if you like.' But Kus-Kus recalled that the idea hadn't struck Aunt Eugenia as all that brilliant, and that she'd smiled rather dutifully and changed the subject. That must have been shortly before Julian came. It must have been during the summer, in August ... She'd been right in a way, that stupid woman, the unfortunate Villacantero woman (it was Aunt Eugenia's idea to call her 'that unfortunate woman'), she'd been right in a way the other afternoon in his grandmother's house, when she'd talked about the funny turns and the manias women had. And he seemed suddenly to remember that all that month of August Aunt Eugenia had seemed odd to him, really odd, somehow more worried than usual about her weight and yet incessantly eating dates and peanuts and toasted almonds between meals, which his grandmother said distended your stomach, one lot of food never getting properly digested before the next was upon it, a disgusting habit, pure gluttony, just awful, and she, Mercedes, had never understood how a beautiful girl with Aunt Eugenia's looks had come to that ... And on top of it all there were the frequent glasses of sherry. Yes, that last August Aunt Eugenia had seemed odd, always complaining about some friends of hers who, in fact, she never saw, accusing them of being stupid and cowardly, just because ... why? Kus-Kus had the feeling that the 'whys' were multiplying, that trying to find answers to them was draining the energy he needed to summon up the memories. He had always preferred remembering things to explaining them; just letting them surface all together, the way remembered things do, and holding them for an instant, just letting them come and go, in fragments. The idea of coming up with an explanation, like in an exam, was something new to Kus-Kus, a disagreeable consequence of his altered relationship with Aunt Eugenia. And the bad thing about it was that once you started to ask why this and why that, you couldn't just enjoy the memories like before. And then that business about Manolo . . . There was no explaining that. And if you couldn't explain it, it must be unforgivable; and if it was unforgivable . . . what then? If only it had been someone else, someone Kus-Kus could talk to. But he couldn't talk to that Manolo. The row there'd be if the priests at school found out; or if his grandmother or the Villacantero woman or anyone found out. And that just proved there was no explaining the business with Manolo, just proved that it was unforgivable. It occurred to Kus-Kus at that point that the reason the situation had no solution was because it was in bad taste; that was why there was no way of talking about it or resolving it, because it was the truth, and telling the truth was in bad taste. He was getting nowhere. It was as if, while still hounded by memories of Aunt Eugenia that struggled to the surface, he now found himself obliged, because of this abstract web of questions that beset him, to suppress his memories in some way, make them less bright, less important.

It was Thursday afternoon; he'd been in this state of mind for a couple of days now, going over and over it all, just making matters worse all the time, and moving further and further away from any interpretation or comforting explanation. He went out, telling Miss Hart that he was going to play football at school; once outside, he wandered by the sunny port, up to the end of the jetty, where there are railings to stop people getting as far as the marker beacon. He sat down next to some men who were fishing. The oily edges of the sea licked and slid about the base of the jetty. It was high tide. That was when he said the word out loud: 'blackmailer'.

It didn't sound bad, didn't sound like anything very serious. It sounded a little like 'fire-eater' or 'juggler', like a circus act, a conjuror perhaps. It occurred to him that he'd never known a blackmailer, which must prove that no one did it seriously, only now and then, in order to get something. It wasn't a profession, it wasn't anything. Someone who, in order to get a hold on another person, threatens to reveal that person's shameful secret. The precision of the sentence surprised him. That it contained an allusion to himself surprised him too, and he suddenly blushed to the roots of his hair – he could feel his ears burning – as if he'd overheard two friends laughing at him behind his back.

17

Julian woke up the next day with a bad taste in his mouth and a headache. His eyes were watering profusely. He lit a cigarette as soon as he got up. It was too early for breakfast; he smiled to think how quickly he'd adapted to the routine of Aunt Eugenia's apartment. It was pleasant not to have to think about cooking, not having to work, being waited on. His good mood, however, didn't last long; yesterday evening's conversation had upset him. Out of sheer habit he stood for a long while contemplating the glittering sea and the tiny port, which at that hour looked like a coloured print; the yellow, the blue, the slightly antique look, the delicate watercolour greys which made one think of something painted from memory, a familiar landscape evoked rather than actually perceived. But he couldn't now easily recover the mood of the previous days. He was in the hands of a cruel and irresponsible child. Asking Kus-Kus for help now seemed complete madness, the only explanation for which could be a desire to hand himself over to the victims of his crime. He reflected bitterly on how little importance the police – and, therefore, the people involved – must have given the matter, 'They've got more than enough money, it's all the same to them, as long as it doesn't cause them any bother.' On the other hand the kid had, half-jokingly, given him the impression that the amount stolen, even in his employers' eyes, was considerable. What would happen if, as he'd said to the boy, he went to talk to the master and mistress? Would they take him back, even if it was without pay, or on half pay? He'd have to work for nothing for two years to pay back all the money. And how could he stand two years like that? He lay down on the bed and thought about Rafael, about Esther, compounding them into one painful, erotic image. Was Esther still in the city? The front doorbell rang. He heard Aunt Eugenia's footsteps.

He thought: 'This is it, the kid must have informed on me last night, he phoned the police, they're here.' He got dressed. Where were his glasses? The visitor and Miss Eugenia seemed to be holding a hurried, whispered conference by the door to the living room. There was no doubt now, it must be the police. He had to find those wretched glasses. He went round the room checking everything meticulously. He stopped when he heard Miss Eugenia talking to him through the door. He said, in rather a quiet voice: 'I'm just coming,' and then said, almost shouting this time, 'I'll be right there!' He needed a moment to think. He turned his back to the door, looked round the room and sighed with relief. Suddenly he felt much better. It was the end of Esther, the end of Rafael, the end of his own miserable existence. They would arrest him, take him to court, put him in prison . . . He closed his eyes. It was a great relief. Then he opened the door.

'There's a visitor to see you in the living room,' Miss

Eugenia announced, adding: 'Would you like your breakfast now, sir? I can bring your tray there if you want . . .'

'I'm not sure, don't go to any bother . . .' said Julian, looking inquisitively at Miss Eugenia. 'A visitor, you said?' he asked at last.

'Yes, sir, in the living room, waiting for you. Shall I take your breakfast in there?'

He opened the living-room door slowly, looking back at Miss Eugenia before going in, as if to say goodbye to her. Her expression was blank, the respectfully restrained expression of a servant: that was all he could read on her pale, distant face.

The visitor was Esther. He closed the door and went towards her, thinking that he hadn't said if he wanted to have his breakfast in the living room or not. He wasn't surprised; just worried, uncomfortable.

'How did you know I was here?'

'Rafael phoned last night. It was his idea, in fact. A brilliant idea really. I always said Rafael should have been a policeman. Manolo didn't say a word, you'd never think he was my brother. It's very like you, by the way, to come back and hide at the scene of the crime . . . You're in the boy's hands now, always in someone's hands . . .'

'What's that got to do with it?'

'It's the truth.'

'Have you got the money?'

'What money?'

'The money, the money Rafael was going to send me, I need it.'

'I don't know anything about any money. Did Rafael say he was going to send you some money?' asked Esther, putting all the malice she could into the question.

'Yes,' said Julian, without looking at her.

'When has Rafael sent money to anyone? You're so naïve. Anyway, what do you need money for? You're all right here. This is some apartment!'

Desperation made him clench his jaws. Shame made him blush. He trembled with rage. To hide the trembling, he asked: 'How did you know I was here?'

'I've just told you: through Rafael. He phoned me last night telling me to come and see you here. And here I am. You should be pleased.'

Julian thought of Miss Eugenia coming and going silently about the apartment, serving him his three meals a day, tidying his room, ironing his clothes, opening the door every afternoon to her unknown visitor; he thought of her shut up in the kitchen for a couple of hours every afternoon with the unknown visitor, someone, perhaps, as strange and unknown to her as Julian himself was. His eyes felt gritty and began to water. Esther had installed herself on the sofa and was looking round the room with curiosity. Julian felt like beating her brains out.

'It was a brilliant idea to come and look for you here. A brilliant idea,' she said at last.

'Not that brilliant. It was me who gave him the address, the master and mistress's address. I told him to send the money here, in a letter addressed to the kid. I would have passed by here anyway . . . So it wasn't such a brilliant idea.'

'What do you think you'll do, supposing the money does arrive? Do you trust the boy? He'll end up telling the whole story, at school, or to his grandmother . . . You've fallen into a trap.'

'Whilst trying to escape from another.'

'I don't know what you mean. Rafael loves you, only yesterday he was saying so. Only yesterday, on the phone, he said it again, that you're the only friend he has in the world, and that he'd shoot himself if they arrested you now and sent you down for twenty years. He absolutely insisted on me coming to see you in case you needed anything.'

'I don't need anything, thanks. Just the money.'

'Aren't you going to go back?' asked Esther. 'Aren't you

going to go back to Rafael? He's your only friend, the only one you have in the whole world. And me, of course, I'm your best woman friend, the only woman who's ever understood you. I mean you do have rather unusual tastes, don't you, darling, a little bit too strong for any decent woman ... Do you really not want to go back to Rafael? It won't be easy for you to abandon him altogether ...'

'No, I'm not going back. Not this time. Anyway, I can't. Not without money ... what would Rafael want with me, without money. This time it will be easy to leave the two of you. I won't get out of prison so soon this time ... not as soon as last time, not for a second offence, committed whilst employed in a private house. I don't think you'll see me again for a long time. It's a relief really.'

'How can you be so sure? You could probably escape to France. I don't see why not.'

'What were you two talking about?'

'What were who talking about?'

'What were you talking about with her?'

'With her? With who?'

'With her. Who do you think? With Miss Eugenia.'

'Oh, her!'

'Don't you want to tell me?'

'I had to introduce myself, didn't I? I enjoyed it. Miss Eugenia, as you call her, went quite pale. Well, I assume she went pale because she certainly went very quiet, staring at me with those mad eyes of hers. That useless brother of mine hadn't told her anything about me at all, and I've been here three months! It would seem he doesn't like to talk about his family. And we're a decent family, all of us, except me perhaps. I'm an actress, and what can you expect from an actress? Reds, the lot of us, red through and through. I can't remember what we were talking about! Give me a cigarette. You should have asked me if I wanted a cigarette or a drink ages ago. You've no manners, darling. In a place like this, surrounded by luxury, with such neighbours, you should pick up a few tips, sweetheart. It isn't difficult, you're an actor too, after all, and this place has got everything. If you just got away with the silver you'd make yourself a bit of money. Have you got a ration card? You probably wouldn't have here, here you probably eat black market stuff. You can tell they're rich, all of them, and they beat us, the bastards. You can tell they've got money, it's the little touches that give it away. You've got the soul of a servant though, no eye for detail...'

'Servants *do* notice details. They notice them a lot,' said Julian, interrupting her and sitting down next to her on the sofa, feeling victorious for having interrupted her, for having dented her vain belief that she always knew what was and what wasn't in good taste. 'It's true,' he thought with satisfaction, 'servants do have an eye for detail. But only people who've had servants know that, and that's exactly what they pay us for, so that they don't have to worry about details.' For a moment he almost wanted to say, almost did say, all that out loud. He wanted, just once, to make her feel false and ridiculous, even if it *was* only over an insignificant detail. But he didn't say anything because it was always like that with Esther. She wore her small victories like ornaments, highlighting and adorning her total triumph over Julian's will. There was no point in beating around the bush. Why had she really come? He knew there was no point asking her, and smiled to think that everything had already been decided, except for small details of staging, dialogue, costume and plot, which would end exactly as foreseen from the very start.

'Esther, I'd like you to tell me what you and Miss Eugenia were talking about... out of simple curiosity. I hardly ever speak to her, hardly even see her. I was curious, that's all. You were talking for some time in the corridor. I was listening because I thought it was the police, I thought they'd finally come to arrest me. Or release me, if you prefer...'

'When I came in, I said: "Good afternoon, Eugenia, I'm Esther, the sister of Manolo, the shop assistant who's been keeping you company recently. A good-looking boy, my brother, especially in the parts that matter. Do you know what I mean, Eugenia? The masculine equipment. Very superior tackle, but then all the men in my family have got pricks as big as donkeys' on them. Well, I'm his older sister and I've come to see what you do to the boy in the evenings, because he's wasting away to a shadow, poor child, you ought to be ashamed of yourself," I said. Do you think I wouldn't say that?'

'I'm sure you're capable of even greater cruelty than that. In this case, though, I don't think you'd dare. In your own way you're naïve, even decent, even conventional, and this place impresses you, don't deny it, it excites your theatrical instincts, awakens your failed dreams of belonging to high society; this house makes you feel humiliated, Esther, deny it if you like, I know it's true because I know you very well, because I loved you, incredible as it may seem, I was in love with you . . . in my own way, of course.'

'Like a pansy, you mean.'

'You liked it . . .' said Julian, suddenly caught up on the same old helterskelter of aggression and triumph. Thinking that things were the same as before, he added, almost in a whisper: 'I don't think you were pretending; you weren't pretending all the time, you couldn't have been, I don't care what you say now, you wanted me.'

'Julian, don't start. It'll only end up the way it always does. I know what you are, let's get that straight, and I know what you like, apart from little boys that is, you disgusting pervert. Do you want to know why I'm here? Do you really want to know? To get money out of this whore of an aunt, this Aunt Eugenia, or whatever she's called. That's what I've come for. Now you know.'

'I'd already guessed it was something like that, because I've loved you and I know you. I know both of you well, Esther. Rafael, you and me, we're all the same really . . . But you can count me out of this one.'

'No one's mentioned counting you in, as far as I know. You got yourself into this on your own, sweetheart, all on your own. Whether you like it or not, we may have to count you in, because you're already in up to your neck.'

'What are you planning to do?' he asked, thinking it better to know; as he listened to Esther talk, it began to seem to him both a necessity and a duty to warn Aunt Eugenia of the couple's plans, and to protect her, this woman he hardly knew. If, that is, there was any likelihood of the plan being put into action. Julian wasn't sure about that yet. All their plans became unrealisable as soon as they were anything more than talk. Sometimes he thought this failing in his friends was symptomatic of something. Esther was still talking, loudly, languidly, elegantly, with the artificial attractiveness of a mannequin.

'We're thinking about it. A lot depends on her, on the importance she gives to her "lapse", on the importance her friends and family give it. It depends on a lot of things, it depends on that idiot brother of mine; if he didn't want to be involved, it would be much more difficult. He's like you that way. Come on, Julian, don't tell me you've never noticed my little brother, I find that hard to believe. He's just your type, a bit thick!'

'Yes, I know who he is. He's a good-looking boy. You haven't got anything planned. Admit you've got nothing planned. It's all talk, as usual. You're addicted to words.'

'If my brother won't play along, we can always steal the silver, the jewels, any little things she might have, that she must have, they all have them, hundreds of valuable objects all over the place, the bastards. And, of course, with your police record, if they find you and find out you've been living here . . . I must tell Rafael this, I've only just thought of it.

Since no one knows I've been here today, how's anyone to know if I've been here or not on other days. Your word won't count for much. It won't make a blind bit of difference what you say . . .'

'You're right there. It won't make any difference what I say. A previous offender and living in the house . . . They won't have to think very hard. You're right. That's why it doesn't matter what you tell me, any accusation I make will be used against me. You're both covered, well covered.'

Aunt Eugenia came in at that point. Julian had heard a couple of light knocks on the door. Esther, on the other hand, turned round, startled. 'Don't you want breakfast, sir?'

'No, thank you very much. It's too late now. Thank you, Miss Eugenia.'

Esther watched them with her eyes half-closed, her head on one side, like someone studying a painting in an exaggeratedly contemplative attitude. Aunt Eugenia removed the full ashtray which Esther had placed on the sofa between Julian and herself. Julian had noticed that when she came in Aunt Eugenia was carrying a clean ashtray in her hand, and she exchanged it for the dirty one. Julian thought that if this was an act, or a joke intended to make them think that Aunt Eugenia had become the servant in the house, then it was a perfect performance; only an actress of genius could have imitated so perfectly the efficient, silent orderliness of a maidservant, brought to life a minor character with such exactitude; if it wasn't genius it was a miracle. When Aunt Eugenia left, Esther asked exactly the question Julian was asking himself: 'What the hell's wrong with her? Why is she behaving in that idiotic fashion? She looks like the maid. Is she always like that?'

Julian didn't know what to say. He remembered Aunt Eugenia drinking a little glass of Marie Brizard in the master and mistress's house, talking to two people at once, wearing her hair in the extravagant style she'd adopted for that day.

And he remembered too the still-extravagant Aunt Eugenia of the night Kus-Kus first brought him there. She must be acting, Julian decided. But why?

'Who the hell does she think she's fooling?' Esther's voice resounded like an explosion. Resentful, common and tactless, thought Julian. But, even so, it could hardly be denied that on this point she was right. Again the desire to protect Miss Eugenia at all costs rose in Julian, like an imperious, unbidden wave of emotion.

'She's not trying to fool us,' he said. 'She means it. I don't know why, but she does.'

'Do you like her? You do, don't you! I can't make you out. You obviously want to protect her. I suppose you know she's a tart, a dirty tart, ask my brother. Fat women, I don't know how they do it, but they always attract queers. They say they're good at handjobs. Does she do that for you? You've got plenty of time and space up here. You want to protect her because you like her.'

'Don't be childish. Why are you so childish sometimes, Esther?'

He was trembling. He became aware of it suddenly, as one does when one has mislaid a parcel. The sick cramps in the pit of his stomach, the urgent, disconcerting tug of tenderness. 'This is awful,' he thought, 'like being in hell. It can't possibly get worse.' The past flashed up like a clip of film, a single polyphonic note of music. 'They weren't like this before,' he thought, believing he could remember them as he had seen them the first time, the very first day, and he was ashamed to remember them so affectionately, in spite of their being a thousand times younger, as if, somehow, the simple act of remembering them was also to forgive them, to love them again, to absolve them. He knew it was useless. He would always remember them as lovingly as now, however unlovable they had become. And to remember them like that, he knew, was to deliver himself – a defenceless accomplice to their corruption – back into their hands. Esther was looking at him. Julian looked away and buried his face in his hands. He felt her hands between his legs, awkwardly caressing him, as if unsure of herself. Without moving, he murmured: 'You weren't like this before, we weren't like this . . . Esther, say something. Why don't you say something? Promise me you'll leave the poor stupid woman in peace. Swear it, Esther, swear it. You were lying to me, weren't you? Before, I mean. I swear there's nothing between me and that poor foolish woman.'

He looked up. Esther, who had ceased her caresses, had sprung to her feet like a cat. He remained seated, raising his head a little to see her. He thought she looked like a film star, faded but still triumphant, more triumphant than ever, now that time had left its marks on her face, enriching and beautifying it. Yes, more triumphant than ever. As usual.

'You look like a film star, Esther. You really do. Like a real celebrity. You do still love me, don't you?'

'You mean to stay here, don't you? You had it all worked out. You're lying, of course. You'll tell her everything as soon as I'm gone. You miserable little prick!' Esther's tone changed, she seemed a different person. Although he'd often seen such changes before, Julian was surprised again, feeling himself trapped and happy in hell. Esther had already taken a few steps towards the door.

He got up to follow her. 'When are you coming back?' he asked.

'Soon, don't worry. You haven't told me how you came to be here . . .'

'The boy brought me. It was his idea.'

'You should watch him! He's a bad sort, he's got the face of a devil. He's worse than we are. I can smell it. You just watch him!'

Julian had the impression that she ran out, because the front door slammed violently shut just as he reached the door of the living room. He thought: 'Will they really do it?'

18

'My beloved children: In this mass I would like to consider briefly the meaning of the sentence from the Catechism that you all learned when you were little and which yesterday, as I was walking through the school rooms, I heard you reciting to your colleagues in the primary school. The ten commandments can be reduced to just two: Love God above all else and your neighbour as yourself.' The Father Provincial's head and shoulders and his two small white hands, held together, could just be seen over the pulpit. He reminded one of a bird, though Kus-Kus could not have said what kind. 'I wonder how much the Father Provincial weighs?' Kus-Kus had thought during the tour of inspection. It now occurred to him that the birdlike appearance came from that, from his appearing to weigh about forty-five pounds and from the jerky way he walked and gestured and moved his head. 'My children, does not the second part of the sentence seem strange to you? Does it not seem to you that the part about loving God above all else is all well and good but that the part about loving your neighbour as yourself, on the other hand, seems too little to ask?' Kus-Kus nodded his head several times in agreement, in short sharp jerks, as if infected by the birdlike movements of the Father Provincial. It was true, very true, he'd often thought the same himself; it had struck Kus-Kus too that loving one's neighbour only as much as oneself was mean-spirited. After all, if instead of having ten commandments to obey, from now on there were only going to be two, the least they could do was to think things out properly from the start, grandly, even magnificently, none of that mean, limited business about caring for one's neighbour as one did for oneself. The Father Provincial was right to think that this was too little; not just too little, but far too little, Kus-Kus decided. Now he was repeating himself, only in different words, the way they do in sermons, so as not to bore the faithful. The Father Provincial slightly raised his right hand and stretched out his arm, like a bird's thin leg: 'I say that we should love our neighbour more, more than ourselves, at least as much as we love God. Because, dearly beloved, how are you to love above all else a God whom you cannot see, if you do not love above all else, more than yourselves, *more* than yourselves,' he repeated, lowering his arm and gripping the rail again with both hands, 'your neighbour, whom you can see?'

Kus-Kus was distracted at this point. A boy on his pew was desperately trying to get out, in spite of the fact that any movement during the sermon was strictly forbidden; even to go to the toilet, even to confess, however strongly and suddenly repentance came upon one. But the boy, his neighbour, insisted on getting out and whispered to them that he wanted to get out, that they should let him past, his face all red and his shirt-tails coming out of his trousers. Kus-Kus, who had slightly turned his head towards the priest in charge of their year, discovered to his satisfaction that the man (a young priest with long legs and blonde hair) was bearing down on them with long, tiptoeing strides, his face quite green with rage and threats of bad marks. The restless boy had managed to reach the place next to Kus-Kus, who was sitting almost at the end of the pew that gave on to the central aisle. It was a tense situation, with the young priest standing there and the boy, like a tightrope-walker edging one foot in front of the other, moving down the kneeling rail. Above them the small voice of the Father Provincial went on and on, like the fragile warblings of a goldfinch. 'You'll be for it if you don't sit down!' whispered Kus-Kus, pulling at the boy's shirt-tails. After Kus-Kus there were only two boys between him and the aisle. 'Yes, my children, your neighbour, your colleague, your friend, your brothers and sisters, your parents, your grand-parents, your aunts and uncles, can all be seen much more closely and clearly than we can see God, but they can be seen more easily too than we see ourselves. And although we can see ourselves quite clearly, often much of what we see is our sinful nature, whilst in others, in our neighbour, although we see less, we can see, overlooking his sins, a clearer reflection of the image and likeness of God our Father . . .' Kus-Kus tugged at the boy's shirt-tails again. The incident had made him lose his thread and he felt irritated. Thinking about it afterwards, Kus-Kus didn't think he'd pulled that hard, but he must have done because the boy stumbled and fell head first into the aisle. There was a considerable stir. The Father Provincial interrupted his speech and the young priest whisked the fallen boy off to the rear of the chapel. Kus-Kus felt the hostility of the other boys in his year prickle around him. 'I didn't do it on purpose,' he thought. 'I didn't mean to, it was his fault for wanting to leave when it's not allowed, it's his fault.' But the pricks of something, half remorse and half pride, which mingled with the acute discomfort caused by the disapproval of his classmates, stayed with Kus-Kus for the rest of the sermon. And so he didn't really understand what the Father Provincial meant when he said that one saw one's own sins more clearly than those of others. 'I see other people's sins much more clearly than my own, whatever the Father Provincial says, because in the case of other people, I'm not both judge and accuser,' Kus-Kus was thinking as he left the chapel. He kept turning it round in his head during the study period and the following class, which was the last that day. He went home alone, thinking about it, and about what the Father Provincial would, no doubt, call 'the sins' of Aunt Eugenia. At home he found that Aunt Eugenia had spoken to Miss Hart on the phone and had asked if Kus-Kus would please go up to see her. He went straight up, without stopping to have tea, not daring to ask Miss Hart anything, not daring to think anything. He arrived breathless at the door to the mansards. While he was waiting for the door to be opened, he could see the clear evening sky through the big skylight above the stairs, already dotted with cold, ambivalent stars. He felt misunderstood, abused and profoundly alone. When Aunt Eugenia opened the door, smiling and apologising for making him come up with so little warning, and took him into the kitchen, instead of the sitting room or the bedroom as on other occasions, Kus-Kus started crying, as he had when he was a child and he and Aunt Eugenia were playmates.

Aunt Eugenia wanted to know if he was crying about something they'd said to him at school, and if so he should tell her, because sometimes she understood things very clearly, with an almost eerie clarity, and probably by talking about it, getting it off his chest, crying all he wanted to, between them they could understand the problem, solve it, and that sometimes in life it was impossible not to cry and sometimes it was best just to let oneself cry, however embarrassed one felt, rather than to dig one's heels in and cut oneself off and not talk to anyone. And if it was something to do with school, something to do with those frightful exams that Aunt Eugenia couldn't understand how he had time to study so much for, and so many different subjects, like a real scholar . . .

'It's nothing to do with school,' said Kus-Kus, looking at Aunt Eugenia with reddened eyes but no longer crying. 'It was just when I got here, I don't know why, when you opened the door . . .'

'You're probably remembering, now that you're grown up, when you used to come up before, when you used to come up as a child to spend the afternoons, sometimes you cry about that, because life can't be the same as it was, now you're older, not as much fun as it was when we were young...'

'No, it wasn't that.'

Where was Julian? He hadn't dared to ask because that stupid crying fit had put him in an inferior position. He felt bad-tempered now, like after taking a spoonful of cough medicine. Why had she asked him up? The fact that Aunt Eugenia had found him crying when she opened the door started to irritate him after only a few minutes in the kitchen. And Aunt Eugenia's remarks on crying and tears in general, instead of calming him, added to his irritation, and made him armour himself in his coldest feelings. Why didn't Aunt Eugenia just come out with what she wanted to say? At that moment there was the sound of a door opening inside the apartment, and immediately afterwards Julian came into the kitchen. 'I'm just going out for a walk,' he announced. He was wearing a jacket and secondhand maroon tie which Kus-Kus didn't remember having seen him wear before. He looked well. Attractive. He seemed to be waiting for a sign of approval or permission from one of them. But neither Kus-Kus nor Aunt Eugenia, who, after exchanging a confused look when Julian entered, now regarded him in silence as if waiting for him to take the initiative, made any sign which could be interpreted as either approval or disapproval of his announcement. 'It's nearly dark. I haven't been out for ten days. It's just to stretch my legs a bit. I won't be long.' And with that he went out of the kitchen, and, after a moment, to judge by the sound of the front door being carefully closed, out of the house.

'I didn't know what to say...' said Aunt Eugenia, 'and as you didn't say anything...'

'Does he go out for a walk every day?'

'Today's the first time,' said Aunt Eugenia.

It was an embarrassing situation. Kus-Kus had the impression that Aunt Eugenia was waiting for instructions from him. Or perhaps he himself felt that he should be issuing them, since, after all, he was the one who had installed Julian in the house. But what instructions could he give when he could hardly remember what it was all about anyway? Aunt Eugenia had a quiet, foolish air about her, a look of distraction.

'Why did you want me to come up? I thought something was wrong . . .'

'You must forgive me, Kus-Kus. If you don't forgive me, I won't be able . . . I'm not going to be able . . .' Aunt Eugenia's voice trembled slightly, 'I'll never be able to find any peace.'

'Forgive you, why? Have you done something wrong?'

'Don't make fun of your poor aunt, Kus-Kus. You make me feel old and foolish. You know perfectly well what I'm talking about.'

'No, I don't know. Not unless you explain more clearly. I don't know what you're talking about, honestly.'

'Manolo doesn't come up any more. I've told him not to come up . . . It's better like that . . . The best thing I could do, best for both of us. And for you too.'

'For me? Why? It doesn't make any difference to me whether Manolo comes up or not. Why have you told him not to come up? Does that mean that before you did tell him to come up? What goings-on, Aunt Eugenia!'

It was like a door slamming violently shut. Suddenly Aunt Eugenia looked very gaunt. She was, thought Kus-Kus, quite a lot thinner than before. Haggard and ashen. But now it seemed that her eyes bulged like a madwoman's.

'You're trying to trick me,' muttered Aunt Eugenia, 'you're laughing at me. Have pity on me . . .'

'I'm not laughing at anyone. Besides, you haven't said anything funny. What is there to laugh at? You look different, you know. It's a bore coming up here now. I used to enjoy coming up, you know I did, but now it's always like it is today

... Since that Manolo business.'

'I've asked him not to come up again, ever again, and for him to forgive me . . .'

'Manolo too? What does Manolo have to forgive you for?'

'Yes, Manolo too. He must forgive me too. All of you, all of you . . .'

'Have you done something wrong, Aunt?' Kus-Kus asked again, this time without looking at her. He heard a sharp whistle. At that precise moment. Just for a split second.

It was a whistling sound. But not like a whistle would make. Or any musical instrument. It wasn't anything like a sound that could come from the passing of air through the human windpipe. Kus-Kus thought he heard the sound, unpleasant, sharp, but not very loud, just as he was speaking. And he seemed to remember a sudden shiver that had preceded his last question: he could still feel the strange effect, as if a bizarre kind of echo were still prolonging his words. And the fact was that he couldn't remember what it was he had asked; he couldn't recall having asked Aunt Eugenia anything special at that moment. Or at least nothing which corresponded, in significance or intention, to a whistling sound. They were sitting in darkness now, facing each other across the kitchen table, looking at but not seeing each other, or at least not clearly. Kus-Kus thought that not much more than half an hour could have passed since his arrival in the house. But when Aunt Eugenia got up and put the light on, he was surprised to find it was almost midnight.

Aunt Eugenia didn't sit down again after putting the light on; she remained standing in front of her nephew with her arms by her side, looking down at him with the absent look expectant mothers get. Kus-Kus, who was still seated, was on the point of asking his aunt if her remaining standing was a way of telling him that it was time to go, but he didn't say anything, because at that moment he heard a key turn in the front door, and he thought it must be Julian back from his walk. He felt shivery again; the sort of chill one feels in midwinter, on an icy day, when a window suddenly opens. He got up to leave, thinking that the whole meeting, from beginning to end, had been a waste of time.

'I'm going, Aunt Eugenia,' he said, 'It's very late. Has Julian got a front-door key? I just heard him come in.'

Aunt Eugenia seemed surprised, although unworried, as she assured him that he didn't, that during those ten days the need to give her guest a key hadn't arisen, he was such a charming person who scarcely asked for anything, but, of course, it was only natural that he should have a key and there would be no problem at all in letting him have one if Kus-Kus thought it proper.

'It's just that I heard someone open the front door . . . they opened the front door with a key . . .' stuttered Kus-Kus. But he didn't stop to hear what Aunt Eugenia was saying, because suddenly he was terrified by the thought that Aunt Eugenia might calmly assure him once more that she was the only person in the world, the only one, no, not even Manolo, to have the key to her apartment. Already in the hall, Kus-Kus said goodbye, trying to hide the inexplicable nervousness he was feeling. He opened the door himself, and there, with the unmistakable appearance of someone who has just arrived breathless at the top of a flight of stairs, they found Manolo, who said he had run up the stairs, that he hadn't realised how late it was, that the street door was open and he hadn't had to call the nightwatchman . . .

Kus-Kus didn't sleep all night; he shivered with terror, not wanting to sleep, not letting Miss Hart put out the light or leave his side. He couldn't explain to her what had happened, didn't dare admit to himself that nothing had happened . . . except the things that had happened while seeming not really to happen at all, that sudden whistle, that turning of the key in the front door, the icy chill of something or someone stealing into the house.

19

All that spring Maria del Carmen Villacantero's mother, apart from being her usual crippled self, was more than usually finicky. From January on she was continuously ill with some kind of influenza or influenzas, complicated in May by a spectacular (and, in Maria del Carmen's view, deliberate) fall from her wicker armchair, in which chair and invalid ended up on the living-room floor. She lay buried, like a little rabbit, beneath the armchair for the whole morning, not making a sound, not a peep, until Maria del Carmen came back from mass and doing the shopping and then, as soon as she heard her daughter come in the front door, she let out a howl that lasted until the doctor's assistant, who thank God happened to live on the third floor, arrived and gave her an injection, and by this time it was getting terribly late, and neither of them had had a bite to eat, all the fault of her poor father, God rest his soul, who always indulged her every whim, nothing had been too good for her, and on top of her disability to have 'flu all winter and all spring, with high temperatures every evening, never for one day going above or below 100. Maria del Carmen Villacantero then, although with a good general idea of what was going on, couldn't help missing some of the details, especially after her mother's accident. And so, not until two days later, not for two whole days, did she know that Kus-Kus was confined to bed, that one night he had come down from the mansards feeling ill and acting strangely, that he hadn't wanted any supper that night and couldn't sleep and that Miss Hart had sat up with him until six in the morning and then had made him some limeflower tea and the doctor had come at midday, at lunch time, and that the child had had a fever for no apparent reason, according to information given by Josefa over the phone, immediately after Maria del Carmen Villacantero had been informed of the essential details, also over the phone, by his grandmother, Mercedes, who had in fact phoned about something else and mentioned in passing that little Nicolas was not well, at his age boys get colds all the time, you can't pay too much attention every time the maid phones to say the child's at death's door just because he's got a headache. Anyway, declared Mercedes, Maria del Carmen was just being ignorant and stupid, getting in a state about nothing, no better than a peasant woman, a peasant, making such a fuss every time a boy grazed his knee but then not caring about them when they were older, Maria del Carmen was like a broody hen, like a cow, mooning over children when it wasn't necessary and losing all interest later when it was, she showed about as much refinement and education as a village woman but, anyway, she'd better go and find out what the devil was wrong with the boy, she should phone at midday, then go and find out what it was all about, and talk to Miss Hart, because though Mercedes had no intention of treating her grandsons or granddaughters any differently from her own children, or fussing over them about trivialities like colds in the head, Maria del Carmen had better go and see what was wrong, after all, she couldn't leave the boy to die . . .

Maria del Carmen arrived at the house fearing the worst and, wearing the expression of concerned sadness that she saved, together with a black tailored suit and black suede shoes, for the more eminent funerals and obsequies, got as much information as she could out of Josefa almost before she got in the door. What Josefa said about Kus-Kus, although horrifying, was nothing compared to what she left unsaid about Aunt Eugenia, except for incomprehensible hints. Maria del Carmen Villacantero went in to see Kus-Kus like someone going to visit a dying man. (It was no use Miss Hart insisting that the boy was almost well, had got up for lunch, had eaten well and wanted to go to school the next day. It was no use; it only made things worse.)

Kus-Kus felt like talking. Even Maria del Carmen was surprised to find him so ready to chatter away nineteen to the dozen. He seemed a different child, with not a trace of the old sarcasm, the usual brusqueness; he was open, attentive, affectionate with her, even recalling the little present Maria del Carmen had brought him from Belgium and Paris, even saying that 'Ferdinand' was, to this day, his best friend, his favourite toy. But later she realised why. Of course, after what Josefa had told her, Maria del Carmen knew, more or less, exactly what he was talking about, although the poor child didn't actually put it into words, not clearly anyway. But reading between the lines she, Maria del Carmen Villacantero, who had suffered and knew how to read what the heart cannot speak, read a story the equal of *Wuthering Heights* . . .

'Maria del Carmen, let's see if I've got this straight, I get lost when you talk . . . I don't know which I lose first, the thread or my patience, so let's see. What's wrong with Nicolas? Is he or is he not ill?' interrupted Mercedes, having difficulty in controlling her temper.

For once in her life, Maria del Carmen Villacantero, who had by then spent an emotional three-quarters of an hour on the phone, spoke concisely: 'He's desperately ill, Mercedes, desperately ill!'

This, to Mercedes's ears, sounded like foolishness; but if it were true, she thought, which it might be, then what was that idiot Maria del Carmen thinking of? If it was what the grandmother thought it was — which it could be, to judge by the symptoms – and the boy had gone a bit crazy, which was, after all, typical of the family, it wasn't something to go shouting down the phone with the *domestiques* listening in, getting quite the wrong idea; and anyway, there was no need to shout, she had half-deafened her. Maria del Carmen was to come up today to see her. She sounded like a fishwife shouting like that. If she had any doubts it was better to whisper than to go shouting down the phone. She must come up at once, she'd expect her for tea, and stop shouting, she'd wear the receiver out . . .

Time passed, and Maria del Carmen Villacantero didn't come. She didn't phone, there was no answer at her house, no one knew were she was. Teatime came. Mercedes took tea. Teatime passed. Seven o'clock struck. Half past seven. The Capuchin monks rang the bell for rosary. About a mile away the bells in the monastery belltower sounded dully. Eight o'clock struck. Genoveva came in to ask if Mercedes would see Ramon, who was in the kitchen with the whole week's egg accounts. The night, smooth and hard as glass, cast mossy shadows over the fields. Genoveva came in again to ask if she should draw the curtains. It was five to nine. Outside in the garden, in the beds of asparagus set in straight, even lines like tombstones, the light became watery, flickering like the candle flames. Then came the sudden braking of a car. The long beams of light threw the monotonous shadows of the tall privet hedge into a frenzy. Genoveva went running out without a sweater. The noise of the engine gradually stopped. The garden was in complete darkness; by the light of the little lantern by the door, Genoveva could be seen returning, taking short steps, her arm supporting Maria del Carmen Villacantero, who walked with a slight stoop. When they came into the dining room, they had the wasted look of refugees.

Once installed in her seat near the door, and once Genoveva had gone, Maria del Carmen Villacantero, staring fixedly into Mercedes's eyes, said: 'I came by taxi, Mercedes.'

'By mule more likely! Do you know what time it is?'

'No. Frankly, Mercedes, I don't, and I don't know if I care. There are times in one's life, Mercedes . . .'

'It's twenty-seven, nearly twenty-eight minutes past nine at night and you sit there looking distinctly drunk and tell me that you don't care what time it is . . . and you stink, let's see, come here, what do you smell of? Anis I suppose. Do you think you can turn up here at this hour, drunk as a lord, and tell me you don't care what time it is? Where have you been?'

'I've just come from the church,' Maria del Carmen Villacantero declared with a sublime little smile, half-closing her eyes. 'From the church. That's where I've just come from.'

'And what have you been doing in church since teatime? What were you doing there?'

'Talking to Father Secundino. That's what I was doing.'

'And you're telling me that you've been chatting away with Father Secundino until heaven knows what hour, knowing full well that I was expecting you for tea, without thinking to phone or send a message, without . . . ?' Mercedes was so surprised, so utterly indignant, that she rang the bell eighteen times. Genoveva reappeared wild-eyed. Maria del Carmen, wrapped in the equilibrium of self-assurance and placid dignity, smiled again and raised her hand to her head with the gesture of one adjusting the veil she had worn to mass. But Mercedes returned to the attack as soon as Genoveva had disappeared with urgent instructions to get supper ready and to stop daydreaming and get on with things.

'I've told her to make some fried potatoes and fried eggs, Maria del Carmen, and some noodle soup to start with, because I assume you'll want some supper, and this is no time to start messing around with tea . . . let's see if I've understood you correctly: you say you've been talking to Father Secundino, whoever he is, that from the time you spoke to me on the phone until now, ten o'clock, because it's about to strike ten, I don't know if you care or not, but it's nearly ten o'clock, you've been chatting away with this Father Secundino up from Zamora . . . Who is Father Secundino?'

'He's my spiritual adviser,' replied Maria del Carmen, drawing closer to Mercedes, though without getting up, so that she had to drag her chair forward with both hands.

'What are you doing? Now what's wrong with you?'

'And first,' whispered Maria del Carmen, hissing as she talked, gripping the arm of Mercedes's armchair with her right hand, 'and first, before talking to Father Secundino, after talking to you, I talked to the hotel manageress, that's the first thing I did, I'll talk to her first, I thought, and then afterwards with Father Secundino because it's a matter of conscience, a matter of conscience, that's what I thought, and Luisa agreed with me entirely, but then what she told me, imagine, she was even thinking of phoning you herself, if she hadn't talked to me, she'd decided she would have to phone you, and what Father Secundino said to me was, the soul's the important thing, when I told him about it that's what he said, look, Maria del Carmen, the welfare of an innocent soul, the salvation of a soul, is the first thing you must consider, tell that to his parents or his legal guardians, he said that, Mercedes, the legal guardians, you see how far things have gone, tell them that from me, he said, just think of that soul, and I said to Luisa, we must act, we must get moving, take the appropriate steps and she, well, after the way she's treated him, been like a mother to him, and for him to turn out like this and on top of it all to be Manolo's sister's boyfriend, and it was only to be expected, that's what Father Secundino said to me . . . Are you listening, Mercedes? You haven't gone to sleep, have you? Things have even gone missing lately, things have gone missing, believe it or not, and as for the beryl necklace, really it's too awful, Montoya has it for valuing and every bit of the trousseau, all in white linen right down to the camisole, or rather camisoles, because she had a dozen made, with hand-embroidered trims . . .'

Mercedes opened her eyes and then, half-closing them, observed Maria del Carmen in silence. A silence that seemed to last for hours, although in fact barely a couple of minutes passed. Maria del Carmen moved her chair still closer to Mercedes's armchair. Mercedes had closed her eyes again. It was a thrilling moment. Maria del Carmen Villacantero's great moment, although she herself, absorbed in the details of her story, hadn't fully realised it. A triumphant dénouement, bringing in all the characters of a lifetime, proving her to have been right all along. She was sure that Mercedes's motionlessness was a sculptural tribute, after so many years of contradicting and shouting at her, to Maria del Carmen Villacantero's good judgement. It was enough to turn one's head.

'Things have gone missing. Valuable things. Two different sources told me that, two people who don't know each other and who have been at the house. And Chusin Montoya has got the beryl necklace for valuing.'

'Who told you all that? Father Secundino?'

For a fraction of a second, Mercedes's dry, sharp tone almost put a brake on Maria del Carmen's eloquence. But the story was out now and bore the narrator along, like an ocean current, irretrievably carrying her away from her spectators or listeners. She had to keep going, let the narrative take her; that's the secret of a great story. But Maria del Carmen Villacantero let herself be taken a little too far when she added: 'Even the camisole, the whole trousseau, all of it, all in white linen, the camisole too, hand-embroidered!'

'I suppose the detail about the camisole is something Father Secundino told you. Look, Maria del Carmen, I've known and had to deal with a lot of imbeciles in my time. My husband attracted imbeciles and we always had imbeciles in this house to lunch and to dinner. But you beat them all, my husband included, you beat them all, Maria del Carmen, and believe you me, I know all there is to know about imbeciles and their imbecilities.'

Genoveva came in with supper. Disconcerted, Maria del Carmen Villacantero returned to her place, this time standing up to move her chair. They dined in silence. Mercedes didn't ask about anything else, not even her grandson's health. Maria del Carmen, whose mouth was dry and who would have preferred a cup of tea, didn't dare speak. She sipped the noodle soup (which she detested) with tears in her eyes. The fried eggs arrived cold and greasy and the potatoes burned because Genoveva had at first rushed to get things done in the kitchen and then, since Maria del Carmen didn't stop talking and the mistress didn't call, she hadn't dared enter the dining room. Unusually, Mercedes accepted her explanation without comment. And, which surprised and alarmed Maria del Carmen Villacantero even more, she ate those disgusting fried eggs without a murmur of complaint. Mercedes only opened her mouth twice during the rest of the evening. Once to offer Maria del Carmen an apple ('That's all there is for dessert'); and once to tell Genoveva, who had already cleared the dessert plates and removed the table cloth, that Miss Maria del Carmen was leaving now and to tell Fermin to drive her home.

But Maria del Carmen hadn't told the half of it, certainly not the worst part, the essential part; while the brief ritual of saying goodbye and settling herself in the rear seat of Mercedes's black limousine rushed by, Maria del Carmen was thinking that she'd barely had time to go into what Nicolas had told her and what he had merely hinted at; she'd scarcely begun to relate what the manageress had told her (and there was plenty of that); she'd only just managed to mention the beryl necklace and Chusin Montoya; she'd not even had a chance to mention (and in Maria del Carmen's opinion it was worth doing so even if it was only gossip and not, like everything else, proven fact, because, even if it weren't true, it somehow rounded off and confirmed the true part), she'd not even had a chance to mention the possibility of Eugenia and

Manolo's wedding. Maria del Carmen Villacantero went into her house still unable to understand why Mercedes should have insulted her like that. She had said nothing that wasn't true, confirmed by distinguished local figures. She thought that perhaps Mercedes, who, like all her family, was a snob, had taken offence at her talking to Luisa, a remarkable woman and a good friend, who had, moreover, contributed some really indispensable information; that's what it must have been, because of Luisa; Mercedes had got on her high horse on learning that the manageress of a hotel, however luxurious it might be and regardless of its being the Principe Alfonso, had intervened and given her opinion on family matters. Maria del Carmen began to breathe more easily and calmly at this thought. What did it matter? It was just the natural snobbery of a great lady like Mercedes. How few of them, how very few, were left now, like her great grandmother Maria Francisca de la Villa, another great lady, like Mercedes; and, naturally, like Mercedes, a terrible snob. As she was about to fall asleep, lulled by the simplicity and rightness of her explanation, it occurred to Maria del Carmen Villacantero (and the idea kept her awake all night) that it was because of Mercedes's snobbery that they hadn't done the most important thing, hadn't acted on Father Secundino's advice, and he wasn't from Zamora, why would Mercedes think he was from Zamora? That night she and Mercedes had scarcely taken one step, none at all really, towards saving the soul of poor Nicolas, of Mercedes's grandson . . .

20

That same night Mercedes decided to forget about the whole affair, thinking that clearly Maria del Carmen was a busybody and was becoming a nasty scandalmonger in her old age. It was obvious that the business about the boy was an excuse, the Father Secundino story was just absurd, and that new character, that Luisa, had been an indiscretion; and as for Eugenia, the poor creature, it was the same old thing: involved in tangled love affairs and foolish marriages all because as a young woman she'd been a beauty and, now that she was older, was becoming a monster and found herself abandoned and alone. Eugenia had always been a source of gossip and would be until she died. The affair, Mercedes decided, provincial envy and malice apart, was of no importance. Consequently the only sensible thing to do was to pretend she knew nothing about it and to go to bed. But, next morning, things seemed to have become less clear, to have become unpleasantly plausible while she slept. After all, in her own absurd way, Maria del Carmen Villacantero was quite capable of being right, as she had shown on other occasions. Looked at in the calm, cold light of the dining room at breakfast time, it seemed possible that Maria del Carmen might have been telling the truth the previous night. But what was it she'd been saying? Mercedes tried in vain to remember. Apart from exclamations, confusions, and four or five names, there was not, it seemed to her, a single hard fact or piece of indisputable evidence to get hold of. And what was her grandson doing tangled up in all that? Had he really been ill? Both those things could easily be checked later on. That very afternoon she would ring Miss Hart. The only thing Mercedes could remember now, and the only thing that, at that time in the morning, it seemed vital to confirm or deny immediately, was what had been said about the beryl necklace. What had Maria del Carmen said exactly? However hard she tried to remember, she couldn't recall whether she'd said that Eugenia had sold the necklace already, or that Chusin Montoya was just valuing it, with no talk of selling it as yet. If it was for sale, she would buy it. It was all clear now: if Eugenia needed money, wedding or no wedding, if she really needed money, she would sell the necklace. It was the most valuable thing she had. And if she sold the necklace, Mercedes would buy it. There was nothing more to be said. She telephoned Chusin. At first he gave the impression that he knew something but was maintaining a shrewd silence. But, after a relentless interrogation, he ended up swearing that he knew nothing about the matter, and that if the necklace came into his hands for any reason, Doña Mercedes would be the first to know. Mercedes calmed down, and on feeling calmer became rather bored with the necklace story. She decided to go out to the garden to see the new asparagus plants, and, for her still greater peace of mind, applied Chusin Montoya's emphatic denial about the wretched necklace to the validity and likelihood of everything else. She was not one for endlessly going over everything she was told, and what Maria del Carmen had said the previous night rapidly slipped out of existence.

But neither Maria del Carmen Villacantero, nor the manageress at the Hotel Principe Alfonso, nor Father Secundino, nor Kus-Kus could leave things like that.

The manageress had broken the news about the theft; she had found out about it from the kitchen maid, who in her turn had heard it from Manolo himself one night when she went round to borrow a clove of garlic from his parents, who were neighbours of hers. According to the kitchen maid, the four of them were having supper there, the old couple, the famous sister with blonde hair who had been living there for six months without contributing a penny, and Manolo, in his undershirt. Manolo was talking about it when the kitchen maid came in, and he went on talking about it, because the kitchen maid was considered trustworthy. Although Manolo didn't visit as often as before because Miss Eugenia was suffering badly with her nerves, he still went every other day, and the last time he went he noticed that an old clock was missing from the mantelpiece in the living room, as well as all the silver, even the ashtrays and the coffee spoons, and a diamond necklace which it seems Miss Eugenia wore around the house. Questioned by the manageress, the kitchen maid added that Manolo seemed very worried because he cared about Miss Eugenia and also, perhaps more, because of what would happen when the family found out, since he was, after all, the only visitor to the apartment. 'And what did the sister say? She must have said something, girl, try and remember, what did the sister say?' asked the manageress again and again, until the kitchen maid, fed up with trying to remember, finally invented what to her seemed, aesthetically speaking, most appropriate, whether it was true or not. And that was that Manolo's sister had laughed like a hyena, laughed and laughed, so much that she'd started coughing and had to get up for a drink of water; and, to drive the point home, the kitchen maid added that the sister didn't actually say anything, just laughed like a mad thing. If she had only had that wild laugh to go on, the manageress might well have come to the conclusion that Esther was the perpetrator of the mysterious thefts from the mansards, always supposing she didn't have any suspects other than Manolo and Esther herself to hand. But, fortunately, the manageress also had on her list the most suspicious suspect of all: she had Julian, who, though he didn't know it yet, during his outing on the night that Kus-Kus had heard the whistle in the kitchen and invisible keys opening and closing doors, had been seen in the Parque Aguero, in compromising circumstances, by the same ex-workmate from the hotel who, months before, on a rainy night, long before the present calamity had struck, had so thoughtlessly startled him and made him run away. This time Julian didn't get the chance to jump up or be startled or run away because his workmate from the Principe Alfonso, a frequent visitor to the spot, saw him first, and this time, instead of shouting to him, chose to watch him from his hiding place among the box hedges. And what he observed must have interested him, not only because he had hardly expected to see Julian in such a place after he had stolen that cheque (news of which had, of course, reached the ears of all the staff at the Principe Alfonso via the manageress), but also because Julian was not alone and was, as the manageress would hear that same night with thinly disguised glee, clinging like a limpet to his companion; and, as if such brazenness and disregard for public decency were not enough, the two of them were seated on the semi-circular Egyptian-style marble seat round the fountain dedicated to Constancia Leal, poetess and mother, who, with a book half-open on her motherly lap, presides until the small hours over the villainous doings of the riff-raff. But, from this whole report, only the fact that Julian was back had any impact on the manageress. An impact all the more telling because she, informed months ago of Esther's presence in the city, and of her relationship with Manolo, of Manolo's relationship with Miss Eugenia and of Julian's relationship with them all, now had not the slightest doubt that, somehow or other, Julian was hidden in the mansards, having returned to the scene of the crime and (as the manageress, who had been like a mother to him, had always feared would happen) to his old ways. Now, in her opinion, all that remained to be done was to hand him over to the police and to entrust his soul to God as a hardened criminal, a thief, an ungrateful wretch and 'one of them'. This last charge the manageress, when talking to Maria del Carmen Villacantero the day after the latter's fruitless visit to Mercedes, had only dared mention euphemistically as 'unnatural practices', which, to Maria del Carmen's decent and avid ears, conjured up visions of the exterminating angel, the final cataclysm and the last judgement. As a result, she again went to talk to Father Secundino (who had been most disagreeably surprised by Mercedes's reaction and her indifference to the salvation of her grandson's soul), and he again insisted on the soul, the boy's soul being the prime thing; but this time, to Maria del Carmen's despair, he seemed inclined to leave the matter there, believing, apparently, that, the boy's soul apart, the matter was the responsibility of the parents, or relatives, or whoever was in charge of the child. Thus Maria del Carmen Villacantero, frustrated and without the necessary support from Father Secundino, found herself obliged to halt the campaign she had already launched for the soul of Mercedes's grandson (suspecting anyway that, given her snobbery, Mercedes's collaboration would inevitably be slight or even non-existent). But she did not abandon it entirely; partly because of what she believed to be in the interests of everyone involved in the long term, and partly because, as one delicious implication of the projected campaign, Maria del Carmen could still just glimpse the possibility of carrying out the longed-for division of the mansards, since it was clear from all the evidence that poor Eugenia could not manage to live on her own, or keep the opposite sex at bay, or look after herself decently. Ensconced, then, among her turbulent discoveries and desires, Maria del Carmen Villacantero resigned herself to waiting patiently.

After having been on the point of telephoning the police herself and informing them of Julian's hiding-place, the manageress thought better of it and did nothing (although for less noble motives than those that had stopped Maria del Carmen), deciding that at this stage just handing him over would neither sufficiently punish Julian's wickedness nor adequately satisfy her own desire for revenge. Probably, she thought, the longer Julian stayed in Aunt Eugenia's house the worse things would get. And he had to stay there, for lack of anywhere else to go and for lack of money (the story of the money promised by Rafael had also reached the manageress's ears; it was clear that Julian had no escape).

When Kus-Kus went back to school after his violent and (so far) unexplained illness, not only was his health better than ever, but he also felt, as he did after taking communion, set apart by invisible forces – the power of grace among them – from everything that had gone before; as smooth, calm and whole as an innocent child. It was a state of mind as absolute as it was astonishing. And the most notable thing, Kus-Kus reflected, was the torrent of forgetting which he felt battering his consciousness. However hard he tried to remember, there was nothing in his memory, absolutely nothing, either horrifying or commonplace; not even the tiniest recognisable trace of the past. He told Miss Hart about it. He said: 'Miss Hart, I've forgotten everything, absolutely everything. I can't remember a thing.' And Miss Hart had looked at him doubtfully and, when she answered, advised him not to exaggerate because it was impossible to forget *everything* and, if it were possible and it happened to him, it would be a dreadful misfortune, a horrible tragedy.

'You wouldn't know how to talk, not even that.'

'I mean *things*, Miss,' insisted Kus-Kus, 'Talking isn't a thing! I mean the things, all the things that I used to remember, I can't remember them at all now.' This forgetting was accompanied by a deep sense of happiness and well-being, almost as astonishing and absolute as the forgetting itself. Unfortunately it didn't last long. It began to dissolve and lose its brilliance almost as soon as Kus-Kus meticulously and persistently set himself the task of compiling a list of all the things he'd forgotten. He discovered, to his now embittered astonishment, that it is not actually possible to enumerate what one has forgotten; what he had enumerated were in fact the memories of the things that came back to him. Except that now they seemed more precise, more appalling and unavoidable than they had been before he'd forgotten them, as if that passing shadow of oblivion had nourished, renewed and magnified them. Of his feeling of happiness, as it too became a memory, there now remained only one thing, the last on Kus-Kus's list of things forgotten, which he had never dared add to the list. And now he remembered it, his realisation that he was a blackmailer and that he had used blackmail to hide Julian in Aunt Eugenia's house. He remembered that he had felt ashamed, but had continued to treat his aunt cruelly (like the time when he heard that spine-chilling whistle); he remembered that Maria del Carmen Villacantero had come to visit him when he fell ill; and he remembered feeling happy about the visit, chatty and spiteful and carefree, and he remembered having talked his head off. And above all he remembered himself disfigured by the impetuousness of his ideas and words, his mouth full of thoughts that demanded to be spoken, and that escaped and were spoken almost before they came to be thought. He remembered having talked a lot, much more than he ever believed he could have talked to Maria del Carmen Villacantero or to anyone. He did not, however, remember what he had said, and thanks to that he was on the point of recovering the absolute happiness of forgetting. Except that it was impossible to recover it now, because although he could swear that he did not remember what, exactly, he had said, neither could he free himself from the feeling that he had revealed things (about Aunt Eugenia especially) which were, by their very nature, secret and not to be told; things kept back which, once let out in that fit of diabolical garrulousness, would acquire a significance which he himself felt they did not merit. Perhaps it was because of that, because he felt guilty and because happiness and guilt are rarely compatible, or perhaps just because he felt like it, because in spite of all his plotting and wickedness, he was still a child, that Kus-Kus found himself once more outside Aunt Eugenia's door, and that when he rang the bell, when he heard the approaching footsteps, muffled by the deep red hall carpet, when the door opened, he felt his eyes fill with tears.

21

Julian opened the door to him. Kus-Kus's tears gave way to irritation with the suddenness of an explosion.

'What are you doing opening the door?' he asked, still hesitating before entering, as if the unexpected presence of the ex-servant, who indicated with professional ease that he should come in, was something shameful, an insult directed at Kus-Kus personally. At last he entered the hall and, without looking at Julian, who had not yet spoken and was still standing to one side a few steps away, asked him: 'How did you know it was me?' Kus-Kus noticed that his voice was hoarse and trembled a little. He didn't feel irritated now, just cold, hostile, wanting to put this unscrupulous thief, this fool for whom he had once felt such incomprehensible admiration, even affection, in his place.

'I didn't know it was you, how could I? I heard the bell ring and I opened the door,' replied Julian calmly.

'It might have been the police.'

'Yes, that's true. I didn't think of that. Or rather I probably did think of it without realising and opened the door just to make things easier, hoping it would be them at last . . . but the truth is that I wasn't thinking about the police when I opened the door. I wasn't thinking about anything. Except that the bell had just rung, that's all . . .'

'You never think about anything; you don't have to. I do your thinking for you, we all do; my parents, me, and now Aunt Eugenia. Isn't Aunt Eugenia in?'

'She's lying down, I think. I haven't seen her all day. She left my breakfast tray and my lunch tray in the living room, on the usual table . . . I don't know how she manages to come and go without making any noise, not a sound; that's what I find really strange: you'd think she'd been doing it all her life like me, serving in houses, anticipating the needs of a master and mistress . . . or, in this case, me. She must be in her bedroom. I listened outside her door a little while ago, but I couldn't hear a sound; I was beginning to get worried when the bell went; that's probably why I opened it without thinking. It didn't even occur to me that probably the police . . .'

'Why should it be the police?' asked Kus-Kus, turned towards Julian now, but still without raising his eyes or looking directly at him. Then he added, as if putting into words an idea that had been silently growing and swelling: 'You've got a nerve. You really have got a lot of nerve; you fool people at first, before they get to know you. I mean, at first you seem very humble, even kind – to me, my parents, Miss Hart – but once people get to know you, they see you for what you really are. It's a line you throw everyone, a lie you tell, but you don't fool me any more . . .'

'No, not you. And I'm glad. Really, I'm glad . . . although you won't believe me.'

'What does it matter if I believe you or not? Where's Aunt Eugenia?'

'She's here of course. She never leaves the house; she must be in her room now. Shall I tell her you're here?'

'Who does the shopping if she doesn't go out?'

Julian started to tell him something he already knew, which he only half believed, if that. He was inclined to think his aunt was just pretending, playing at being a servant because she wanted to. That was perhaps the most irritating thing: she liked doing it. She wasn't doing it just to make amends to Kus-Kus and to make him forget the painful spectacle of her sluttish behaviour with the boy from the shop, but because she enjoyed humbling herself like that, putting herself on the same level as her lover by playing the servant. He and Aunt Eugenia and the servants had always been mad about acting. Putting on costumes, dressing and undressing, trying on odd secondhand clothes in front of the narrow mirrors in the bedroom with two beds, in the rooms at the back of the house. Kus-Kus used to enjoy it too. Putting on different clothes, putting on a different life, or, like on that Sunday afternoon, slipping on Josefa's shiny stockings, sliding his hands right up to his groin. Aunt Eugenia was the same. What other reason could there be for her dressing like a nun lately; in dark brown or black woollen stockings, long sleeves, no low necklines, no make-up, no hair dye, no rings, not one, not even a bracelet or earrings, or the beryl necklace or the gypsy necklace of gold coins, nothing, none of the paste jewellery which looked like birds, or Red Indian decorations, only more realistic, much more splendid, that fitted her closer than her own skin; why did she no longer wear those lovely paste jewels, so much lovelier than real precious stones? It had to be because she was in disguise; and not dressing or making herself up like the person she really was, was to pretend, to lie, to play the fool for the benefit of who knows which sordid busybodies, for Manolo's benefit, for her own, out of vanity, pride, because she still believed herself to be as imaginative as ever, still the tennis champion she had been when the King and Queen, the Court and all the Ministers came in the summer, and Don Alfonso XIII charmed the fisherwomen, regardless of whether they were reds or not, by eating sardines with his fingers; and Aunt Eugenia was there, whether it was in championships, or for the national tennis tournament cup sponsored by the Queen herself, so dull and so pretty, Doña Victoria Eugenia, like in Aunt Eugenia's photo albums that year after year she and Kus-Kus had leafed through on wintry afternoons, when there wasn't a soul in the streets, on maritime evenings, with the rain licking and smacking against the quay ... just like, only even harsher and more precise, just like in the engraving, but more deeply etched in the memory than any engraving ... the clouds blackening the boats, the dinghies, the motorboats, the sails of the coal barges, the two lighters; and Aunt Eugenia would draw the living-room curtains after a while, just long enough to leave the two of them in the dark to watch the approach, as if it were the invention of the mortuary jet-black of the far-off sea, behind, within, far beyond the lighthouse and the island of La Cabra, of the fierce north-east wind ... '*L'approche de l'orage*,' Aunt Eugenia would say, her voice trembling slightly. And Kus-Kus from his place on the sofa could see the yellowing French engraving, flecked as if with nicotine stains or mildew, which bore that title and which in its turn roared behind its glass, grew dark like the firmament watched over now by the green velvet curtains, and the word '*orage*' seemed almost to mean 'orange', but lacked the courage to be the whole word, and signified not only storms but also disasters, not just the north-east wind but also misfortunes, the reversals of fortune, as Aunt Eugenia called bad luck. Aunt Eugenia said it in French, all in French, just as one would in Bariloche, and read out the little spidery letters of the names of the engraver and the publisher and the seller and of Paris, all in the beautiful French which she spoke like a native, along with English and Italian and even Russian, a little; better than anyone, better even than Miss Hart, better than anyone did at school, explaining everything in all its detail, like a perfumed, bilingual bird of paradise . . .

'What's wrong? What are you staring at?' asked Kus-Kus suddenly, realising that he had asked Julian a question without listening to the answer.

'You went so quiet . . . you haven't spoken for ages. You asked me who did the shopping and I told you and you weren't even listening. What's wrong?'

'Nothing. Why should anything be wrong?'

'You haven't spoken for ages.'

'You've told me that already. You repeat everything twenty times.'

Still quite distracted, Kus-Kus had sat down on the sofa, settling himself like a small animal in his usual place, answering Julian's questions like an automaton. The series of impressions he had just had of Aunt Eugenia, what did they mean? His thoughts, too, seemed to accumulate, as confused and random as if he were suffering a sudden bout of fever. What was going to happen now? What did he have to do? What came next? What was the next step? Was there a next step? He felt upset, anxious and bewildered, as if somehow the creation of the whole world depended on him. The odd thing was that at the same time he felt strong, simultaneously capable and incapable, like God. And if, when the earth had ceased to be in confusion, emptiness and darkness, and on the face of the vast oceans mountain ranges and plains were being hatched, God had realised that He could not stop now, could not leave things as they were, to take care of themselves, but that He had to go on and on, like Kus-Kus now, endlessly creating the world, with no precedents, no examples, so fast and fraught with danger was it that He couldn't even perceive the origin of each conclusion He reached. What, for example, was the origin of the last topic he and Julian had spoken about? What had been concluded just a moment before? Perhaps Aunt Eugenia was ill and that was why she didn't leave her room; or lying dead, on her bed, with only her face uncovered, with her eyes and mouth open. Without ever having explained things, even at the end. And, dead, she would think in the next life that she had said she would leave no explanation, which only proved that she always kept her word. Kus-Kus shivered. The room seemed unreal to him, and Julian's face, his erect body, his feet, which seemed to not quite reach the ground, appeared like a monster in a film which keeps breaking down amidst the stamping and shouts of all the boys in school. Then, just at that moment, like an inspiration from on high, from the highest, most ethereal and crystalline of hell's abysses, came the saving idea. It was simple. Very simple. He looked at Julian, whose blurred, slight figure had grown solid now, and said sharply, with the crisp, casual precision he knew one could use with servants: 'Go and knock at the door, wait to hear what Miss Eugenia says, then tell her that I'm here in the living room and that I've already been waiting quite a while.'

He felt strong again when he said that, using that perfect, authoritarian tone. But when, after bowing slightly and leaving the room without a word, Julian left him alone with himself, Kus-Kus felt weaker than ever, unnerved: giving that order, giving it the way he did, had clearly been a way of hiding and stopping up his fear of going to fetch Aunt Eugenia himself, of going to the door, knocking, waiting for a moment, hearing her voice, or not hearing it, or its being not hers but another's voice, waiting for a moment, turning the doorknob, entering and seeing her, or not seeing her. What was happening now? Who else was in the room? Because someone else was certainly there breathing, was there at that moment; it was like thinking one was alone when one wasn't, like that time he was masturbating in the lavatories – why remember that just now? – and suddenly discovered out of the corner of his eye that he was being watched . . .

Then Kus-Kus saw the cat. Everything else, the room, the furniture, the curtains, was the same; only the cat, there in the middle of it all, spoiled everything. It seemed to take up the whole of the middle of the room, although, in fact, it was sitting at the back, to one side, at the foot of the big French windows that gave on to the terrace. It was a black cat, not very big, not very young, or at least it didn't seem young because it was so still. Its tail was very long, and curled round its front legs, neatly together as if made of stone, like a question mark. And Kus-Kus thought that the cat was looking at him with the intense fixity of a snake (like the snakes in his natural history book, that horrendous 'boa constrictor' in the photo, showing only its head because all its coils wouldn't fit in, just the reptilian fixity of that impassive snout and scarcely a third of its coils). It was a yellowish gaze, two round eyes, as wide open as possible, the pupils narrow, slanted, like buttonholes, like sphincters. And so evil was the yellow of that infernal cat that Kus-Kus didn't dare go near it. A short, though infinite, time passed, like one afternoon on his way home from school when he'd stood absorbed watching for the first time in his life two dogs coupling. Behind him he heard Julian say that Miss Eugenia was just coming and that one morning they had found the cat sitting right where it was now, in the same position, in fact it was the morning of the day Kus-Kus had fallen ill; and Julian added, in the tone of someone telling an amusing anecdote, that there it had stayed without sleeping, without moving, without making a sound, without touching a mouthful of food, ever since. Julian was of the opinion that it had come in through the window from the terrace, across the roofs, fleeing its own home, which was probably on the same block; the only strange thing was that it didn't eat and never appeared to close its eyes or to want to be near people, which, said Julian, was a pity since it was such a pretty animal, so young . . .

'I'm so glad,' Aunt Eugenia said as she came in, 'so glad that you've met each other and are already such good friends, Glufez and you, you can't imagine how pleased I am to see you so friendly already. Julian gets on well with Glufez too, not as well as I do though, isn't that true? Admit it, Julian, he doesn't take half as much notice of you as he does of me, not half as much; cats have always liked me. People haven't, but cats always have; they're so ancient, they even appear in Egyptian tomb paintings, a whole hieroglyphic for a cat with little ears just like the real ones, Kus-Kus, imagine that, it represents fidelity in marriage, or they protect it, I can't remember which, that's why in the pyramids they embalmed the pharaohs' wives, with their maids and their children, each with their own cat, so they wouldn't go off on a spree with the Nubian slaves who served them supper; the cats are little mummies bandaged up just like the Pharaoh, and Isis herself was a cat, she-cat and he-cat, as you'd expect, the Egyptians being what they were, Isis was bound to be both so as to have everything close to hand, and you're the same, Kus-Kus, the same, like me, she-cat and he-cat like Isis, with no Calvinist bourgeois affectations, not going about believing that man alone is the male animal and woman, the poor idiot, can go to blazes, stay at home and never see anyone handsome, or stimulating, not criticising her, Isis . . . Isis' – Kus-Kus thought rapidly that Aunt Eugenia's openness now, although it seemed the same, wasn't like the frivolity, the fun of other times – 'There was no question of anyone going to Isis and reproaching her, because, although she was unmarried, she went about holding hands with the gods, with Osiris. I'm talking nonsense, I don't know what I'm saying, nothing can ever be the same with you again, nor with anyone, and I promise you that I really do try, I scarcely see Manolo, I swear, I swear I hardly see him and he wants to come up and I tell him not to, the poor thing, I tell him to wait and not come up, it breaks my heart to see the poor love, he telephones every day, it's getting him into so much trouble and it's all my fault . . . I swear, Kus-Kus . . .'

'Don't bloody well swear; I'm up to here with you, I'm fed

up, fed up, do you hear? I'm sick to death of you, just shut up once and for all, why don't you just get on with it and die!' Kus-Kus screamed, standing up now, very pale, his arms thrown back and his two furious fists like stones; the final scream, when he said that he wanted her to die, came out like a shriek, changing his voice as it changed his anger. Had he heard it, he himself would have said it sounded like the shriek of a queer.

That was when Señor Don Cat got up on his four legs, arched his back, making a giant, human hump, and left the room without a word, with something of the same air Julian had when he'd bowed and gone off silently on Kus-Kus's orders to get Aunt Eugenia. The three of them stood there dumbfounded. And Julian said: 'It had to happen. Sooner or later it had to happen. You could see it coming, I could see it coming.'

Just then the bell rang, two consecutive rings, the second twice as long as the first. And the police came into the room. Two policemen in single file, one taller than the other, both wearing ties, both middle-aged, one doing the talking and one saying nothing except 'Good evening' when he arrived and when he left. Aunt Eugenia, who was standing up, turned towards them a little without saying anything, remaining in profile, equidistant between the police and Kus-Kus. And she remained standing. The policemen took their cue from her, hesitating whether to sit down but not doing so because Aunt Eugenia, presenting her clear profile, refused to sit. At last she asked them to do so, and sat down herself in a straight-backed chair which proved inadequate to contain her vast buttocks. Kus-Kus remained seated. He felt like a mere spectator. Where had Julian got to? While the police wandered indecisively about, he had time to go over what had happened before. It had consisted of Aunt Eugenia coming in, talking and chattering, Kus-Kus shouting, the black cat suddenly leaving . . . and then, apparently, two rings at the door bell as

Julian went off, either to hide or to open the door and come face to face with the forces of law and order. Kus-Kus had the feeling that he must have left out a scene; because of the cat he now found himself plunged into a confusion of time and space.

The policeman who did the talking apologised twice and explained that the reason for their visit was that they had heard there was a thief hidden in the mansards: a certain Julian from Madrid, one of the servants, with a criminal record . . . 'It's all over,' thought Kus-Kus, and he really felt that it was. It didn't, however, finish just then, because, after stating that she did in fact know the delinquent mentioned, and the circumstances of the theft and of his flight, and after ending her statement with a 'you don't know how sorry I am' that recalled the Bariloche tone of voice, Aunt Eugenia surprised Kus-Kus by declaring that she knew nothing more about Julian, nor indeed did she wish to, not today or ever. On hearing this, the policeman who did the talking told the one who just said 'Good evening' to take notes. The silent policeman took a ballpoint pen from the top pocket of his jacket. However, perhaps because, after her initial declaration Aunt Eugenia had gone on talking, almost more brilliantly and prodigally than ever, the policeman who didn't speak had obviously understood that in such cases it was the thought that counted and consequently wrote nothing but, to show willing, kept his pen at the ready. Just where – Aunt Eugenia had gone on – just where had they got the idea that there were thieves in the mansards of the house and where had they got the idea that they could come in and search them without the occupants either authorising such a search or themselves asking the police to do it? and was that how it was done, was it the usual method of going about things or was it just a custom among provincial police? if it was a custom among them it was an ugly one and if it was the usual method, it was rather a crude one, all the cruder for being usual; she had travelled all over the world and only under Hitler and the Nazis had she seen such a thing ... Aunt Eugenia was splendid. Almost her old self. The policeman who didn't speak watched her fixedly, frowning, and the one who did the talking stared open-mouthed. But Kus-Kus, although he almost believed for a fraction of a second that Aunt Eugenia had been reborn from her ashes, was not entirely taken in. The moment she stops talking, he thought, she's lost. Aunt Eugenia stopped a few minutes after the thought had occurred to Kus-Kus. The policeman who did the talking apologised again, several times, as if, by sheer weight of repetition, he could force quality out of quantity. Each time he apologised his partner nodded. At times Kus-Kus could barely keep himself from laughing. The lady, said the policeman, was quite right. The visit was very far from being strictly official. To tell the truth, explained the policeman, who had regained his confidence, they had on several occasions received confidential information about the presence in the town of the criminal in question, a lot of information about his friends and associates, all of whom were prowling around the neighbourhood. They had carried out investigations in Madrid. They knew without a shadow of a doubt that Julian had left the capital with no known destination and without a penny. The policeman assured her, in all modesty, that he himself had followed up certain clues 'of a mainly psychological nature' based on what he had heard about the said criminal. To cap it all, late yesterday afternoon there had been a telephone tip-off (placing his hand on his heart, he assured her that it was quite impossible, at least for the moment, for him to reveal the identity of the informant). It was nevertheless clear that if Miss Eugenia said that Julian was not hidden in her house, then he was not. Still with hand on heart (or now not quite over his heart, but over his tiepin, which seemed, by the little tugs he was giving it, to have become caught on his undershirt) the inspector assured Aunt Eugenia that at all costs he wanted Miss Eugenia in her heart of hearts to be sure that no one doubted her or her word, because of who she was, where she came from, where she lived and just because. They all got up. Where's that bloody cat got to? thought Kus-Kus. The two policemen were ceremoniously shown to the hall. Kus-Kus went in front, followed by the policeman who only said 'Good evening'. Behind him came the policeman who did the talking, and finally Aunt Eugenia.

'Why did you lie to them?' asked Kus-Kus.

'And why shouldn't I have lied to them, Pichusqui?' replied Aunt Eugenia vigorously. After all, she had earned the right to reply with a certain vehemence, and even with a certain flamboyance. She had won, she had broken the law (which is always invigorating), she had lied with all, or almost all, the brilliance of the poets. She spoiled her victory, however, by asking, or rather by pleading more than asking: 'That's what you wanted me to do, isn't it?'

'*I* don't particularly care. After all, he is a thief, isn't he? I don't know if you understand, Aunt Eugenia, that Julian is a thief and that we're all his victims. He robbed our family so his friend, that fairy in Madrid, would take notice of him. Or is there something else? I can never tell with you, Aunt Eugenia, probably there was something else, you probably didn't fool the police for my sake but for your own, for Julian and you more than for anyone else, because probably after so long, almost a month it's been, almost a month, day after day washing his clothes and cooking his meals, well, you've always liked men, Aunt . . . I realise now that you never talked about anything but men all the time, you used to go into all the details, making use of me a bit, at least a little bit, eh, Aunt Eugenia, wouldn't you say so? Didn't you use me a little bit, just a bit, ever since I was a child? Because what difference did it make to me if it was Gattucci or Josema or Manolo or whoever? Yes, you always used me a bit, because you enjoy talking about that, even my grandmother knows it, everyone knows you do, we all know; my parents know, Miss Hart knows, my friends at school know, we all know how you love that kind of talk and going on and on about it, about whether men are like this or like that, about the men you've known, about your gigolos, your boyfriends; I remember once I came up to see you without telephoning first, about two years ago, at least two years, before the famous Manolo, quite a bit before, and you came to the door half-naked, you opened the door in your nightdress, that was some nightdress, and you were drunk that afternoon, we laughed a lot because when you're drunk you're funny, much funnier than now, now you've turned saint you're almost boring, anyway, that afternoon you talked of nothing except how boys with long legs are less passionate than ones with fat legs, how tight Italian boys wear their trousers, so you can really see their bums when they walk, I'm just repeating what you said, Aunt Eugenia, just repeating it, I was only a child, even now I'm still almost a child, still in junior school, they call us, the juniors, the 'little ones', and we have a separate playground, separate lavatories, the priests at school even take that into consideration because we're so young, they even give us different lavatories so that we don't see the disgusting things the older boys get up to, and then you come along with your talk of slim hips and how short, strong legs are nicer than long, slim ones, sometimes I just stopped listening to you, always going on and on about the same old thing, just as well the priests at school don't know about it, my confessor does, of course, he knows everything down to the last detail, when I confessed I had to tell him, I mean, when I went to confession I had no option but to explain it all because the things you tell me, especially about the kind of legs you do and don't like, well, naturally I get troubled by temptations, because I just take anything you say as gospel and then, inevitably, temptation follows, I don't expect you realise, I doubt it even matters much to you, but this last year at school, the whole year since October, I haven't been able to concentrate because of you, and I'm not exaggerating, my confessor says that if you're not pure you won't grow or develop properly, he says God help you if you start too young, and it's worst at my age, you should have known that I'm just not old enough yet for the kind of things you talk about, the bathing suits, I even know what the bathing suit of the Russian duchess's gigolo was like, how it fitted skin-tight when it got wet, and anyway it's all lies what you told me about Bariloche, it was all a lie, in the third year Geography text book I borrowed it says Bariloche is under snow for half the year or more and no one's going to go around in a bathing suit in the snow, so that was a lie too; it doesn't surprise me in the least that you should be able to fool the police so brilliantly, not when you've had me to practise on, and other things, I remember other things, I remember loads of things. I bet you don't know what I do sometimes in the last lesson, the afternoon one, Aunt Eugenia. I bet you don't know what I do. You'd do the same, you'd do just the same, guess what I do? I ask the priest in charge if I can please go and borrow a Latin dictionary from a friend of mine in the fifth year; he always lets me; and I go up to the fifth form and do you know what I do? Well, I pretend I've dropped a pencil underneath the desks and I crawl around looking at the fifth formers' legs, they're the older boys, and do you know why I do it? Because I've learned all there is to know about legs, the hairy ones and the not so hairy, from you, Aunt Eugenia, and other things, I do other things too . . .' Kus-Kus stopped, breathless. They were face to face. Aunt Eugenia reminded him of the piles of sacks in a warehouse, in a bakery, yielding and porous. She had a vacant look in her eyes, as if she hadn't quite grasped everything that Kus-Kus was saying, or everything that was happening. '. . . and another thing, Aunt Eugenia, shall I tell you why you lied to the police, which is a crime, by the way, only I've forgotten the name, shall I tell you why you said Julian wasn't hiding here? You said it because you're tired of Manolo and now it's Julian you want, isn't that the real reason? Come on, tell me, am I right or not?'

'I did it because I feel sorry for Julian and for you too, and it's all my fault, it's my fault. I know there's no God, I don't believe in God, but I'd like there to be one so that he might never forgive me ... Have pity on me, have pity on me!'

At that moment, simultaneously, Julian came in through the window and the black cat came in through the door which led to the hall and which all through the preceding conversation had stood open. Contrary to its usual habit, the cat installed itself on the sofa, in exactly the place where Kus-Kus had always sat; it turned round and round, the way cats do, turning and turning until they're comfortable, then it curled up into a ball, an innocent, homely circle of cat, and its eyes, seemingly heavy with sleep, closed, green, blue, black, until it fell sound asleep.

'Thank you so much, Miss Eugenia,' said Julian effusively, his sincere expression of gratitude breaking the leaden silence that followed the boy's terrible monologue and Aunt Eugenia's vain plea. 'Thank you so much,' he repeated, and, sensing perhaps rather more than it's reasonable to assume he knew about the relationship between aunt and nephew, added, 'I know you're doing it for the boy, because you love him, but I'm grateful too because, without meaning to, by hiding me, by making excuses for me, you're doing it for me too. It was a mistake. We might have to invent something ... though it probably won't be necessary; the police want results, the motive is the least important thing, and when they arrest me, there'll be no need to give any more explanations, but thank you very much, no one has ever ...'

'I'm going to my room, I'm going to lie down for a while, if I may ...' Aunt Eugenia's voice was paradoxically firm and calm, though very weak. Someone sitting at the back of the room, near the windows, probably wouldn't have been able to hear what she said. Nor what she added after having gone a few steps in the direction of the door. What she said was: 'Manolo is due to arrive, it was his day to visit, he must be about to arrive, it's better to tell him a lie, at least today, that will be easy for him to accept, something that will seem unquestionable, something ... Julian, would you mind telling Manolo when he arrives that I have had to go out unexpectedly and that I'm at the house of Doña Mercedes, the boy's grandmother, that Doña Mercedes called me urgently because she has fallen ill. Will you remember all that?'

'Don't worry, Miss Eugenia. I'm very good at remembering messages, it's my job. Don't worry, I'll tell him exactly what you said.'

'And that I'm staying there to look after her, please tell Manolo that too, and that I'll phone him.'

Kus-Kus left almost immediately after Aunt Eugenia did. But he had time to ask Julian how the hell he'd managed to give the police the slip. He had time to feel a sharp prick of envy at the brief description Julian gave of his escape.

'I opened the door myself. Well, why not? I'm the servant here, it's my job to open the door ... So I opened it, and when I saw them I knew they were policemen even before they told me who they were. "So they've found me at last," I thought, and I felt quite calm about it. Then I thought I'd make it a bit hard for them, just a bit, because my crimes are such ordinary ones, not worth giving them too much trouble, but just a bit, yes, a bit of cat and mouse would add a touch of excitement. I remember that the thought of playing cops and robbers for real made me think of you ...'

'Just tell me what you did, get on with it, I've got to go, it's late ...' Kus-Kus's voice reminded Julian of that of an irritable old man.

'Well, what I did was bow respectfully and say "Please come in, gentlemen, Miss Eugenia and Master Nicolas are in the living room." That's what I did. They did the rest, they believed it, they probably assumed that your aunt had someone in her service, or maybe my act worked like a spell, like a charm that took them from the hall to the living room without looking at me or really seeing me or making the connection between the servant and me . . . By the way, I left when you started screaming like a madman. The cat and I went out together. I felt ashamed for you. I'm sorry, but that's the truth . . .'

'And then what? You came in through the window when they left. And wipe that imbecilic smug look off your face. You're a thief and here you're the servant, so look like one and finish your story quick!'

'Then I went to my room. I didn't pack up my things, because there isn't much and I don't really need any of it. I didn't feel a bit tempted to try and escape while you were talking. I went out on to the roof through my window, the one in the little study, and jumped over the other side on to the living-room terrace and opened the window a little so I could hear everything, although I couldn't see you . . . I'm really very grateful . . .'

Kus-Kus slammed the door, cutting him off short, and Julian thought: 'The poor kid has turned out to be a real bastard, and it's mainly my fault, it's my fault for having let him down . . .'

22

Several days passed, almost a week. Every day Julian thought: 'It can only be a matter of days.' It was a sober, comforting thought, which came to him in the mornings and grew gradually less intense as the day wore on, becoming almost melancholic by sunset. Now that he knew for sure that Miss Eugenia was prepared to protect him and keep him hidden in her apartment, the idea of finding himself shut up there was less appealing than it had been when it merely meant being free of Rafael and Esther. Julian didn't believe that the police would simply accept her false statement of the other day; it was clear, though, that her resounding lie had brought the investigation up short. If she held firm whatever happened, sooner or later they would end up by dropping the matter. In a couple of months – perhaps one month – they would have forgotten it. 'I'm easy to forget,' Julian said to himself, a little ashamed of his own insignificance. 'What's more, I'm an actor: I've learned how to be invisible. An actor is simply a servant who's learned how to be invisible on cue. And I'm a good servant.' The fact that despite all this he should melancholically think of his detention as 'only a matter of days' often made Julian smile. An essential characteristic of such melancholia is the strong attachment the melancholic feels to the very thing from which he is about to free himself. That was how Julian felt about having to leave that place, perched among the chimneys like a monastery among fir trees, whose rooms, though he knew them by heart, like a liturgy, continued to hold surprises for him; he and Miss Eugenia scarcely ever saw each other. There was not a single day on which Julian could recall having exchanged more than half a dozen commonplaces with his strange hostess. The only change he had managed to impose on the routine established on the first day was having his meals in the kitchen rather than in the living room. Now he sat in the kitchen when mealtimes approached. And there, seated at the table, he pretended to be plunged in a state of deep meditation until Miss Eugenia, not daring to disturb him, left the tray on the table and withdrew in silence.

He had heard nothing more from Esther. And now the cat came and went about the house, utterly calm, its blackness somehow less profound. Perhaps, in the eyes of that unfathomable cat, what had happened between Miss Eugenia and her nephew the other day had rendered superfluous its initial hieratic manner. It no longer sat by the window. It scrupulously devoured three or even four helpings of food a day. Now it could always be found close to Julian; sitting on him or near him. It purred quite frequently and miaowed if Julian absentmindedly left it shut out of a room, and miaowed again once inside if Julian, distracted again, neglected to leave the door ajar. It didn't seem the same cat, although it retained its distinguished air.

Julian had heard nothing more of Manolo. Miss Eugenia – who had not asked about him once – was taking on the indecisive, fragile, obstinate look of people who suffer from ill-defined, not very serious chronic illnesses. She didn't appear to suffer; you couldn't have said that she looked unhappy; although never inattentive or indifferent to her guest, she was simply not there. Julian couldn't help comparing her with memories of his own mother, diverse fragments of two women which fitted poorly together.

One morning, very early, it had only just struck half past seven, Esther phoned to tell him that she was clearing out.

'Julian, Julian,' she repeated in the speeded up, demented tones of a bad farce, 'You should get out too, with the money or without it, just get out as soon as possible!' Julian had the feeling he'd heard that sentence a million times already when he decided to interrupt Esther and ask her what the hell she was talking about. 'This business, the whole business,' Esther repeated, 'now everyone's talking about it, they talk of nothing else, it's a public scandal, a terrible scandal...' Julian was invaded by indolence and passivity. Esther's voice seemed to come from a world of tiny anxieties that didn't concern him. That's why he didn't even bother to ask if by the wretched 'business' she meant just one thing or several, and if it included among its scandalous properties the fact that he was hiding where he was. It was, in fact, a very short conversation, given the usual length of her telephone conversations. They said goodbye hurriedly, as if someone were listening to them or watching them.

'It's a matter of days now, Chati, a matter of days,' he said to the cat when he hung up. The rest of that day passed without incident. Kus-Kus appeared on the following day, at noon. There he was standing before Julian, hesitating whether to enter the hall or not, inquiring about his aunt's health like someone reciting a text from memory. Julian could have sworn the child's head had grown enormously in the past few days. He seemed to have got thinner; a muddy down darkened his cheeks. And Julian, involuntarily looking him up and down, felt overcome by nausea at those pale corduroy short trousers, which were too tight for him and revealed the joints of his knees, the murky joints of a large, evil-smelling animal. He managed to hide his feelings and told him that Miss Eugenia was well, thank God, that she was resting and that he had orders to tell the young master so. That seemed to satisfy Kus-Kus, who withdrew almost immediately with the exaggerated flourish of one who has just filled out a form perfectly. What goes on in his head? thought Julian when he was alone again. What will he do with me in the end? The truth is that Kus-Kus had become impenetrable again; perhaps he himself knew it and took advantage of it. Nevertheless, he returned two days later, at more or less the same time; and when, convinced now that another encounter between aunt and nephew could only have disastrous consequences, Julian was on the point of repeating what he had said on the previous occasion, Miss Eugenia appeared in the hall and ushered Kus-Kus in.

'Are you better, Aunt? You look better.' Kus-Kus had sat down in his old place on the sofa, after energetically shaking the cushion, which was covered in hairs from the cat's siestas, the cat, by the way, having disappeared.

'I'm much better, Pichusqui, thank you. Much, much better, though why I don't know. Julian told me you'd come up to ask after me. I was most grateful.'

'I'm not all bad, Aunt. I'm not as bad as you think, not nearly so bad . . .'

'I don't believe you're bad, I don't believe it now, and I never have. It's true you're very imaginative, like me, I'm imaginative too . . . People think we're bad just because we're imaginative, they think it's bad to imagine things . . . I don't know how to explain, but strange things, very strange things, which if other people thought them would even be considered sinful, because they just couldn't endure them; that's why, I'm sure that's why it is that the things that you and I think of, they . . . they wouldn't be able . . .' Aunt Eugenia was stuttering now, or rather it was just that she felt unsure about something and her hesitation came across as a stammer.

'What wouldn't they be able to do, Aunt Eugenia? You were going to say what and you stopped in mid-sentence. It was very interesting. Why is it, do you think, that they wouldn't be able to but we would? What wouldn't they be able to do?'

'Do you know I can't remember what we were talking

about! One of these days we'll go on a trip to La Cabra, the three of us, Manolo, you and me. What do you think? I was thinking about it all day yesterday, we could take our tea with us, it doesn't matter that it's still winter . . .'

'It's not winter now, Aunt; it's spring, it's been spring for more than a month, it's nearly June . . . haven't you noticed? It's almost time for the exams . . .'

'If Manolo won't go, I'll have to go alone; he won't admit it, but I think he's afraid of sailing. But I tell you I can understand him being afraid, the sea is frightening sometimes, however calm it is, however close you stay to the shore, it's frightening sometimes. I think that's what's wrong with him . . .'

'He's probably a bit of a poof,' Kus-Kus said, just for something to say.

This time it was true that Kus-Kus simply said it for the sake of saying something, simply because that remark rather than any other came into his head. Aunt Eugenia had gone very quiet. Kus-Kus felt drowsy, sure of himself. His aunt's slightly trembly voice lulled the whole room that stood poised on the splendid edge of summer. Kus-Kus looked around him, thinking he could smell spikenards. He yawned a couple of times. He wished that nothing had ever happened and that nothing would happen from now on. It was a diffuse, floating sensation, similar to the feeling you get after passing an exam, or after undressing on the beach. Like a shiver down the spine. And he looked at his aunt who, frowning a little as if trying to remember something, was staring at him. 'She needs to be protected,' thought Kus-Kus, 'looked after and protected, and after all I'm her natural protector, the only one she has.' And he felt inflamed and purified to think that. And he smiled, not noticing that the cat, phosphorescent, pushing with its head and one of its front paws at the living-room door, was entering the room.

'Why do you say that?' asked Aunt Eugenia suddenly.

'Say what? Why do I say what? I don't know what you mean . . .' purred Kus-Kus, who felt sure he'd asked those questions in the correct tone: of light benevolence, like a mature man, a calm, wise man.

'What you said, what you said Manolo probably is . . . about him being a poof . . . Why do you say those things?'

'Because he probably is; there's nothing unusual about it, there are masses of them; there are even some at school, to take an obvious example; I've seen them in the lavatories, between classes; they get thrown out of school, of course, don't go thinking they allow that sort of thing, they've thrown some out, quite a few . . . Manolo could be too, he could be queer like Julian, why not?'

'Not Manolo, no. Leave him out of it . . . Don't say that about Manolo,' murmured Aunt Eugenia.

'But isn't Manolo a pretty boy, like they all are? I thought that was why you liked him . . .'

'You're a cruel child, I don't know if you realise it. I don't know if it's your fault, or whose it is, but you are. You're very cruel,' said Aunt Eugenia sharply, though hardly raising her voice.

Kus-Kus had gone pale; and when she repeated the word 'cruel' it sounded more and more unjust, harder and more hateful. Kus-Kus had gone very quiet, as if crouching within his soul. A long time passed. Aunt Eugenia, with her eyes closed, rested her head on the back of the sofa; she had the exhausted, heavy look of a woman who has fainted. Kus-Kus had reached the door by the time she opened her eyes. At her feet was the cat, like a vigorously wrought porcelain figure. They looked at each other. For an instant it seemed that nothing would happen, that Kus-Kus was simply going to say goodbye from the doorway and go. Instead, he said: 'You'll soon see how cruel I am. Very soon.'

Kus-Kus thought when he went out that his resentment, his desire to hurt Aunt Eugenia and to avenge himself, could not bear interruption; there would be an unbearable vacuum in his life until he had carried out the action he'd announced. But what happened was that he stopped on the landing outside the apartment just below Aunt Eugenia's. He stopped as if someone had forced him to, and he found himself compelled to hide his feelings, his rage, out of simple courtesy. He stopped outside the door of an apartment that seemed the distillation of many memories; it was a beautiful apartment, too, even more beautiful than Aunt Eugenia's. It belonged to his grandmother, Mercedes, who let it in the summer by putting an advertisement in one of the weeklies, never the same advertisement, and never – as far as he knew – the same tenants two summers running, and never the same rent: always double, despite the fact that, abandoned for nine months of the year and full to bursting for three, both of which took their toll on the chintz, the apartment didn't increase its charms in line with its rent. All this information, which came almost exclusively from memories of Aunt Eugenia's descriptions, instantly imposed itself on Kus-Kus with the force of an inescapable obligation. Yes, they were only memories, but there they were, and Kus-Kus felt obliged to recall them, and through them to remember Aunt Eugenia and himself. It was the story about the rent that always doubled that Aunt Eugenia never tired of telling; and the stories about the notices and instructions in his grandmother's own handwriting, pinned up with drawing pins, like edicts, like verses from the Koran; and the broken taps that his grandmother swore she'd repaired, without ever having had the least intention of doing so, and which either dripped incessantly or spat out gouts of rust-coloured water ... Things that Aunt Eugenia talked about in the afternoons, when autumn filled everything and the apartment downstairs was empty again and the problems the last summer tenants had and the latest news about them began to dwindle, only to proliferate again through telling and retelling, as if the summer, like a much-read book, were inexhaustible, intensified by the high, polished, sad blue of the first autumn days, the anemone-coloured jerseys and the classes and the smell of mothballs and new books, with more time spent at home and fewer boats in the harbour; when at nightfall prowling souls drummed on the eaves, on the black windows, and Aunt Eugenia threw over her shoulders a man's navy jacket that she wore indoors and the two of them together, he and Aunt Eugenia, would scour the atlas in search of archipelagos or the Sargasso Sea or the Sea of Turtles through which Aunt Eugenia said she herself had sailed, and the smell of freshly baked apples at teatime . . . in Aunt Eugenia's apartment.

At that moment Manolo collided with Kus-Kus; Kus-Kus, knocked off balance, fell on his backside; Manolo sat down next to him, both of them with their backs resting against the door of Mercedes's apartment. Through the skylight slipped the silky, nodding reflections of a tide that had been slowly rising like the slow dusk.

'God, you really came down hard!' said Manolo. 'Didn't you see me coming up? You must have!'

'I didn't notice. I thought it was someone coming down. It could have been someone coming down, couldn't it? My mind was on something else, thinking about something else. I heard the noise but I didn't pay any attention. All noises are the same . . .' concluded Kus-Kus loftily.

'Well, it depends . . .' commented Manolo.

'It doesn't depend on anything. They're all the same. Noise is the lowest thing there is, the lowest; making a noise is for animals, for pigs; pigs make an incredible amount of noise . . .'

'And canaries, what about them! There are a lot of different kinds of noise. My father says that even fleas make a noise when they jump; my father says that even a hair falling makes a noise, even a hair from your head, imagine that . . . !'

'He must be consumptive, your father. Only consumptives can hear things like that.'

'He's not consumptive, I don't think. What he does have is an ulcer that he got in the war from eating so many rats and other crap . . .' Manolo suddenly interrupted the conversation that Kus-Kus's fall had spontaneously opened between them to say in a more serious, more conventional and cautious tone of voice that didn't entirely match his appearance: 'Listen, we can talk man to man here . . . I mean because of your aunt, I mean Miss Eugenia.'

'You can if you want. Why should I?'

'I don't know! I meant because of your aunt, I mean because of her, since we both know her . . .'

'I've got nothing to say to you; not to anybody, but least of all to you.'

Kus-Kus was enjoying himself. He had to tell himself so quickly, because it seemed to him quite contrary to what he would have expected to feel on such an occasion. Manolo amused him. And, he thought, he really was handsome. Although he could scarcely make him out by the light from the skylight. He thought it was a shame they'd met the way they had, with Aunt Eugenia always between them, confusing everything, turning everything into women's business. These ideas, together with the memories of Aunt Eugenia and of other times and the desire to avenge himself and to hurt her (which had not diminished), made Kus-Kus repeat in a casual, almost coquettish tone: 'I've got nothing to say to you. Least of all to you, so there . . .'

'God, why are you like that? What have I done to you? I've never done anything to you that I know of. Come on, what have I ever done to you?'

'To me, nothing. And that's exactly it, because you've got nothing to do with me, that's it . . . what I just said. You're absolutely the last person I'd talk to . . .'

'You've quarrelled because of me,' said Manolo, who was

totally thrown by Kus-Kus's new tone. For want of anything more brilliant to say, he added: 'That's why you're angry, you've quarrelled because of me.'

'Who do you think you are? You even think my aunt and me are running after you like all the others do. Is it true, by the way, that they all chase you, the girls I mean? I don't see what the fuss is about.'

'Women are pretty brainless,' said Manolo thoughtfully.

'What were you going up there for now? To see her?'

'Yes, I was going up to see her. Anything wrong with that?'

'Why should there be? If you were going up, you were going up. Or aren't you going up there after all? We're getting nowhere sitting here . . .'

'You're all wrong about your aunt and me, I mean me and Miss Eugenia. It isn't what you think, really. I don't know what the hell you think she and I do . . . I swear we never do anything . . . We weren't doing anything the other day either, honest.'

'Do you go out with other girls? You must go out with other girls, because otherwise why would there be so much talk?'

'I don't go out with anyone, honest. I'll swear it if you want.'

'You must be a fairy then. Only queers don't have girlfriends.'

'Hey, mind your language. If you go on like that you'll be sorry, I'll knock your teeth out . . . Oh, forget it. You don't know what you're talking about.'

'That's fine by me. We can forget it if you want. But on the clear understanding that I'd be quite happy to continue. I've been known to argue for hours. And I never lose, never, not if it goes on long enough. It's always the others who lose. I can go on for hours, I'm used to it . . .'

'You seem older than you are when you talk. How old are you? About thirteen . . . no, never, you can't be!'

'What the hell has my age got to do with it? Hasn't my aunt told you that it's common to ask people their age?'

'No.'

'Of course not, she's too busy showing you her cunt.'

'Jesus, you're foul! Honestly, I've never met such a foul-mouthed kid.'

'There are worse, I can tell you; much worse. And girls too, there are girls who are twice as bad as me; twice as bad.'

'Well they must be really bad then.'

'What were you going up there now for? I'm asking you because I'd like to know. What's the first thing you do with women? A boy in seventh grade was telling me that the first thing he did, before anything else, was show them his cock. Is that what you do first? Seriously. After all, we are talking man to man, aren't we?'

Kus-Kus felt unable to stop himself. He felt that he had to talk about all that with Manolo. It was the first time he'd spoken like this with anyone. To his confessor he just said: 'I confess to having had bad thoughts,' and that was enough. He put his arm awkwardly round Manolo's neck, feeling his way in the dark, almost kissing him as his lips sought his ear. Now his desire for vengeance really had disappeared. All that remained was a mixture of curiosity and self-pity ... and a need to talk about it all with Manolo, who knew all about those things, according to Josefa, according to all the girls. He sat there almost embracing him, the warmth from Manolo's body giving him courage. He smelled of sweat. He noticed how Manolo turned within his embrace, how within his hand Manolo's face, his head, his nose, his whole neck turned like the great neck of an animal that stands quietly and allows itself to be stroked, without uttering a sound, without running away ...

'Do you know, Manolo, once on the pier, one time when we were fishing, me and someone else ... he was some way away and I'd got my fishing tackle tangled, and this other person came over and sat down next to me, he said he could help me with the tackle, it had rained quite heavily in the morning, so there was just him and me, the others had left, you don't bear me any grudge, do you, Manolo? if you like you can come to my house whenever you want to and sleep in my bed and lie there very quiet, as quiet as you are now, breathing really softly, when I'm older I'll be like my grandfather, the richest man in Spain, I bet you didn't know that, did you? I'm not joking, you can ask my aunt if you want, you've moved away a bit, just let me tell you about this then you can go if you want, if I'm so disgusting, then you can punch me in the mouth or whatever you want, I don't care what you do and I've never told anyone since it happened, there on the pier, you've moved again, you've moved your legs, nobody loves me, did you know that, Manolo? whatever I do, that's why I let him sit near me, just a little at first and then gradually getting closer and it was time I went, it was one evening last summer, it must have been about six o'clock, although it seemed later because of the rain, it was almost low tide and it came on to rain, that very fine drenching drizzle, my rod was brand new and long, really long, you could use it for deep-sea fishing, to catch mullet, anything, just by changing hooks, I think it got tangled because of the bait, because I put too much in, I kept throwing it in, after I'd managed to convince Miss Hart, she looks after me, she's English, she's been with me since I was born, I'd convinced her that dull days were the best for fishing, I must have snatched at it or something, and that's why I got tangled up, Manolo, don't go thinking I don't know how to fish, and don't bear me any grudge because I like you a lot, really, ah, but you've moved again, at first I hardly noticed how close he'd come, it was on the pier underneath the crane they red-leaded this April and that still hasn't been painted, you know the one I mean? what I didn't want, the way it was getting jerked about, was to lose the sinker which was new, brand new, do you know which crane I mean, Manolo?'

'More or less. So what happened? You keep chopping and changing, I don't know why. What happened between you?'

'It's because you want to go, you want to go and that's why you ask me that, to get it over with and leave, that's why . . .'

'You can tell me anything you want, kid, I won't go. Talk as much as you want to, I won't move; but don't mess my hair up like that, damn it, you'll make me look like I don't know what . . . what happened with the guy?'

'Now you'll probably laugh, because well, I don't know, probably nothing much happened, that's why I asked you if you knew exactly where the place was, because the place . . . the place made an impression on me too; he was an older man, much older than you, twice as old, with a belted raincoat, an old raincoat, and he helped me with the line, he did it really well, hardly moving, just moving his arms from one side to the other, in circles, until the hook and the sinker came out cleanly, shining, dripping water, and I thanked him and sat down next to him, with my feet hanging, watching it rain, the water was all green, it went all bottle green, the fish came to the surface to breathe, you could see their silver backs as they went back down, the air was cool, really cool, and he took some baby sea bream out of a basket, they'd just been caught and were still flailing about, and he said, look, the baby bream are alive, they're alive, look, and he put one in my shorts, it lay between my legs and I expect I moved a bit and then with his left hand he grabbed my shorts and my cock, I didn't feel anything, that's what shocked me most, not to have felt anything then, afterwards I did, of course, I wanted to get up but I couldn't really, not there, I told him I had to go because they were expecting me at home, and he spoke so softly I couldn't hear him and I said I'm sorry, sir, I didn't hear what you said because of the noise the rain was making and he came even closer, without taking his hand away and he undid a button and the one below was missing and he said tell them at home to sew that button on, you can't go around with your willy hanging out, some rough guy might cut it off, castrate you, and then you'd bleed to death, that's what he said, and I wanted to go and he said I can't find it, did you look this morning to see if it was still there, women can buy removable ones you know, you probably haven't got one, he said, and I was beginning to feel sick but I didn't leave either because . . . the rain got much heavier just then and he said, you're big for your age, and I didn't feel anything and that shocked me, and then the coastguards' motorboat came round the pier head and he took his hand away fast and said he was going, and that if I came there on other evenings we could see each other again if I wanted, in a doorway near his house, and then the boat was almost underneath us by the steps of the landing-stage and I was alone.'

They remained in the same position as at the start, except that Kus-Kus noticed (he'd noticed it as the story came more and more to resemble their present situation, the two of them in the dark whispering together like lovers) that Manolo was following the oscillations and undulations of his story less closely. 'Your neck's stiff, Manolo, really stiff,' murmured Kus-Kus, still affectionately, but losing confidence in his ability to fascinate, or rather already feeling, already sensing, Manolo's rebuff. It's very likely that such situations of mutual fascination depend, as does any situation, on certain chronologies and rhythms. And it's probable that the situation in which Kus-Kus and Manolo found themselves had, objectively speaking, already begun its decline. What actually happened was that Manolo suddenly sat up, cross-legged, with his hands on his knees. For an instant Kus-Kus found himself with his arm around nothing. From here on Kus-Kus's feelings and emotions began to grow cooler, more brittle. At that moment, without warning, Manolo lit a match. It felt like an explosion. Kus-Kus (though he scarcely moved) shrank in on himself like a crab or a sea urchin. By the light of the match you could see how very close they were, like two lovers driven apart by circumstances. Manolo let the flame burn out and then lit another match and a cigarette. It was over. But Kus-Kus — and quite probably Manolo too — had little experience of endings. He thought, therefore, that it would be possible for him to recover the lost enchantment without difficulty. He leaned against Manolo's shoulder. Manolo's shirt smelled clean. Manolo pushed him off, vigorously lifting both his arms as if in a gymnastic exercise.

'What time is it? It's dark already,' said Manolo.

'It was dark before, but it didn't bother you then,' said Kus-Kus tearfully. Or, perhaps, pale and stiffening again at the suggestion that Manolo was ready to leave.

'We've been here nearly an hour. Maybe more. I have to go. I wonder if it's too late to call on Miss Eugenia.'

Manolo almost jumped to his feet; Kus-Kus also stood, only more slowly. Standing up they were more or less the same height, although Kus-Kus was, or at least appeared to be, bulkier than Manolo.

'I smoke too. Julian showed me how . . .' said Kus-Kus, with a certain wheedling, monotonous charm. And since Manolo said nothing, he continued in the same tone, 'Only now and then, the odd cigarette. I inhale though. At my age, you know, it's not usual to inhale, out of all the boys in my class who smoke not one inhales . . .'

'I'm going to have to go. Now I really must go . . .' interrupted Manolo, without moving. The fact that he didn't move and that his voice sounded a little hoarse, as if he were unsure of himself, encouraged Kus-Kus. He thought: 'I'm sure he wants me to go on talking about myself; I'm sure he wants to tell me something, well, it would be only natural and logical after the things I've told him, but, coming from the family he does, he's uncultivated, uneducated, he doesn't know how to begin or what to do. And that's why he doesn't go.' He felt his limbs invaded by tenderness again, felt again the desire to touch Manolo like he had before; he felt excited.

It was like being in class and wanting to masturbate and come. It was an interesting state of mind to be in, like an instantaneous, shining sense of elation. He grabbed Manolo's arm with both hands; he felt the rapid movement of Manolo's muscles, his biceps; he thought that later, when they were together in his house (Kus-Kus felt an urgent need to take Manolo to his own house, to his playroom, to his bedroom), when they were alone, he would tell him to show him his biceps, like they did at school; there wasn't a boy in school, Kus-Kus thought, not even the strongest of them all, as strong as Manolo; he'd take him to the cinema one Thursday and the others would see, then they'd see . . .

'What I just told you, I've never told anyone before, it's the first time; if you like we can go down to my house and I'll tell you more things, we're getting nowhere here . . .' Kus-Kus moved towards Manolo, still gripping his arm with both hands, until he was almost pressed against his side. And he thought it was lovely being like that, almost better in the dark than with the lights on.

'Damn it, don't paw me like that, can't you talk to me without pawing me? Come on, men don't need to paw each other like that . . . that's for queers . . .'

'I tell you all about myself and you go and insult me. I don't mind being a queer. With you, that is. But there's no reason for you to insult me, no reason for you to get angry. After all I've told you, you get angry. You should feel sorry for me after what happened . . .'

'But nothing much happened. The guy ran off, didn't he, as soon as he saw the coastguards' boat. Why should I feel sorry for you?'

'I've been perverted because of that. In the Exercises this Easter they said a sin like that is unforgivable; if they knew about it at school they'd probably expel me, the Rector would probably write a letter to my father and then what? My father told me that you only have to be touched by dishonour once to be dishonoured forever, that's what he said. And it's touched me, so that's why you should feel sorry for me, you must feel sorry for me . . .'

'It happens to lots of people. The thing is that because your family's got money, you think everyone should jump to attention . . . but things aren't like that. It happens to a lot of people. If I feel sorry for anyone, it's for the other guy.'

'And Aunt Eugenia! You feel sorry for her, don't you?'

'Well, yes, I do, to be honest. After all, Miss Eugenia is more alone than you, much more, and it upsets me, well, because it does, because I'd like to see her on another footing, with me, poor woman, but what can I do? We can't go to the cinema together, or go out together . . . people can be such shits, that's why I feel sorry for her . . .'

'You go up to my aunt's house to steal her money, and to touch her up and take advantage of the fact that she's sex-mad. But I'll make you pay for it. You won't forget me in a hurry. If you want to make a fool of somebody pick on your own mother, but don't try it with my family, not my family. Perhaps you don't realise that my family are the richest in all Spain, and the police are going to beat the living daylights out of you, and quite right too, for having taken advantage of a half-mad woman, you're a bastard, that's what you are . . .'

'Just piss off, kid, all right, and watch what you go telling your family. I'm warning you. You'd better be careful and leave her alone, leave her alone or . . .'

'It's her fault. You know that as well as I do. It's all her fault. She's the one who's messed everything up. She's messed everything up, she has, it's her fault, she's ruined everything . . .'

'Well, damn it, forgive her and bloody well forget about it. Can't you just forgive her?'

'I won't forgive any of you, you bastards.'

Three floors down the lift stopped, and the lights went on. They heard several people talking at once; at least two couples. They fell silent. Almost immediately afterwards they heard a door close and there were fewer people down below, and two or three people coming up the stairs, stopping on the landing and putting on the light. They could hear the rattle of keys on a key-ring. Manolo and Kus-Kus could make each other out almost perfectly now. Kus-Kus began to go down the stairs very slowly, and Manolo very slowly went up the remaining flight to the top floor, to the mansards.

At first they didn't understand him; they couldn't make out what he was talking about or who he was; the story that the unexpected informer insisted on telling them at seven o'clock that morning was passed from extension to extension for fifteen minutes; it seemed an eternity. What had happened to his desire for revenge? Still dressed, but without his shoes, Kus-Kus had spent the night with his eyes wide open, fixed on himself, so strong an impression had Manolo's coldness made on him, so intense was the jealousy he had felt on seeing him go up to Aunt Eugenia's apartment. His apartment was so empty, the empty playroom so sordid with the crude vestiges of his childhood still there in the engineless trains, the broken-backed books, the children's edition of *A Tale of Two Cities*, the complete collection of William books. During the night, he got up once to pee and to have a drink of water; when he came back, he leafed through his complete collection of *The Adventures of Roberto Alcazar and Pedrin*. He thought: those two have got more to answer for than ... those two are the worst of all; he thought: I'm no hero and I don't bloody need to be; but the ominous vacuity of his room and of his childhood without stories, without excitement, without wonder, didn't give him any coherent answers. Probably, he thought, some people's heroism consists in not being able to fool themselves however hard they try, and I'm one of those, and my heroism doesn't consist in believing that Aunt Eugenia is good, but in believing the exact opposite and living with the consequences; that's the kind of hero I am . . . At night solitude is paralysing, any idea becomes an itch that no changing of position, no consolation can relieve; years later Kus-Kus would remember that night with horror. At the last moment, as dawn broke, he was overcome by an uncontrollable fit of shivering . . . Five minutes before phoning the police station, his desire for revenge was like a kind of chill, like the early symptoms of 'flu.

He got his own name wrong; they wanted to know both his family names, his address, his age . . . his age, how old he was, that's what they wanted to know in every office. They asked him where he was at that moment, where he was phoning from. At last a fuller, calmer voice than the others took hold of Kus-Kus's consciousness and he managed to explain himself clearly. The voice begged him not to hang up and to wait a moment, just a moment, the superintendent was due any minute. At the other end of the phone, in the overheard police station, which would shortly see the invisible consequences of an act long contemplated but never carried out as irreversibly as now, he could hear voices, see the empty desks of eight o'clock in the morning like endless interrogations. At last he heard: 'Stay where you are. Don't move from there, and don't try calling your aunt, we're on our way, a car is just leaving, don't move from there, Nicolas, don't move . . .' He slammed down the receiver. For a moment he felt happy. It had been exciting. 'It's over now, it's finally over,' he said out loud. And then he felt cold. As if his happiness, which had made him feel like a god for a moment, withdrew, sucked up in a twinkling by Lucifer himself.

They arrived less than ten minutes later. In silence they cordoned off the whole block. From the balcony of the study Kus-Kus saw the Plaza de San Andres becoming crowded with curious onlookers, despite the early hour. The crowd, diffuse and brilliant as an impressionist painting amongst the greenness of the plane trees . . . They were both arrested.

Manolo too. He must have spent the night upstairs. Kus-Kus went out on to the landing to watch them as they went down. And he saw them both, Julian and Manolo, go down one after the other, their hands behind their backs. They were escorted by policemen. Several men from the Armed Police. And Julian followed Manolo, almost smiling, with, Kus-Kus thought, the same wry expression he used to have when he smiled in the old days. And his eyes, without his dark glasses, were watering, as if he were crying, though Kus-Kus knew very well that Julian wasn't crying then. And Julian turned to look at him, and seemed to want to tell him something without the policeman behind him hearing. And as there wasn't much time, Julian stopped abruptly and said: 'Forgive me if you can, I let you down.' And he looked straight into his eyes and then the policeman pushed him down the stairs, so as not to complicate things or cause a scene, at least not too much of one, at that hour.

Several days passed; then in June the exams started . . . It was as if he had dreamed it; Kus-Kus couldn't rid himself of a vacuous somnolence. And he couldn't sit still. He couldn't think of anything else. After the first exam, Geography and History, he went straight up to Aunt Eugenia's apartment; he had left the paper blank. The front door was ajar. In that unrecognisable, damp apartment, which recalled the corridors, the bleak rooms of a boarding house, all the doors were either standing ajar or wide open, as if they had come off their hinges. It looked like an empty apartment. He found Aunt Eugenia in her room lying on the bed fully clothed, quite still. When he came in she opened her eyes. Kus-Kus, feeling guilty, greeted her feebly. Covered with an eiderdown, as if she had just gone to bed for the first time in a month, Aunt Eugenia stared at him. Kus-Kus recognised now, in her gaunt features, the likeness of the Aunt Eugenia he had loved. Only her eyes reflected the profound changes in both their lives. The eyes that looked at him, bright and dark, from the other side of the room, from that face at once familiar and strange, were the eyes of a madwoman. The oddest thing was that they looked a little beyond him; never leaving him, but not quite resting on him; and the other curious and the most terrible thing was the sweetness with which they looked at him . . . Screwing up his courage, he went over to the bed, suppressing as he did so a desire to run away and forget all about it. He went nearer, stifling the desire to escape because he thought he heard the sound of a human voice. But when he got nearer still, he saw only that Aunt Eugenia's lips were moving a little. He felt his whole being fill with the desire to run away and forget those images. 'It's not my fault she's like this,' he thought. 'It's not my fault.' And a shiver ran through him like a bolt of lightning. He had the feeling that, although innocent, he was in the wrong, and he hurriedly searched his memories, among the polite formulae they had taught him to use, for something unequivocally superficial to say, but could find nothing. Aunt Eugenia helped things a lot by sitting up and saying something herself. He couldn't hear properly and he had to go a little closer. 'She smells bad,' he thought, 'she smells of several days' sweat.' The disagreeable presence of that unwonted smell left him, once more, speechless.

'When I return to Bariloche,' Aunt Eugenia said, almost in a whisper, 'I'm never coming back. Not this time.'

'Never? That can't be, Aunt Eugenia. I'd miss you a lot. And Manolo. We'd miss you a lot, Manolo and me . . .'

'Probably this time you would. Darling Kus-Kus, adío . . .'

They found the body at low tide; drowned in the small inner harbour, floating by the steps where Josema used to tie up in the summer. She must have slipped going down the steps. Everyone was thunderstruck. How thin she'd got, just like when she was young. And it was true that Aunt Eugenia did look thin, very thin, dead in Bariloche.

The master and mistress were away. It was considered an

elegant end. The morning of the funeral was a real summer's day. We all went in our Sunday best. The parish church was full; it was all as it should be; everyone was there; we all knew each other. I led the mourning. At the end they expressed their condolences to me. Maria del Carmen Villacantero, the poor thing, made an entrance but, for once in her life, discreetly, so that none of us noticed. It seems that for two days and nights Maria del Carmen had struggled with the temptation not to go to Eugenia's funeral. She did attend, though, because of what people might say, and also out of the affection she had always felt for the family. She did not, however, occupy her usual place at Mercedes's side in the first row of the pews. She felt hurt and rejected (especially after having learned from the hotel manageress that not even after Eugenia's suicide would the mansards be divided. Instead, the manageress assured her, accompanying the information with a clearing of the throat and a cough, they were to be renovated and painted in order to be rented out that very summer to a family from Madrid). She felt hurt, and so she should, in the manageress's opinion, hurt and stunned by that affront, after so many years of friendship. But what really wounded Maria del Carmen Villacantero (and not only in her conscience) was when Mercedes, who had arrived in the parish church half an hour early ('To make sure,' as she said to Genoveva on leaving the house, 'that the coadjutor doesn't make a fool of himself this time'), after running her eyes impatiently over the whole congregation, left her seat and came over to Maria del Carmen, who had placed herself modestly at the end of one of the last pews. Maria del Carmen was still standing because the funeral had not yet begun. Mercedes gave her a shove and knelt down next to her as if nothing had happened. Giving in to the habit of many years of submission, Maria del Carmen Villacantero made room for her, and, after a moment's hesitation, knelt down next to her friend. The funeral service was beginning now. Given the circumstances, they had decided to have three priests but no singing. So all one heard, intermingled with prayers in Latin, was murmuring and the scraping of chairs and feet.

'I'm sorry, Maria del Carmen,' Mercedes whispered firmly, without looking at her friend. Her voice trembled a little on the 'Carmen,' as if Mercedes were on the point of bursting into tears because she couldn't find the Mass for the Dead in her missal.

'It doesn't matter, Mercedes,' Maria del Carmen Villacantero whispered in turn, 'it doesn't matter in the least. I'm a humble person, as you well know. It's my duty to forgive wrongs, it's my duty to forget everything, if I can . . .'

'Forgive me, Maria del Carmen, if you can,' answered Mercedes, almost out loud.

The two remained kneeling until the end; everyone saw them leave the church together, but after that day they never saw each other again.

It was a magnificent funeral. All in Latin, as is only proper, but without music. When they left everyone was deeply moved, or so they said. Yes, it was a magnificent funeral, worthy of that French-style building with vast mansards that rose up among the clumps of chimneys, the bronze statues lending an additional elegance to the balcony parapets and the six glittering glassed-in balconies, perched high above the trees in the Plaza de San Andres, almost as elegant and dashing as the masts of the sailing ships moored by the yacht club in the shelter of the port.